	DATE DUE		

SEP - - 2001

ALL
LOVES
EXCELLING

Also by Josiah Bunting III

The Lionheads
The Advent of Frederick Giles
An Education for Our Time

ALL LOVES EXCELLING

Josiah Bunting III

Bridge Works Publishing
Bridgehampton, New York

Published in the United States by Bridge Works Publishing Company, Bridgehampton, New York. Distributed in the United States by National Book Network, Lanham, Maryland.

For descriptions of this and other Bridge Works books visit the Web site of National Book Network at www.nbnbooks.com.

FIRST EDITION

The characters and events in this book are fictitious. Any similarity to actual persons, living or dead, is coincidental and not intended by the author.

Library of Congress Cataloging-in-Publication Data

Bunting, Josiah, 1939–
    All loves excelling : a novel / Josiah Bunting, III.
       p. cm.
    ISBN 1-882593-40-5 (alk. paper)
    1. Universities and colleges — Admission — Fiction. 2. Preparatory school students — Fiction. 3. Mothers and daughters — Fiction. 4. New York (State) — Fiction. 5. Teenage girls — Fiction. I. Title.

    PS3552.U48 A79 2001
    813'.54 — dc21

                     00-050756

10 9 8 7 6 5 4 3 2 1

Book and jacket design by Eva Auchincloss

Printed in the United States of America

I am especially indebted to my editor, Barbara Phillips. Several other friends were particularly helpful: Tina Bennett, Rita Brown, Patricia Cantlay, Dr. David Copeland, Leita Hamill, Dr. Jane Horton, Dr. Robin Karpf, Lori Parrent, Kathryn Popenoe, Stephanie Schragger, Arthur S. Thomas.

To Diana
and to my children
Elizabeth, Josiah, Charlie and Alexandra

To My Daughter

Bright clasp of her whole hand around my finger,
My daughter, as we walk together now,
All my life I'll feel a ring invisibly
Circle this bone with shining: when she is grown
Far from today as her eyes are far already.

— Stephen Spender

PART ONE

CHAPTER ONE

Just before 11:00, on a warm and feathery September morning, one of the Bahringer family vehicles arrived at the Alumni Gates of St. Matthew's School. "Look at the sign," said Joey Bahringer, who was driving. "Look at it." WE COME AS BOYS WE LEAVE AS MEN, it proclaimed.

"Well, it used to be a school just for boys," said his daughter Amanda, more nervous now than she had been on the long drive from home.

"But you know," her father declared, "these places went co-ed much better than girls schools did. The thing is, a lot of nice girls will come here. But you can't get a good cross-section of boys to go to a girls' school. You know what I mean? Look at that one kid over there. Big kid!" There appeared, on Mrs. Bahringer's side of the Land Rover, a tow-headed boy, tall and muscular. He looked in on them. "Welcome," he said. "Welcome to St. Matthew's. What's your name?" A silver nametape on his blazer identified him as Toby.

Tess Bahringer turned around and looked at her daughter, who stammered her reply: "Amanda. Amanda Bahringer."

The boy looked at his clipboard. He looked up at the mother, then at Amanda. "All right. Amanda Bahringer.

Post Graduate — a P.G. Morison Dormitory, Room 23, third building on the left. Good luck, O.K?" He withdrew, shuffling to the next car in line. Joey Bahringer eased the car forward. Tess and Amanda stared at the larger scene that now unfolded before them.

It was a bright tumult of purposeful activity, set in a large oblong quadrangle enclosed by eight three-story buildings and a chapel, or some sort of assembly hall, at the far end. Within this broad space of grass, in luminous array, lay the pride of the automobile manufactory of three continents. Hundreds of cars were being unloaded. Smart gleaming Grand Cherokees and burnished Land Cruisers, bulbous Expeditions, wolfish silver Lexuses alongside chunky Suburbans and Tahoes large enough to hold the contents of a small house. There were gigantic Navigators, understated Saabs, Jaguars, Explorers, Audi A-6s and a single scarlet Durango, all with their doors and bays agape, disgorging the cargo of American adolescents: bright blankets, stacked luggage, wicker hampers, lap-tops, lacrosse sticks, skates, speakers large and powerful enough to electrify gymnasiums; dangling irons, bins full of notebooks, blow-dryers, wastebaskets with horses painted on them, North Face jackets . . .

Immediately in front of the Bahringers, getting out of their cars at the same time, two fathers talked into cell phones, one small enough to be concealed in the man's palm. Both fathers looked out over the dormitories at the hazy smudges of the Tuscaroras in the distance. One barked angrily into his phone, consulting a gigantic gold wristwatch. The other gesticulated suddenly, then clapped his phone shut and waved weakly at the Bahringers — who, he saw, had been looking at him.

"Imagine if it rained opening day!"

"Imagine! What're you, a sadist? This is bad enough." Joey Bahringer had begun thinking about the labor of unloading and carrying and listening that lay before him, not to mention the long drive back to Long Island later, perhaps much later, that afternoon.

"Can you make it down to Westchester by 6:30, you leave here by 3:00?"

"I don't know," Joey answered. "We're out on the Island."

"They got a program, too. We have to go to that."

Tess and Amanda were at the rear of the Land Rover, taking things out. Two boys, one of them Toby, helped.

"My daughter's scared to death," Joey confided to the other father. "Hi. Joey Bahringer."

"Max Buck. Mine too. I don't care. She makes it into Princeton, Penn, this time next year, I'm easy with it. You like the Land Rover?"

"Yeah, I do. It's the Four Point Six. A real mountain goat."

"Sure is."

"See you later," said Joey. "We still got a lot of stuff to move."

"Twenty-six grand a year, and they got her in a tiger cage. You see the room, Tess?"

Amanda's assigned room in Morison was a single, austere and meager in its furnishings. A fire ordinance on the inside of the door warned against hanging flammable materials on the walls; another, signed by a student council two years earlier, forbade any decoration of a racist, sexist, or otherwise demeaning character. There was a battered desk, and, tucked under it, a straight-backed chair. The bed was narrow, like a nun's, its mattress thin, lumpy, and stained. An odd mullioned window — odd because the window began at the floor and rose almost to the high ceiling of the room — offered a narrow view of athletic fields, and, beyond them, woodland and hazy grey skyline. The room smelled like pine disinfectant.

It struck Tess Bahringer as spartan and purposive: appropriate to its place and function, perfectly suited to Amanda's need in her new venture. The Bahringers were enrolling their daughter at St. Matthew's to recoup a disappointing senior year at Lawrence High School.

Tess liked the room, approved of the narrow chamber stripped down to its essentials, unencumbered by any of the girlish clutter of Amanda's second-floor room at home. This was not all. The building itself was almost as old as St. Matthew's, founded in 1844. Generations of students had lived here, had sent their own children, indeed their grandchildren, to live and learn here. Tess sensed that simply living in such surroundings would do something more for Amanda then merely teaching her how to concentrate and helping to get her into Dartmouth College. It would confer some dim if inarticulable advantage, some membership, some network . . . well, Tess didn't know exactly what it was, but it was an opportunity that she had never had, and she and Joey did not intend to pay over large amounts for their daughter to live in circumstances of luxury.

They carried up the last of her things: a cello, a scale, her new computer and printer, a crate full of running shoes and athletic gear.

"I'll get as aerobic as you are, I keep this up. Where you want the desk, baby?"

"Right where it is, Daddy, it's O.K. where it is."

"I can put it in front of the window. This is some view."

"Joey" — Tess cut in — "she'll concentrate better with the desk where it is."

There was a rattle at the door and a bustling sound out in the hallway. Max Buck, the father who had wondered how long it took to get to Westchester, appeared with his daughter Sumner and his wife.

"We've got to get over to the Chapel. They have a welcoming address from the headmaster in five minutes."

The six of them walked down the corridor of the third floor of Morison, in self-conscious silence. Joey and Tess walked on either side of their daughter, at the rear of the little party, Joey with his hand at the small of Amanda's back, in a gesture of reassurance and sadness at the separation that would come at the end of the day.

"Hymn 125, The St. Matthew's School Hymn. All please rise."

> *Love Divine, all loves excelling, Joy of Heav'n*
> *To earth come down*
> *Fix in us thy humble dwelling, All thy faithful*
> *Mercies crown.*

The sound, Amanda thought, was beautiful and radiant — reassuring in an unexpected way. The hymn had a sweetness to it. She felt a silky rustle at her elbow and realized that it was the touch of the loose sleeve of a member of the choir brushing by her as the procession passed her pew. It moved forward at a gentle pace, the choir's faces ardent and full of hope. Minutes seemed to pass. On they came until, at the very end, alone and without a hymnal, an older man passed by. He looked directly at Amanda and smiled, and such a smile, she believed, she had never seen: it was illuminated by delighted surprise, as if in recognition of an old friend. The man was strong-looking, even under his white surplice; his face, ruddy with health and crowned with thick grey hair immaculately parted. But in fact she had only a second or two to study him. He had passed on, and now she felt a spiky touch at her other side: her mother's.

"That's him," she said. "That's Dr. Passmore."

And now he stood facing them, or, rather, looking down at them from the pulpit.

"Dear Friends, I want to preach, not a sermon, not a homily, but to offer simply a message of welcome to St. Matthew's. Later in the term, in our annual candle-light ceremony of Ingathering, the whole school will come together for the beginning convocation of our literary year. Then I will talk at rather more length than today — and, I fear, in the mode that the late president at Yale, Dr. Giamatti, called 'High Institutional.' We will summon ourselves from our summer diversions and rededicate our energies . . ."

This is how they talk up here, Tess thought. The man certainly knows what he's doing. It sounded as though he was using a broad *A,* like an Englishman.

". . . that all here this day, in this venerable house of God, take deeply to their hearts the words of the School Hymn: 'All Loves Excelling.' For can there be any love, other than the love of God, that excels that of a mother, of a father, for her child? Yes, we acknowledge our mission and our work. But our consecration must be to higher duties: to works of sacrifice, of giving, of self-forgetfulness . . ."

Joey wondered whether they would ask everyone to give the peace sign to each other, which he always found awkward. He remembered his commissioning ceremony in the Marines, just at the end of Vietnam, when the general had said, "You're Marines now, and will be 'til the day you die." A sardonic, communal grunt from the new lieutenants reflected their knowledge that they might indeed die soon. But now, at forty-nine, he was giving his only child, their daughter, to this headmaster. He looked over at Amanda, at her mother sitting between them in the pew, saw them both in rapt and vivid profile, as tensely attentive as perched falcons.

They had to go to some kind of a reception, Tess saw, a tea. She led her party towards the University Advisement Office, "U.A." It had become very hot. The breezes that had dandled and refreshed her earlier in the morning had subsided; the trios of new students and parents no longer strode from one fixture to another but began to trudge. Some began to worry about their clothes. Max Buck re-appeared just ahead of them, his heliotrope shirt soaked through at the back. "U.A.'s the real business of St. Matthew's, isn't it? It's why they call it a prep school — right?"

A cool and immaculate young man appeared. "Please take out your academic schedules. O.K. — what's it say? How many here are P.G.s?" There was a reluctant show of six or seven hands. "O.K., I'll direct my first comments to you, because you're going to squeeze us like a sponge, and you got literally about five months, tops, to make your nut. You 'P.G.' to do what you failed to do last year: get into a college that you couldn't get into then. St. Matthew's can help you! It's what we're in business to do. Brown's still a tough ticket, O.K.? Ditto Stanford, Princeton, Dartmouth. About twenty of them are. The rest of them basically want you and want your money. Buyer's market.

"Of course, most of you don't want *them*, am I right?"

Absently Tess wondered why no academic person, a dean or something, had greeted her before they stuck this university advisement man in front of them. "I don't know how many of you are going to be recruited athletes. That'll skew the process." Tess wondered what "skew" meant. It sounded like splitting a suckling pig at a barbecue. "How many are going to do SAT UP? All right. For those who don't know, SAT UP is a program we contract here at the school. They send out a man from Gloversville, twice a week. He runs it for us. It will help get your SATs up, no question about it. All right. Take your curriculum sheet out of your folders, if you will, and look at your fall and spring schedules. All right?"

Tess pulled the form out of the folder and laid it on the armrest between her daughter and herself. In her last phone conversation with someone from the Dean's Office they had considered Amanda's best curriculum for the post-graduate year. Now it lay before them.

FALL TERM	SPRING TERM
U. S. History A.P.	U. S. History A.P.
Biology A.P.	Biology A.P.
Latin IV A.P.	Latin V A.P.
Pre-college Algebra I	Pre-college Algebra II
Hopkins & Housman	Hopkins & Housman

Only a month earlier, Tess and an associate dean had fashioned the schedule of courses in which Amanda would be enrolled. The Advanced Placements (A.P.s), were a necessity: success in them demonstrated seriousness of purpose and the ability to perform in a demanding college curriculum. Yet the courses must not overmatch the new pupil. "I don't know what her current school is like," the dean had admitted, "but St. Matthew's is rigorous and demanding. The workload is truly formidable" — words that evoked in Tess's imagination a rock-bound fastness, a monastery on a remote coast, where all sat over benches in rigorous and demanding work. It pleased her to think of Amanda laboring like this. The courses chosen must prove her smart; the circumstances in which she studied and learned must aid in her development of concentration.

The young man was finishing. "Let me say something about college recommendations and SATs. First, recommendations. Usually one of our department chairmen will take a P.G. section. These men and women write good recs. Middlebury has dealt with Mrs. Cadwallader for nineteen years. That's the kind of thing a place like this can do for you. But you can't get around the big verbal number. They all want it, no matter what they say. You want the good places, you better put up the big numbers."

Tess was riveted. She and Joey and Amanda were sitting in a horseshoe around the briefer, in those little plastic chairs that remind adults of everything they hate about schools. An immense bulletin board, twenty feet long, stretched along the front of the room like an old Cinemascope screen, covered by dozens of bright pictures and posters representing American universities and colleges. Tess studied them. They had a curious sameness: reddish-brown towers and huge overhanging boughs of trees; clusters of smiling students carrying books. Great care had been taken to populate each poster with certain numbers of Hispanic, Black, and Asian students. There were dazzling snow scenes; huge throngs in football stadiums; earnest scientists in white coats looking at translucent tubes they held up to the light; cityscapes to suggest the cultural resources of the urban schools. Tess searched vainly for a photograph of Dartmouth's lovely campus. She heard the briefer call for questions.

Max Buck spoke up: "Class rank mean anything? Because if it does, a lot of these kids may go down. Very bright youngster here, she may get lower grades than she did at a public school."

"No, Sir. You're wrong on that one. Halfway down the class here is top ten per cent anywhere else. The point is, they know us. They know Bronx Science and Horace Mann, Exeter. St. Matthew's. Last year we got nine into Harvard, eight into Duke. One of the Duke kids was second quintile here. See my point?"

Joey whispered to Amanda, "Anything else you want to know? Now's your chance."

But she shook her head. No.

During the long drive up the New York State Thruway Tess Bahringer had been considering her clothes for the tea. You get only one chance to make a first impression. All that she was prepared to show the world was calculated for effect and detail. Depth and mystery must be communicated to those meeting her for the first time; she liked to imagine people saying to one another, "Who is that woman over there, who is she?" Already her mind's eye had framed the scene: a lustrous lawn, willows at its boundaries, the house of the headmaster at its far flank; a soft afternoon of early, gauzy autumn haze. A few men and women, vaguely Nordic in appearance, the women with their jaws slightly overslung, would be murmuring private witticisms to one another. Tess couldn't tell whether the children would attend the tea; she was in fact uncertain whether they were to be called children or young people or students, or what. She hoped they would not be present, as Amanda did not do well in such settings. There would be faculty. They would be called masters, all in their fifties, their faces rubicund and etched, all with thick salt-and-pepper hair. And at their center would be the famous Dr. Passmore, formidable in appearance yet engaging and witty. She had read about him in the school literature and, from time to time, in

Town and Country. He would take her by the hand and "My Dear" her, and she would give good daughter. How old was he — 65? She would captivate him.

Tess's imagination, if a trifle superheated, was at least within stalking distance of what the Bahringers actually encountered. She wore a lavender silk Vittadini dress, moderately scooped at the neck, a tiny ocelot pin with citrines and diamonds as its only garnish. She stood, however, in a rubbernecking line of sweaty parents drinking warm tea out of plastic cups, and waiting to meet one of the deans, Dr. Passmore having left for the West Coast it was said, to raise money in Pasadena. They drank their tea, and now they walked silently, Amanda between Tess and Joey, towards the dwindling ranks of automobiles parked on the grass inside the quadrangle. A rough band of football players huffed by in their silver and garnet. The rear windows of the remaining cars were filled up like trophy cases with testimonials to the academic successes of the older children of their owners. Tess considered them. A solitary YALE had a simple authority to it. PRINCETON was to die for, though the colors were jarring. There was an eccentric flag of OBERLIN, but no DARTMOUTH.

They came to their own car. Tess turned to her daughter, to frail, frightened Amanda, whom she and Joey had put into St. Matthew's for her own good. She kissed her, and she offered her this parting advice:

"Don't let us down." She pressed a fifty-dollar bill into Amanda's hand. "Call us."

CHAPTER TWO

The long hallway of Third Floor Morison bore the signs of recent and unsuccessful rehabilitation: an industrial-strength carpet the color of moleskin, already mottled by spilled drinks and muddy athletic shoes; automatic doors that could be kept open only by door jambs. Amanda could see the names of all her hallmates affixed to the doors, just under the room numbers. Only first names were given. The effect of walking down the hall, seeing them all at one passage, was like looking at the names of horses in a row of stalls. It was a suggestive, intimidating array of names. Arrogant-sounding names. Page, Sumner, Constance, Laurence. Some struck her as fakey and pretentious: Simone, Joelle, Fiona. There were two Jennifers, two Kates, an Ashley, and a Daniella, and the last of these made Amanda think of her mother, and how she would react to such a name: Daniella? What kind of a name is that?

Under each name, affixed to the door, was a dark cork bulletin board in a garnet-colored frame. The boards and their frames smelled of fresh paint. E-mail had not displaced their function. In their upper left-hand corners were small grey cards stamped identically: OBLIGATIONS MESSAGES FIXTURES DO NOT REMOVE. Amanda walked back to look at her own board. There was a note, written in bright red scrawl. *Welcome lean mean running machine. First practice 4 P.M., Penrith Field. Coach Kellam.* Amanda wondered what day he meant.

There was a cloudy quiet all about, the sound of a large old house in winter, a house full of people in quiet distant conversation, an old furnace in the basement. But it was late summer at St. Matthew's. Obedient to an instruction found in a note left on her bed, Amanda now made her way back down the hallway to the hall-master's apartment — a Miss Rodman — whose coaching duties had kept her from meeting several of the new and returning girls.

She joined a ragged assembly, five or six of them sitting on the hallway floor just outside the apartment, all waiting for beginning-of-term interviews. In a silent terror of self-consciousness Amanda understood at once that what she had worn was horribly wrong: her pleated fawn-colored pants of crushed silk, what Tess had told her would be ideal for evening visits in the dormitory, perfect with a white silk blouse. Such a shirt would hang well on Amanda's frame, she had said; it would have a kind of off-hand glamour to it.

But all the other girls were in battered jeans and T-shirts with Absolut logos, *Lochsa Whitewater* labels on them, things like that. Their body language disclosed long familiarity and easy friendship; their greetings and banter were off-hand, affectionate, oddly inflected: "Hey, Page, looking good!" or "Complain about food — your first night back — Come on! There's a Stairmaster here, just like home!"

Amanda heard an authoritative, older voice: "You never, *never* come in here dressed like that. I'm surprised at you, Testy Tilden. You go and change. Then I'll see you."

A girl pushed past, her hands straight out in front of her and balled into little fists. "What a bitch. What an uptight bitch!" She was wearing decrepit jeans ripped horizontally at both knees and a man's basketball jersey that said BULLS.

Another girl, squat and chirpy, and wearing seed-pearl earrings, asked Amanda where she lived.

"Room Twenty-three, right down there."

"No, home."

"Oh, home. Long Island."

"Where in Long Island? Locust Valley? Do you know the Demerays?"

"No. Lawrence."

"Lawrence?" The girl accentuated the first syllable. Amanda looked away from her, towards the door. She could hear Frank Sinatra from inside.

"Are you the first girl from Lawrence to go here?"

But now a voice from the apartment severed their exchange. "Miss Bahringer, Miss A. Bahringer, you're next. Are you there?" The chirpy girl lowered her eyes, quite deliberately and maliciously, to show that she was staring at Amanda's pants, and Amanda walked past her into the apartment.

All here was dull, the light dim, the rugs dingy and sepia — almost, Amanda thought, like the rugs in a kennel. The furniture was boxy and generic. Over a sofa covered in green chintz hung an engraving, quite large, of a medieval knight on an uprearing armored horse. The desk Miss Rodman sat behind held irregular piles, tottering humps of folders, hillocks of paperbacks, examination blue-books; there were framed photos of girls' teams with big ST. Ms on the singlets, and a large colored photograph of the Queen Mother of England. Behind the hallmaster, against the wall, sat an old console television with a circular picture tube.

Amanda and Miss Rodman were not alone. A fat black Labrador lay alongside the desk, its chin on the edge of a wicker dog-basket. It was chewing the edge of its red bandana.

"Do sit down, my *dear* Amanda, do sit down. How has your first day gone? You've seen everything? Met everyone? Yes, yes, that's right. Been to U.A.? Been to Chapel yet? Made a few chums?"

"No chums yet." Amanda had never said the word before, and associated it with English nannies. Miss Rodman said *bean* for been.

"Well. You'll settle in. The other girls have bean here longer, most of them."

Amanda did not respond, only looked at Miss Rodman, trying to compose her expression, her posture, in ways that might demonstrate eager politeness and gratitude.

"The other girls have bean here longer. You're a maid on a mission, so it means nothing."

Amanda made a little fretful sound at the back of her throat that showed she understood and accepted what she had heard. But of course she did not. As Miss Rodman made her observations sound like incontestable declarations, metallic and complete, Amanda sat helpless and mute.

"A maid with a mission. A post-graduate. Here to plunder the academic resources of St. Matthew's, to lift up all scores, pass to a famous college, and thereafter say, 'I went to St. Matthew's!' — ay?"

"My parents, my mother, they think it's good for me to go here. I got turned down last spring by the colleges I wanted to go to."

"Where?"

"Well, everywhere, really, everywhere I applied to. I got turned down or wait-listed everywhere?"

"No room at the inn, ay? Just say, everywhere I applied, not everywhere I applied to. Don't put a preposition at the end."

"Everywhere I applied. I guess I can see why I didn't get in. I can see *now.*"

"You know," Miss Rodman continued, lighting a cigarette and inhaling with evident relish, "all this college acceptance rigmarole in the States reminds me of Caligula sitting in the Coliseum, turning people down gleefully, or letting them off on a whim. You dear child, how in the world do these places know you from Madame Curie? How old are you, Dear? Seventeen? You throw down a few scribbles on a page and they turn you down. Well, but we shall fix that, won't we? If you want these places, and if you work as hard as you can, well, St. Matthew's is unexcelled. But you must do it between now and January. February at the outside. After that the colleges won't see anything. They decide in February. Five months then — at full steam. But one can stand on her head for five months. What were your SATs?"

"I'll take them again, first week in November."

"But that's not what I asked. Listen to the question, Dear."

"Oh. 570 verbal. 540 math."

"I hated maths too. And where d'you want to go?"

"Dartmouth College."

"You don't mind my smoking, do you? You're all obsessed with smoking. Gretchen doesn't care." Miss Rodman chucked the big lab under the chin. "Whom do you have for U. S. History?"

"Mr. Steele."

"You need at least an A-minus from him. That's an important course here, it's one those colleges look at. A lot of them know Steele. They trust him. You have a heart throb at home, Dear?"

"W-what?"

"A beau. A boy friend."

"No. Did have. I don't have one now."

"I'm surprised, you're a lovely girl."

Miss Rodman seemed to be making an inventory, brisk and frank. She noted the careful attention Amanda had given her hair, how it was trained to shelter her ears and the far indented edges of her cheeks and the high limit of her forehead. Plainly she wanted the world to see of her face only what she allowed. Her expression had a trusting, wistful cast to it — an expression, Miss Rodman decided, of a child who had been bruised in some way. And for so early-on, just at the end of summer, her face seemed rather pale.

"Are you a recruited athlete?"

"No, I don't think I am."

"But you really don't know. They let in some P.G.s just to help St. Matthew's win. Crew's a good example. Dr. Passmore's very keen on crew. He rowed at Princeton. He loves to send crews to Henley."

"My sport is cross-country. Running," Amanda replied. She spoke very quietly, as if making a frail assertion. She looked, not at Miss Rodman's eyes, but at the sides of her face. After each response she made her catching sound at the back of her throat and looked down at her lap.

"Have brothers or sisters?"

"No. Neither one."

"Most problematical thing there is. A single daughter. Triple burden. Parent ambition. Parent protection. Wanted another one."

Amanda understood that "another one" probably meant a boy. She sensed what Miss Rodman was communicating, that she was trying to convey something important, but she couldn't be sure. Problematical?

"Tell me about your family."

"Well, my mother works in New York, for Warfield Stedman, it's a public relations firm? And my father works in Lawrence, in commercial real estate? They, like, want me here to focus better on my academics."

"Are you glad you're here?"

"I think so."

She's been knocked around pretty well, Miss Rodman thought. An unusual child, but with the familiar insignia. Won't look right at you. Statements all end in question marks. No beau. Too thin. And what Dr. Patterson called lack of affect. She saw it quite often. The girls were not hostile; not shy, exactly — just, somehow, lifeless. And yet Amanda, one had to say it, had a certain serenity to her, a composition, her hands folded in her lap, her head primly upright. She had a sweetness to her.

"You must make an effort now, an effort to know the other girls. Don't keep to yourself — you're in a single, and you're a one-year girl, and there'll be that tendency. Do you see? You must go out and meet people. Engage them. That's what Mrs. Thatcher made herself do when she was at Oxford. She became Prime Minister. Solitude is companionable, but make friends, Dear. And this must be lovely country to run in. Do you have questions for me?"

But no, she had no questions. Miss Rodman wondered whether she was taking something. Some of them were. The Arseneau girl last year in number 16, her medicine chest was full of St. John's Wort and Ativan, calmatives.

"Good-bye, Dear. My door is always open to you." Miss Rodman stood up, smoothed her skirt, prodded the dog out of the way and walked towards the door with Amanda. They stood for a moment under a bright light in the entrance foyer.

"We're the same height. And I see you have *green* eyes. That says something, Dear."

"Miss Fitzsimmons. Ashley Fitzsimmons, I will call your name only once! Where is that winsome child?"

Amanda left. Dorothea Rodman read the essay from her admission folder while she waited for Miss Fitzsimmons. Directed to "state honors and awards that you have won, and their significance," the new student had set down the following:

> When people ask me to describe myself in terms of honors I have won and what achievements I have accomplished, it makes me sad. I love to play the piano, and, a little less, the cello. On several occasions I have been given musical honors at my current school, Lawrence High School. I have run on our cross-country team for three years, and two years ago our team won the All-Counties. I finished second out of our girls. I do not have many academic honors or awards, but it seems as though I have spent much time trying to achieve these honors and awards that you speak of. I hope I may continue my progress at St. Matthew's School.
>
> Amanda Bahringer

CHAPTER THREE

Driving in the Land Rover through the rich grey gloaming, the car light and clear now that Amanda's things had been off-loaded — the sensation made Tess Bahringer think of a singer her father had liked — Vaughan Monroe. A man with a deep voice who always sounded like he had a cold: something about racing with the moon, high up in the midnight clouds, high up in something. She knew Joey loved his car and that he felt elevated in its comfort and power. Her husband adored the instrumentation, the computerized artifacts that glowed fluorescently like the dials of a warplane. He seemed to embrace the steering wheel. When he reached over and touched Tess's knee, and said, "Think we did the right thing? Think we were right to put her into boarding school?" she let him have it.

"Whaddyou mean, did we do the right thing?"

"I just wonder . . ."

"Are you kidding, Joey? Crack the window, let out the hot air."

"She can get turned down again."

"I know that. Don't worry about it, O.K.?"

"You like the school, like what you saw?"

"Is that a serious question?"

"It's a beautiful place. You wonder what it costs them to keep it running."

"Twenty-six thousand a year, times 425 tuitions. Am I right?"

"No, " he said. "A lot of it's endowment, old, old, money. That tuition money they take in is small change, school like that. A lot of the teachers, they don't pay them anything — a lot of them are rich. A place like that's the most solid place in the world."

"You asked me about Amanda. She knows exactly what she has to do. I had Dr. Maine take her through visualization and focus, the Monday before we left." Tess had a sense, vague but hopeful, that this technique might be helpful.

"What's that?"

"He's got a friend who wrote a book about it. You actually visualize getting the letter from Dartmouth. The fat one — the thin one only has the rejection slip. She sees herself with the St. Matthew's diploma. It's a kind of motivation. They use it in the Olympics. They visualize the victory."

"Hey. Tess. Go take a Paxil, will you? You're a smart lady. Visualize getting an acceptance letter from a college, for Christ's sake. Give me a break."

Tess made an almost silent noise, somewhere between a wince and a giggle. It was a sound of small surrender, an acknowledgement of the absurdity of the thing she wanted, or what she wanted to believe in, a sound that included the suggestion of an apology. She touched him quietly, the back of her hand against his thigh. He could feel her ring.

"Joey, you don't just take a Paxil, all right? Don't trivialize it. Drug protocols don't work like that. You know that. It's not like taking a tranquilizer when you're stressed."

"You think the Paxil does you more good than the other stuff?"

"The Luvox? Yes, it's better."

"She's our baby."

"Only one."

"At least she won't get shot up there. You can get shot on a train. An I-beam on the L.I.E."

"She won't get shot. She won't do drugs. They supervise the hell out of them."

"She's so sad, you leave her anywhere. She looked sad. She'll be all right, won't she? Most of the kids in her class have been there two or three years."

"You're focussed like she's gotta be, you don't stay sad long. You don't have time for sad. I'm not worried."

"She's got to get her SATs up, you said that."

"I know that. They work with them on that."

The Bahringers ate in a Big Boys on the New York Thruway, Joey reading a column in *USA Today* while Tess peeled the skin off her fried chicken. The dining area was a dull late summer chaos of scraping chairs and angry children.

"Look how fat these people are. Americans, all they do is eat. Look at that one guy."

"Hey, Tess, we can't all define our abs. You can't live on Dannon's and Metamusil. Weight's half-genetic. Look at Amanda, what's she weigh, a hundred eight?"

"She works out all the time. She has to."

"She doesn't have to. Her whole life is have to. It's why she's on that drug."

"He took her off it."

"Yeah — but it's still summer. Frank told me his kid went on Outward Bound, didn't need Ritalin the whole time he was there. Now he's back on it again, big time."

24

Back in the car, the day had grown dark and silent. Joey said, "We get home by 8:30, I can watch Florida-Tennessee, big S.E.C. game. Get some take-out."

Tess didn't answer. Maybe Joey had forgotten their daughter, but she hadn't. She was thinking about Amanda's dormitory room in Morison Hall, how perfect it was for its purpose.

CHAPTER FOUR

Her first night at St. Matthew's, she dreamed. She did not dream often; Amanda's sleep was fragile and shallow — the consequence, they told her, of anxiety. She had been prescribed .25 mg. of Halcion for this, but she did not trust the drug; there was a faint nausea, and with it a kind of fogginess that stuck to her all day. Had she brought the pills with her? She couldn't remember; and then she was asleep somehow, and inside a bleak undimensional dream. She was a little girl, her arms like frozen twigs, as brittle and stiff as a catatonic's; and someone had dressed her in a kilt and black knee socks and a black sweater. She was standing on a grey ice floe, being swept along, hissing and irresistible, some distance from the shore of the river. Along either bank stretched rows of older people, two or three feet apart from each other, most with faces that she recognized — though she couldn't be sure. But she was certain that they were jeering at her, even though she couldn't hear them. They were too far away to touch her, or to be touched; but at their last limit, as the rapids gave way to a churning rush that would carry her over the falls, at the final limit on either side were her mother and father, both shaking their heads: I can't help you now. When she tried to call to them, to

26

call her father's name, no sound came; and even in her dream some other level of consciousness told her that she *could* be heard. He would not let her rush past. He was reaching for her, desperately and finally, and successfully, just as the river was gathering itself into boiling dark foam and began tumbling over the high cliff, its power so immense that she could feel its force, its heavy, frigid doom, throttling her. Shaking her shoulder: Amanda, Amanda. She saw in grainy focus a girl looking down at her, no one she knew or recognized, and heard her say, "Come on, we have to go to breakfast — it's the first day, after that seniors can sleep in. We only have five minutes to get there."

The girl disappeared. The heavy undertow of the dream pulled at Amanda, even as she found herself, elbows propped on the narrow parts of her thighs, her head resting in her hands. She was sitting exactly as her father sat at the edge of his bed every morning before standing. It was a posture Amanda took for resignation: what I will do today is nothing different from what I did yesterday. In the background, almost seismic in her alertness, clattering from bathroom to closet and back, her mother, ready to tear the heart out of the world. Amanda heard classmates running, scampering along the hall, and she rushed to prepare to join their world.

CHAPTER FIVE

Savernake, one of the two interior dining halls in the Penrith Refectory Building, looked like the Hall of the Mountain King. Heavy timbers and ceiling buttresses of dark oak stood out against creamy stucco walls of great height. Old flags hung from the rafters — heraldries representing the founding families of St. Matthew's.

Hanging from a bronze hook on each student's wooden chair in Savernake was a garment, in texture and appearance something like a judge's robe, except that it had no sleeves. Amanda, like every St. Matthew's student, was obliged to "don the messcoat" on arriving at her assigned table; and at the command "All Rise," when meals were finished, had to dis-robe, hang the messcoat on the back of the chair, and leave at once.

A hearty-looking man sat at the head of a table marked Morison One. The man, Mr. Barber, a master, made Amanda think of a set of windup false teeth, the kind that clatter in cartoons: all there was of him above a paisley bow tie.

"Amanda," Mr. Barber almost shouted, "are you a sugar-firster or a sugar-laster, or a non-sugar person? Want eggs, Park sausages, more Park sausages, Mom! — breakfast like a king, lunch like a prince, dinner like a pauper! Not too P.C., a thousand pardons, forgive me. Breakfast like a *queen,* etcetera. The queen was in her parlor, drinking milk and honey, pure saturnian line, I believe. Sugar, Amanda?"

What could he want me to say, Amanda wondered.

"Sink your sails, Todhunter," Barber shouted at a girl near the end of the table; she had failed to place her napkin in her lap. Amanda figured the man thought himself a "character," but she was puzzled. The girl next to her muttered "jackass."

"You gals — eat up! No skinny minnies at this table."

"Thank you." It was all Amanda could manage. She never ate sugar.

Mr. Barber sat bolt upright, utensil in either hand, vertical: the autocrat of the breakfast table. "Everyone, introduce yourselves to your new classmate!"

There were seven of them, all seniors who must have been at St. Matthew's for at least a year. One by one they greeted Amanda, moving clockwise around the table. Hi, Amanda. Kate. Hi, Amanda, Jennifer. Serena, Amanda — Hi. Laurence Emerson. The three boys attached to the table for Fall Term each pronounced his name with a kind of shy confidence. On the wall of the dining-hall, just across from her seat, Amanda looked at two pale impressions, faded patches — spaces where pictures had hung, two of the fifty-six graduates whose names new students had to learn by Thanksgiving. The removed portraits were those of two disgraced alumni. The other portraits rimmed the great room. They were arranged chronologically, from the date of St. Matthew's founding. There were no women, a few war heroes, scholars full of years, their flesh scoured away by penury; a professional tennis player; four U.S. Senators; and all the headmasters, Dr. Passmore included. He looked just as he did in Chapel: sturdy and ruddy and with eyes both kindly and penetrating.

"Stick you in that empty space some day. Why not?"

Mr. Barber had been studying Amanda. "Peculiar thing to remember is that these guys were all failures when they were here. Either failures or rather quiet students. What you do here seems to correlate only unpredictably with what you do later. It's quite Churchillian: the ones you think aren't going anywhere, they wind up running the world. Where're you from?"

"Lawrence, Long Island."

"Return of Thanks!" A commanding, amplified voice boomed suddenly over a public address system. The whole school fell silent.

> *Teach us, Dear Lord, to serve thee as thou*
> *Deservest. To give and not to count the cost.*
> *To fight, and not to heed the wounds.*
> *To labor, and not to seek for rest.*
> *To serve thee, and not to ask for any reward,*
> *Save that of knowing that we do thy will.*

Sound swept over her, the hazy clamor of several hundred people eating together. It began instantly at the end of Return of Thanks, and subsided only after announcements had signified the end of the meal.

"Recognize the prayer, Amanda?"

"I don't think so."

"Aren't you a Roman Catholic?"

"Not that good of a one." How, she wondered, would he know what I was?

"Saint Ignatius Loyola. The Head Jesuit. St. Matthew's is Episcopalian, but Dr. Passmore likes the prayer . . ."

Again, as in the conversation with Miss Rodman, Amanda couldn't think how to reply. They made these statements, and you didn't know what to say, and then they just looked at you.

"All Rise!" Again, the booming voice. Amanda, about to take a small bite of her granola, rose, imitated her tablemates in the brief ritual of dis-robing, and followed them out of Savernake, and into her first day at School.

She felt a gentle, guiding pressure on her elbow — and heard a soft voice before she saw its face, the voice saying, "Hi. Toby. You all right? Don't worry about it. These people are all crazy."

The boy was the one who had helped unload the Land Rover, and now he walked, or rather ambled, next to her, over the stone brim of broad steps leading out of the refectory building. They joined a jostling crowd of students, a moving stream now dividing into smaller clumps as they headed for the several academic buildings and the first morning of classes.

"What do you have?"

"Mr. Steele," Amanda said. "U.S. History. She paused — A.P."

"Good," Toby said. "That's what I have too."

The culture of St. Matthew's was implacably hostile to leisure, to unscheduled time, to solitude. It was a place of furious energy and bustle. Amanda saw this at once and it frightened her. The school had become an institution for the New Millenium — on-line, intense, watchfully competitive. Parents who paid twenty-six grand a year, in Joey Bahringer's phrase, had a right to expect results. Amanda, fed into this maw of ceaseless assessment and pressure, now began an academic week-day that would vary only slightly from any other. She would attend five classes; required School Chapel;

required meals; mandatory athletics; Avocational Pursuit (for Amanda piano and, possibly cello in Winter Term); SAT UP; required study halls each night — for three hours, which, however, Class IVs could satisfy in their own rooms. And there was a breathless welter of counseling sessions, meetings with college reps, cheer rallies, concerts, addresses by alumni. The work never stopped.

United States History A.P. met four times a week, in the Haney building, a structure of singular monstrosity, a glass spaceship with pale blue pillars supporting a maize-colored roof. Passersby could see every class in session at once; could watch striding lecturers, turtle-necked knights of the blackboard, slumping students, alert notetakers, stupefied pupils hunkered at their desks before the gales of academic harangues. When they had seen St. Matthew's the preceding Spring, Amanda and Tess had been fascinated by the Haney building. Everyone was. "Not a lot of places to hide," the mother observed — causing the tour guide to look at her uneasily. "I guess that's the idea, ma'am."

CHAPTER SIX

Roderick Steele, Master of History, had lately become conscious that he was older than his students' parents. Earlier they had condescended to him. Now they began to humor him with contrived solicitudes, occasional gifts, Christmas bibelots from catalogues. On campus the conventional wisdom was that he was a tough grader, unassailably learned and incorruptible. His commitment to his work and to St. Matthew's was absolute. His appearance in its austerity suited his reputation.

Amanda looked before her to see, striding to the center of the classroom, a man of middle height, his complexion as bloodless as a cadaver's, his eyes fixed on the lectern. He deposited a black briefcase next to the lectern, withdrew a pair of gold-rimmed reading glasses, and looked up at his new section. He began reciting their names.

"We are all here. Good morning." Mr. Steele withdrew an old-fashioned mechanical pencil from his pocket and held it before them. "This is my word-processor. Edward Gibbon wrote with a pencil, and so can I. So may you, if you choose. I am interested in your brain, not your means of setting down what is in it, if . . . but let it pass."

"I work on the premise that you know nothing of the history of your own country. I am going to rectify that. You know nothing of our common history. But you are determined to get into, to *get into,* in your telling phrase, Harvard College or perhaps Princeton University. As you say, *what*-ever. A grade of five on your History A.P. will service that ambition. We have therefore a convergence of vocation and ambition. My vocation is to learn and propagate history. Your ambition is advancement.

But you *will* learn our history. Let us begin. Miss Todhunter. Miss Todhunter, what are the principal differences between the duties and powers of the Prime Minister, in England, on the one hand, and the American president, on the other?"

Mr. Steele's question hung before the class like a grenade about to detonate. Oh my God, Amanda thought, oh my God, if he asks me something like that.

No answer was forthcoming.

"Well, Miss Todhunter, do you at least know who the President is?"

"Yes."

Steele did not ask who. Rather he asked whether Miss Todhunter could identify the Prime Minister of Great Britain.

"Churchill?"

"No, it is not Churchill." Mr. Steele informed the section that the famous Briton had been dead since January 1965. He continued. "It is a pertinent and illuminating question. The American president is head of state, head of government, commander-in-chief. The prime minister is head of government only. His name is Mr. Blair, and he is a rather modest personage. He is not expected to be a *moral force* or a symbolical projection of the nation's character. That would be the monarch. Who is the monarch?"

"Princess Diana — until she died in the car crash?"

Steele looked steadily at the woebegone Miss Todhunter. The other students all stared at their desktops or wrote with urgent concentration in their notebooks.

"Always much writing on the first pages of fresh notebooks. Who is that one?" Mr. Steele pointed with his little finger at a president whose portrait hung from the wall. "Miss, let us see, let us find a new face, Miss A. Bahringer. What is your first name, Miss Bahringer?"

"Amanda. Amanda, Sir."

"Miss Bahringer, who is that man?"

Here was terror. Everyone watching her, this master staring right at her. She said what came suddenly into her mind.

"Buchanan?"

"Buchanan!"

"Yes, Sir?"

"Are you asking or telling?"

"Asking, Sir."

"Miss Bahringer, you are an honest child. That is not James Buchanan. It is rather a man who in many ways was his opposite. That is Andrew Jackson. What can you tell me about him?"

"The War of 1812?"

"What was his role in the war?"

"He was this general?"

"Yes, do go on, Miss Bahringer."

"He attacked the English army, but the war had already ended before he attacked them."

"Go on."

"Then he became president."

"Thank you, Miss Bahringer. No, no. There was a lapse of some years between the war and his election. He succeeded John *Quincy* Adams in 1829. So you do not get full marks, but you did bravely, and you know more about Jackson than most of your contemporaries. Well done, Child."

Amanda's heart beat wildly, and she was certain she must have blushed. She could see her fingers trembling. She could feel sweat on her forehead, just beneath her hairline. The relief! But was this what this school was going to be like? These crazy people blazing out at you, I mean, maybe not bad people, but like military drill sergeants, half of them with accents. She had never seen a teacher like this one. He reminded her of an old priest, one that would always know what you were thinking and what you had done, even before your confession.

Towards the end of the period Steele turned to look at something outside the window. When he faced them again, his arms were folded across his chest. He raised one hand to his mouth and briefly drummed his fingers against his lips, as though remembering something. Here it came:

"I disbelieve in the grade of A, or Alpha. Ordinarily the highest grade I confer is A-minus. There is a rare exception, but only a rare one. Here is my theory of grades. An A is for a truly brilliant pupil who works very hard. A B is for a brilliant student who is lazy or an average student who works very hard. A C is for an average student who is lazy or a limited student who is diligent. A D is for an idiot who should not be a Matthewsian." There was the merest, tiniest crinkle at the corners of his eyes, Amanda thought.

This was a famous speech. Each new Class IV history section waited for it. Even Amanda joined the laughter — in relief. She could tell her mother, after all, that this weird man never *gave* straight A's.

Steele was finishing. "You must write clean and vigorous prose. You must convince me that you know what you are talking about. I believe that you can write a brilliant paper, and not be brilliant. I do not believe Charles Darwin was brilliant. But he was relentless in his research, and he wrote a *limber* prose. What is limber, Mr. Carrington?"

"Flexible," Toby replied.

"Very good. One of my lazy bright boys. Darwin had the power *de fixer les objets longtemps sans être fatigué*. He could work for a long time with exactness, and could resist fatigue. He could *deny* himself."

An odd, low hum signaled the end of the period. Amanda looked over at Toby, who made a snapping gesture at her with his forefinger, winking at the same time. His expression said, "Hey, Amanda, you're smart. These teachers act like they're tough, but they're really just characters. Nothing to worry about."

CHAPTER SEVEN

"Amanda, you've got a call" — a girl's voice, almost a shriek, sounded from the landing. She found the phone.

"How'd it go?"

"All right."

"You get the courses we signed up for?"

"Yes."

"Because if you didn't I can call somebody. The Shumakers sued Andover last year."

"Mother."

"Is the hallmaster O.K.?"

"She's a Canadian."

"And. . . . ?"

"Mother. Yes. All right. She's O.K. She has an accent."

"When do you get your first grades?"

"I've been here ninety-six hours. I don't know when I get my first grades."

"You been to SAT UP?"

"No, tomorrow."

"There's a thing about it in the *New York Times*."

Amanda had found the SAT UP brochure on her desk at the opening of school. A boy, about fifteen or sixteen, with red hair and a Howdy-Doody smile, had just come to the full upright position at the end of a sit-up, and, hands folded behind his head, faced the photographer. A cartoon balloon issued from his mouth like a bright blue breath: "I sat up — 120 points!" On the wall behind him in what was obviously a kid's room was an old-fashioned football pennant: COLUMBIA.

"It can raise your score a hundred points if you let it."

"What do you mean, if I let it?"

"You know, work with it, work with the program. Let it help you. Did you run today?"

"No, not yet."

"Don't get that anxiety about anything. We had that talk before. I have to go. Remember what Dr. Maine said about complex carbohydrates."

"O.K. I remember. What else?"

"I love you."

"Bye."

"See you Parents Weekend."

Amanda tried to visualize her mother, the attitude at which she was sitting when she phoned, her desk litter in its profuse orderliness, her office at Warfield Stedman. Her mother squeezed and strangled time, she spent more time trying to figure out how to make more calls, stay more wired, arrange more meetings, than actually doing the work. She couldn't be still. She had a habit of sitting, leaning really, at the edge of the desk, extending a foot before her, rolling it around in the arc of a circle, looking at the shoe, watching how her skirt hung on her calf. She would be wearing, Amanda imagined, Carolina Herrera. The men in her office, and four-fifths of the partners at Warfield were still men, they didn't want you wearing manclothes, Tess had told her. No man likes that. Why try to look like them? You know what I'm saying? They wanted you to be feminine. But the only time she'd been in the new office with her mother, last fall at some kind of event in which mothers were supposed to bring their daughters to the office, she hadn't even seen a male partner.

A voice Amanda connected with the shriek from down the hall asked, "Everything all right at home?"

"Miss Rodman, How *are* you?" Tess had a way of inflecting the "are," that, she believed, made the recipient of her greeting feel special.

"Who is this?"

"It's Tess Bahringer, Miss Rodman. Amanda's mother."

"Mrs. Bahringer."

"Am I getting you at a bad time?"

As far as Miss Rodman was concerned, any time in the evening was a bad time.

"Because if I haven't, I'd like to ask you a question or two about my daughter."

"Yes, Mrs. Bahringer, let me turn the television down." She was watching a documentary about English architecture; a member of the Royal Family was host.

"Please call me Tess."

"Thank you. How can I help?"

"You know, her father and I put her into the school for a post-graduate year. I need accurate advice about her needs and your expectations. I know that your environment's a task-saturated one. I don't argue about this, but I need to know how we measure her progress, what she needs to do Dartmouth. That's the objective."

Amazing. On what planet am I now living, thought the hallmaster. *Task-saturated.*

"She's doing very well. Very purposeful child, keeps to herself, very composed, room neat as a pin, early academic evaluations reasonably good — does that help? Perhaps she's a bit tired."

"I know all that. What about Dartmouth? Is it doable?"

"I should have thought so. She needs a bright row of Alphas and Alpha-minuses, she needs to nudge her SATs into the 1300s, and she needs, I don't know, a couple of other arrows in her quiver. Will she be a candidate for financial aid?"

"Certainly not."

"Does she seem happy to you? Does she call home?"

"Yes. Remember also, she has her piano and her running, and she brought her cello."

"Yes, I've seen the cello, and I've heard her play Jacqueline duPre CDs."

"Have you heard Amanda play the piano? Get her to play for you."

On television they were showing the stout Prince of Wales. They showed how he sneaked out of his apartments near Cambridge when he was an undergraduate in the nineteenth century.

"She has her 5K times in the low 19s."

"I beg your pardon?"

"So her father and I think we can get her a nudge from the cross-country man at Dartmouth. He knows your program and he knows your course has hills on it . . ."

"Mrs. Bahringer, the person you want to talk to is Bobby Arnett, the college counselor. He can help you. I do know these colleges, the ones like Dartmouth, are awfully hard to get into. All our applicants are doing two or three things besides their academic work. I hate to tell you this, but our football captain was turned down by them last year, and he was a double-legacy and had quite decent SATs."

But this was an unprofitable axis of advance to follow. Miss Rodman little understood the *métier* of her new adversary.

"The key," Tess rejoined, "is both communicating intent and demonstrating that you have something they need, something they want. We are not spending twenty-six thousand a year to get her into Colby."

In truth, Tess Bahringer didn't know Colby from Ole Miss. She had read the name that afternoon in an obituary in *Newsday*.

"Colby is a splendid little school."

"Yes, but it's not our objective, or Amanda's either. If you can get into Julliard, why go to Curtis? Can I count on you?"

"I beg your pardon?"

"We can get her all the help and support she needs. If she needs tutors, that's fine. She needs encouragement, and there's something else I'd like to say to you."

"Yes?"

"She says you smoke in front of the girls."

"Thank you, Mrs. Bahringer, thank you. I imagine I'll see you during Parents Weekend. Good night."

The phone call, in a most peculiar way, had exactly the effect Tess intended. As soon as she put the receiver down, Dorothea Rodman walked directly to Amanda's room, knocked, entered, and said, simply — Amanda was sitting erect at her desk, working at her computer — "Are you all right, Dear? You've been quiet as a mouse."

CHAPTER EIGHT

There were several e-mail messages and Obligations Board notes to attend to. *Reminder App Deadlines Colgate Univ and Hamilton College are 1 January, best to get done and mailed even if not app for Early Decision/Early Action, R. J. Arnett. Running Physicals, Room #24, 5 p.m. Amanda Bahringer, poss consideration also Emory Univ., Atlanta — good profile and you'd be attractive to them. R.A.*

In the academic jargon, most Class IV masters "taught to the A.P." That is, the syllabus of their courses and the character of their teaching were dictated by what the Advanced Placement Program prescribed — specifically, by topics on the Advanced Placement Exams. A.P.s "indicated disciplined academic intellect," according to the St. Matthew's Academic Manual. Merely by enrolling in A.P.s, a St. Matthew's senior heightened her chances for admission to competitive universities.

Yet it was in a non-A.P. course, Pre-college Algebra, that Amanda found her most frightening challenge. She had darkly anticipated it. She had never really understood anything in mathematics after arithmetic; she both feared and resented having to engage the subject: because you had to engage it on *its* terms, not *yours,* as you could with English or Art or even Latin. Worse, the St. Matthew's master was a humorless geek who seemed to understand that he terrified her, just as a dog understands when you are afraid of it. Mr. Carnes did all his teaching with his back to the class. He chalked numbers and symbols on the blackboard at a headlong, furious pace, turning around only to fasten on one student, usually a girl, and to pose a question only rarely answered successfully. He seemed to relish his authority over Amanda and all the girls in the class, intimating that most could not really "get" what he was trying to teach them. He was right. However disingenuous, at least the textbook tried. It featured little sidebars and photographs of various mathematicians, all of them French or German, who had discovered or invented certain principles of mathematics. The sidebars confided droll humanizing anecdotes about them, regretting that, almost uniformly, they had died very young. Their early deaths were always described as tragic. Amanda did not think them tragic. Imagine the miseries they might have created had they lived to be eighty!

On this late September day there lay before her two bloodless algebraic problems. To gaze upon them was to be defeated by them. They were like the steel armaments, shiny and impregnable, of an enemy army — one who would never parley or negotiate, and who enjoyed the terror of his opponent. Amanda knew that an hour's determined application would bring her no closer to success than a moment's cheerless reconnaissance. What they appeared to want from Amanda was that she find the inverse function. She thought instead of Toby, and then of her cat at home, Cleopatra. She stared out the window at the greenback rim of the Seneca Forest and heard faint echoes of her favorite piano composer, Schumann. No one listened to him or loved him; he was her secret sharer. Already a few leaves on a gigantic sycamore just outside the window had turned tawny . . . a hand took her paper, sliding it away from her and moving up the aisle, sweeping up all papers as Mr. Carnes advanced towards the front of the room. Still not looking at them, he declared, "You are free to go, boys and girls. I got A.P. Calculus coming in here next period. Miller time!"

She prided herself on an ability to compartmentalize. She knew, at least, that she had to try. She craved solitude and used it almost as a rehabilitating drug, particularly after things that stressed her — like algebra. She never confided her need for this . . . aloneness; she just escaped to it. Solitude brought Amanda not only calm and order; it signified for her the safety of a tiny island of independence: a place and time that she might control, and for herself alone. For as long as she could remember, the world — her world — had worked her over for its purposes; and she had obliged it as best she could, but she craved respite and relief. Once she had watched Yo-Yo Ma play through the slow movement of the Dvořák Concerto, and she was drawn to the expression on his face, an attitude of transforming serenity, calm, of being at one with the music he was celebrating. It was as though he had no sense of audience, of place, of *having* to perform.

"I see you have the nesting instinct, Dear." Dorothea Rodman suddenly stepped into her Morison room. "Nuns fret not at their convent's narrow room, ay? Hello, what's this?" The hallmaster nudged a heavy textbook, *College Algebra,* that lay on the salmon-colored bedspread next to where Amanda stood, putting things onto a shelf. Then she withdrew, striding briskly away down the hall. Amanda did not understand what was meant, except that, by their tone, the words were intended as sympathetic or complimentary. She had returned at mid-morning from Mr. Carnes' class and seen e-mails asking her to CALL YOUR MOM and attend SAT UP SESSION THREE, GASCOIGNE HALL 7:30 P.M.

But it wasn't a nesting instinct, as Miss Rodman called it. It was rather the transforming character of her arranged possessions, and how they could be made to make this tiny narrow place her own island of isolation, of calm, of rehabilitation: all her things arranged, ranked, stacked in colorful symmetries, in linear order, on shelves, chests, glass fixtures, desk, windowsills, the small coffee-table at the foot of her bed. This array of owned things formed a barricading expression of a certain need: to affirm her domain over the meager space that was all she could now be allowed: a skinny room under the eaves of an old dormitory in an upstate boarding school — and, so far as she could, to keep up a few cherished connectors to her room, and the way it looked, at home: an oriental rug little bigger than a prayer rug; a framed print of Christina's World.

On the glass shelves over the sink Amanda had methodically laid out a dense collection of medicines, commercial preparations, cosmetics — the arrangements configured as carefully as a boy's deployment of lead soldiers: vials of Vioxx, Voltaren, jumbo-sized Motrin tablets, all anti-inflammatories used when it was necessary to run through pain; orangey prescription jars of Keflex and Amoxycillin; and of Xanax, Halcion, and Paxil — all anti-anxiety agents, none of which Amanda was "on," but which made up a certain calming reserve. Good to know they were there. And there were other receptacles: Tylenol-PM, Aleve, Caffalert to sustain late study and the herbal potion Valerian, which Amanda believed helped her sleep afterwards. There were some strays, too — she called them to herself: things she had taken from Tess's medicine chest, including Luvox and Fiorinal — which Tess had used for migraines and which Amanda had tried for a tension headache; finally stout little bottles full of herbal concoctions like Ginkgo-Biloba, Picolonate, Time-release St. John's Wort, and *Sambu:* the last promised weight-loss and energy, and internal cleansing, as did another product that assured a *Zit Minimal You.*

At the head of her bed rested two saffron-colored pillows. A Panda Bear (a gift from Tess) sat on the top one. On the floor between bureau and desk Amanda had placed her scale, a simple Harnett model C-300 with digital read-out and available memory: you touched a black button with your toe and the display flashed your weight the last five times you had stood on the scale. Just now it registered 8.22 pounds: the weight of a plumber's bag Tess had given Amanda for her books. It was an elaborate equipage — a muddy-green canvas kidney, the same color as the Land Rover, and covered with hasps, leather gussets, tuck buckles — and with shoulder straps with heavy pads.

Amanda had arranged her desk in perfect order. At its center, covering half the surface, was a blotter with green calf edging, another going-away gift from Tess. Amanda put three silver picture frames along its back edge: one of Joey in a Marine uniform; another showing her parents together at the edge of a translucent sea, goggles and snorkels pushed oddly back over their foreheads, the last of her cat Cleopatra. Next to the blotter was an old copy of *The Federalist* and a *Word for the Day* display.

The day's word was "precipitate."

CHAPTER NINE

It is a law of schools like St. Matthew's, a law timeless and unstated: adults throw scraps — of censure, praise, encouragement, ridicule, sarcasm — and children run after them like cats in a cage: devour them, are nourished or devastated. Robert Arnett, College Counselor, was now to become what the Gospel According to St. Matthew is to a nun: sustenance, a validator of faith. Through him she must learn and tread the path to her goal.

Today, as Amanda walked into his office, Arnett wore an expression of disciplined exasperation, of impatience barely mastered. Already, still early in the term, parents were after him. He waved Amanda into the chair next to his desk.

"Mr. Mitchell, last year they had 14,500 applicants. They had a freshman class of 1,100. They turned down a kid with 1490s. He was our soccer captain, plus he was a terrific bassoonist . . ."

Amanda could hear a tinny, shouted reply from Mr. Mitchell, about a goddamned bassoon.

"I know she has a 3.85 weighted. I know that. I saw her spring grades. All I'm saying is that it won't hurt to have her take a *look* at Northwestern and Tufts. Just take a *look* at them. The president of Tufts has the Nobel Prize! I think it's the Nobel Prize, and have her take a look at Chicago, too. These are fabulous places! You don't have a section man teaching you at Chicago. You have Saul Bellow — he teaches freshman. No. No. I do think she'll get into Princeton. I'm just saying the man there is unpredictable, he loads up on female athletes, that's all I'm saying . . ."

There was more shouting at the other end. Amanda imagined a heavy man at his desk, the thrusting skyline of Dallas or Chicago behind him. A man not used to being thwarted.

"You know we'll do everything we can. Yes, Sir. She's a great kid. I know what you're paying. The Econ Department at Chicago is very conservative. Yes, Sir, I will. No problem."

He hung up. "Hello, Miss Bahringer, hello, Amanda — Robert Arnett. How are you? Everything going well?"

"Everything is fine. I've only been here four days."

"Are you in SAT UP with Mr. Ebrington?"

"I signed up at home. I haven't seen him yet."

"I saw your course schedule. You can clean up with those courses."

"I can?" She thought she understood what he meant.

"Oh, yeah. The math is a lower level program. A.P. Bio no problem, ditto the poetry elective — that's just a couple of poets he studied in grad school. U. S. History A.P. — you want to do well in that, and if Steele likes you, he writes a hell of a rec. Where you want to go?"

"Dartmouth."

"You got denied there last year, right? I saw your folder. But that's all right. Couple reasons. One, you're a local kid, Long Island school they never heard of, they figure you're just naïve, don't know what you're doing, etcetera. Two, they *love* St. Matthew's. We send 'em great kids. Plus that, they're suckers for kids that really want to go there. That's important, Amanda: let them know how bad you want it. You're an athlete, too — right? Runner? They know that?"

The phone rang again.

"Sure. Put him on. Hi, Jack." He put his hand over the receiver and winked at Amanda. "It's a guy at Berkeley. Berkeley's not you. Here. Read this." Arnett pushed a catalogue towards her, across the desk, a scrumptious confection, green and purple embossed on heavy stock. The cover proclaimed: THE UNIVERSITY OF THE SOUTH. "Hey, Jack. No. Talking to a kid. No. No, I don't know — about six five, maybe two forty, two forty-five. He could play in your program, you'd have to redshirt him a year. Call the coach, what am I, Lou Holtz? Lateral movement, what do I know? Yeah, his grades are fine. About a 2.2. He's got 920s on his PSATs. You can do him. Do your image some good here, too. He's not a wonk or a commie. Our head thinks you're all still hippies."

A voice from Berkeley jabbered along on the other end. Amanda lifted the pages in the Sewanee catalogue. There were pictures of a dark cathedral and students in black gowns. There was a noisy direction at the top of one page: HOW TO FIND US. Underneath were directions from Atlanta and Memphis. Arnett hung up.

"Let's see. Amanda. This would be a reasonable presentation for Dartmouth. This would probably get you in, O.K.? Three As, maybe an A-minus, two Bs, around a 3.4. SATs around 1360, you can do that. I saw your old SATs. And you're cross-country. You can run number one or number two here, it says. They like that. Plus this will not be a big year for them here; we'll only have ten, maybe twelve kids applying. They'll take four or five, wait list a couple. You like St. Matthew's so far?"

"It's great."

"Think so?"

"Sure. I'm very busy."

"Well, that's the way. They keep you moving. But there's the pay-off up ahead. Why do you want to go to Dartmouth?"

"I don't know, they have great teachers. Also, because of its size? It's not so large you get lost there, you know? Plus the professors are accessible. They have good running."

"You should list a few back-ups, too." Arnett held up his palm to silence protest or assuage apprehension. They didn't want you to talk about back-ups, but you had to. It was like making them think about their college essays: they didn't want to, even the smartest ones, but they had to. "Amanda, one thing to remember. Back-ups don't always know they're back-ups. You walk onto the campus at Gettysburg, they think they're Williams. We sent a kid there last year on a visit and the admission guy asked him why he was there, and the kid told him he didn't want to go to a large university or a real small college: he just wanted to go to a mediocre one. You believe that? Where'd you apply last year, besides Dartmouth?"

"Hamilton College. Colgate, Trinity."

"And . . . ?"

"Got wait-listed."

"No problem. We can do those places again. They're nice little schools. Hartford, take a gun. What a city."

"The campus is nice. It's self-contained."

It was time to terminate the interview. He gave them all ten, twelve minutes.

51

"We'll meet the week before Parents' Weekend, and then between Thanksgiving and Christmas, O.K.? Start to get your stuff together in the mail, from all four places, and we may want to add a couple. In the essays, think about what you want to say, carry the topics around in the back of your head. That's a tricky mission, deciding what to say to them, you know? Don't force it. Think about it a couple of weeks. You know what you have to do with your grades and SAT UP. Hey, Toby!"

Toby Carrington was standing in the doorway, Arnett's next advisee.

"Amanda — here's a U. VA. boy. In-state, double legacy, a name like that. Just glidin' on through St. Matthew's. Toby, say hi to Amanda."

"I know this girl, Sir" — Toby flashed his easy grin at her — "How you doin', Amanda?"

CHAPTER TEN

Gibbon Gymnasium lay at the western edge of the St. Matthew's campus where, raw, dark, and abrupt, the Seneca Forest began. No contrast could have been more complete or more vivid. All the humming, polished regularity of the school's routines, all its elegance of architecture, of pollarded trees and clipped shrubs and shaved lawns — here all stopped abruptly at the limit of the great forest. The forest floor was honeycombed with running trails, meandering paths, old logging roads, most leading towards, or rather down to the Seneca River, no more than a mile from the campus, but infinitely remote from its enterprise and ambience.

The river was so sluggish that no current, no motion of waters, could be discerned. Even in winter its surface was an onyx-like blackness, an unglistening mirror. Yet the river was also deep enough, and sufficiently broad, that it could accommodate St. Matthew's crews for an uncluttered reach of almost a mile. On the school side of the Seneca, an old berm, perhaps three feet above the river's surface, offered a worn pathway, the longest portion of which served as a main venue for the training and racing of St. Matthew's runners.

Amanda ran like an adolescent American athlete of ordinary gifts. She had started three years earlier, under a new policy that required every Lawrence sophomore to compete in an interscholastic sport. Cross-country running seemed less threatening to her, less competitive, than the only other fall option — field hockey. The high school running coach had said, "You're tall for your age, and pretty thin. You oughtta run." She competed with a modest success that was the product of tenacious training. The transformation of an off-hand avocation into a serious staple of Amanda's daily routine came quickly and unremarked.

Amanda understood that what the coach called serious running also offered serious benefits — a message her mother reinforced. It made you lean and fit. And while you were doing it, it somehow lifted you out of your troubles and worries. You could measure progress. Your success was a function of how you trained — you by yourself, but how you trained was soon transmuted to how *long* you trained, how many miles you ran — and how many miles everyone else ran. She heard coaches gabbing away at meets about runner's highs and endorphins, but the closest she came to them was a feeling of dull exhilaration that seemed to blot out other anxieties for a few hours. Inevitably a new consideration was imposed — opportunity and liability both: Amanda understood that she might attain "times" that would aid her chances to get into an Ivy League college. There was, Amanda began to learn, a kind of system at work; students who were good athletes would be given certain advantages in the admissions process. Coaches were said to have unstated quotas, slots they could fill with the athletes they wanted, provided these athletes were smart enough to do the work after they got in. So Amanda no longer ran to feel free or feel good: she began to run for a purpose — for success in running, and, a year later, success in getting into Dartmouth. By now this had become her mother's goal for her.

The Seneca trailhead was easy to find. Amanda jogged along, descending easily into the forest. On either side she could see no more than a few feet; the canopy above her, lustrously dense, allowed only a meager dappling of the trail. The forest seemed a place of perfect solitude and silence, even a place of enchantment. The path leveled off and widened out. Here and there stood mossy hollows lit by bright slants of light. She sensed a lateral emptiness ahead and, only a moment later, found herself running along the top of an embankment at the edge of the Seneca River. An arrow cut into a huge maple pointed to the left, and she followed the trail along the river for some distance.

Now the path diverged from the river. It began to climb and wander again, at last opening out onto an area of the school campus known as the Far Fields. She saw a group of eight or ten girls in a semi-circle around a man, and ran to join them.

He was whippet-thin, his shins veiny — and his feet, she noticed it at once, encased in bright new Reeboks. He wore a white singlet with ST. MATTHEW'S A D in block garnet letters across the chest. He frowned. "This is it? Nine girls? I thought we had eleven." They looked at each other, back at him, and waited. "All right. Nine. The smaller the number, the greater glory, something like that. All right?

"This is a compacted season, all right? Two months, that's all. I hope you followed your running protocols all summer, I sincerely do. I sent them out in July. You laid down your base, and if you didn't lay down your base you're in trouble.

"Now listen up for a minute. Two things quick. Nutrition and training. One, nutrition. If we don't take *care* of ourselves, we don't win. You cover the ribs, you carry the extra etcetera, you pay the price. Replenish your fluids. I know a man in Albany can get us a deal on B Vitamins. Don't let yourself get depleted. Want you lean like a cheetah.

"Look at me, Melanie. Our distance is 5K — the 3.1 miles. Girl in California ran 16. 32 this year — did it on heart, diet, and training — some things you bring to the table. If you want to add your aquatic runs early in the morning, before class, that's your call. We'll do our ladders and repeats — and you get one solitary a week. Questions?

"No? All right. We have a great running tradition up here. Last year we sent two girls to Division One schools, both full rides. Don't want to hear any P.C. bullshit about doing our best, I tried, Sir, etcetera. We're *in it to win it!* I don't want to see girls sprinting the last hundred meters — shows you didn't really *leave* it on the course. O.K.?

"We have a great tactical course, half the time in the woods, along the Seneca and so on, and let me tell you it's some kind of a beautiful river to run along — it's almost like a *haunted* river."

It was strange, Amanda thought, to hear him say "haunted." The word, like many others she heard at St. Matthew's, seemed insincere. Long distance running was a challenge to self-mastery and discipline, not a subject for reflections about haunted forests and rivers. Coach Kellam wasn't the kind of guy to talk like that.

And then she noticed Dr. Passmore. He had joined the group in silence and was standing behind several of the girls, a well-behaved little black dog at his feet. Every afternoon at four he visited the different team practices. She could see that his pride in Kellam — a St. Matthew's graduate — was very strong. And she thought she saw, too, a glint, a flicker of delighted recognition when he noticed *her,* Amanda, in the group.

She read him accurately. He had recognized her, just as he'd recognized all the girls, and, especially, Coach Kellam. Here was one of the school's best masters, a lovely athlete, an inspired teacher, a coach who had once been one of Passmore's own students. And here he was, Passmore, starting out again in a fresh new year, his backdrop the dusty purple of the Tuscarora hills, far smoky vistas whose changeless skyline and vacant silences bore mute testimony to the legacy of history and legend in which St. Matthew's School had its being.

CHAPTER ELEVEN

T hose are Victorian baluster urns, my mother bought them at Broadway, in the Cotswolds, before the war. They do very well in here, but as a rule I don't like dark things, do you? A dark suit on a woman, yes, a woman of a certain bearing, always looks marvelous — do you remember those wonderful Davidow suits, what they looked like? But how could you? The company went under thirty years ago. You are Amanda Bahringer? Well, sit down, do sit down wherever you want. Hello, Daniella. Hello, Toby. The rest of you fend for yourselves, sit wherever you want. Sit on the floor like Indians if you can't find a seat! Daniella, do forgive me, a thousand pardons! Goodness gracious!" His eyes blazed earnestness and exasperation both.

"Dr. Passmore, I'm turning you in to the thought police. Prepare yourself."

He shuddered inwardly. He loved the girl; she was a marvelous girl — the best at St. Matthew's. She was a Mohawk Indian who had won the Iroquois National Scholarship as a St. Matthew's freshman, and, later, virtually every award and recognition, including several for *character,* that the school had to offer. She would certainly be admitted into the Brown eight-year medical program.

"I am sorry. I am old and halt, not a bigot. I am contemporaneously challenged. I cannot keep up with my culture's expectations of me."

Passmore was moving around his study, handing each student a sheet of paper, looking at each one as he did so. " . . . And, Amanda, that is eight. Good."

On the paper, without title or author, was a short poem.

> *I have desired to go*
> *Where springs not fail*
> *To fields where flies no steep and sided hail*
> *And a few lilies blow.*
>
> *And I have asked to be*
> *Where no storms come*
> *Where the green swell is in the havens dumb*
> *And out of the swing of the sea.*

Passmore read the poem aloud — with a small catch in his voice just after "asked to be." He loved the poem, and he loved what he was doing, teaching it, and teaching it in his own house, where *he* had asked to be. The room was silent, the students rapt. He looked at Amanda with the same gentle directness she remembered from the opening Chapel procession. Behind him on the wall were dozens of framed photographs of St. Matthew's crews and football teams, themselves silent witnesses to a living tradition, the headmaster as chief master, or teacher. This was not a man you would want to disappoint. There was a kindly earnestness in him, learned and earned through forty years' teaching and (as he called it) school-keeping.

"Americans are made nervous by stillness and silence. Have a look at this book *Dakota* — it's an eastern, Mid-Atlantic sort of woman who goes to live on the Great Plains, where people are quiet and thoughtful. When you read the poem I've just given you, by Father Gerard Hopkins, you must be silent when you consider it. The poem is called "Heaven Haven." Look at it, read it tonight, and you will not forget it. You will think about it some day when you are striding down Madison Avenue rushing to a meeting on the Asian currency market. The poem will put everything into perspective. Do you see? Testy, do you see, and can you believe that?"

"Yes, Sir. I can believe that."

Testy was the girl who had offended Miss Rodman on opening day. Passmore tried to imagine her, ten years hence, clattering down the avenue of commercial purpose, right in the middle of New York. "I want you to," he said. But he knew she would forget the poem as soon as she left the seminar.

Carlisle Passmore had offered it for ten years, half his tenure at the school. He taught in his house (Ravenspurgh, it was called on school maps) to a group of seniors with empty spaces (as he put it) on their dance cards. This meant that the seminar was filled with P.G.s or seniors without much academic ambition. There was a great prejudice against taking anything that "isn't A.P."

He taught A. E. Housman because he loved his lyrics. And there was a certain fit between Passmore and the young men, their mettle and thew, whom Housman celebrated. Once, when a friend at the Ausable Club suggested that Housman was probably a homosexual, Passmore's response was quick, and very much in character: "not bloody likely." Thereafter, however, he worried about it. He stayed away from the newest biography after he'd seen a headline over a review that said POET PROBABLY GAY.

Gerard Hopkins, on the other hand, was a ruling passion of Passmore's life, a Victorian priest-poet who, the headmaster believed, united perfectly in his life a triumphant self-discipline, an answered vocation to serve Christ's Church, and a celebratory poetic gift that took for its subjects the physical artifacts of God's creation. He believed that the example of Hopkins's life and the legacy of his poetry were gifts that old Matthewsians might keep with them long after they had left his school: gifts that would inspire and chasten, long after they had ceased to read poetry. "Do not call the Jesuit discipline hard," Cardinal Newman had told the poet. "It will bring you to Heaven." All that Hopkins celebrated and exemplified, Passmore loved: fierce commitments; self-mastery; silent, selfless toil; an absolute willingness to go his own way. "The effect of studying a classic is to make me admire — and do otherwise."

To look at the headmaster, to watch him, to hear his ordinary conversation, to see him eat his meals in Savernake or tramp the muddy sidelines of children's games, was to form an impression that such a passion for poetry was as unlikely as his suddenly leaving his profession, his vocation. But he regarded himself as an agent of transmission, a teacher bearing a priceless gift, this poetry, from one generation to another, the one long dead, the other not yet born.

Early each term, students new to Hopkins and to Dr. Passmore hardly knew what to make of either. They reacted unpredictably. Some responded in disbelief; they tried to get out of the seminar. He let them go. Others thought him soft in the head or a religious zealot. It was believed in the school that he had gone off the deep

61

end after the only woman he had ever loved had thrown him over for a Wall Street mogul in the 1980s. He'd buried himself in poetry: as an idiosyncrasy it was harmless, though it seemed out of character. And he had never given an F. There were many such reactions. Yet every few years Hopkins' poetry, through the head-master's grace and passion for it, really *did,* in fact, change a life. Knowing this, knowing this alone, sustained and rewarded him. What more did a man need?

Amanda discovered that she had virtually memorized the poem — almost without trying. Moreover, she sensed that Dr. Passmore had taken a certain interest in her. She left the seminar so enthusiastic that she called Tess, at work, and told her it had been her best class since high school at home.

"You mean you're in the headmaster's own class? Amanda — you're set!"

Only reluctantly — and sadly — had Carlisle Passmore acceded to the argument that St. Matthew's needed a SAT UP program on campus. They told him it was a matter of competitiveness: that parents demanded it and that his students would have to compete for their acceptances at college with one arm tied behind their backs — if SAT UP was not established at the school.

For *could not* (he was fond of such archaisms), could not the same intellectual benefit be realized by having the students read *Middlemarch* and *Moby Dick* and Keats? What was a liberal education for? Are we to become a cram school? Can't the students build and replenish their stores of words and formulae through the disciplined study of assigned courses? "Dorothea, the idea of hiring these SAT UP people revolts my sensibility," he told Miss Rodman.

But he had yielded. Forces for the future, grim-visaged and ambitious, his own young administrators, had their way with him. He insisted that scholarship boys and girls be allowed to attend the sessions (money would have to be found for them somewhere), and he repeated: muscular reading of great books by engaged minds — that's the way to educate!

The same day he taught "Heaven Haven" to his seminar, Passmore noticed Amanda walking towards Gascoigne, where that afternoon's SAT UP session was to be held. It was a sunny fall day with a fragrant scent of burning leaves in the air. He decided (he did it once or twice a year) to watch the session from the back of the room. Ebrington, the local SAT UP representative, had made no objection before; he wouldn't now. Ebrington was only a flunkey paid by SAT UP, like hundreds of others, to batten on the ambitions of parents and the fears of their adolescent children: particularly, Passmore might have reflected, on children like Amanda. "She does not test well," Tess had told Miss Rodman. "Not a single child in this country got into Stanford last year with a SAT verbal under 500."

Passmore had met Ebrington once or twice. He was a retired life insurance man who lived on a dairy farm near the school. "SAT UP is especially suited to your pupils who do not test well," he asserted. Two fifty-minute sessions a week, for one term, he said, and a sincere study of the materials, would lead reliably to rises in the verbal portion of the SAT of 100 points; and in the math, only slightly less. The work would confer confidence, a serenity even, on the candidate. Ebrington worked from old SATs, and he was convinced that confidence and technique would achieve results. "And it won't hurt St. Matthew's, either, if I may say so." Ebrington then named two or three rival schools whose median SATs had become, in Passmore's own word, *alarmingly* high.

Yes, alarmingly. Passmore did not like smarty pants/quiz kid academic achievers; or, if his students really were brilliant (he did not like this word either), he preferred that their brilliance be of a quiet kind, unforced and unselfconscious. He had a strong prejudice in favor of boys (and girls) who were sound, who were *attractive,* and who were likely to become sound and attractive adults. At the same time, he understood that the famous universities to which they aspired, like his own, Princeton, no longer cared particularly for applicants who might best be described as sound, as attractive. There was not a great deal he could do.

Amanda's back was to him, as were those of fourteen other Class IVs. They were going over long lists of words, Ebrington urging them to "nail down" their precise meanings: pitiable, pitiful; farther, further; precipitate, precipitous; amber, yellow, and so on. Then he had them read gamy passages from difficult texts, newspaper articles or literary criticism, and respond to questions on what they had just read. How well did they *retain* what they had read? And analogies — Passmore looked at one of the hand-outs: *Gray is to Maroon as Indecisive is to (a) Confident (b) Cocksure (c) Diffident (d) Uncertain.* What was one to make of such a question? The answers fuddled and frustrated *him.* What would they do to a child — especially one who was conscientious and interested in words? How could excelling in such an exercise prove or disprove her fitness for admission to, say, Williams or Harvard? The thing was sterile. He'd had friends who were good at crossword puzzles. This exercise reminded him of crossword puzzles. But the friends who were good at them hadn't amounted to anything; one of them was stodgy and peculiar.

He watched a handsome boy from Hong Kong respond instantly, perfectly, to every question Ebrington put to him. He wondered why the boy was even there. He was a nice boy; his hallmaster had simply said that "his parents cannot bear to see him at leisure."

Ebrington was talking about technique, about whether or not to *guess*. One answer was always clearly wrong, he said. Passmore looked down at his analogies sheet and found that in several questions he was unable to decide whether *any* answer was clearly wrong. He took another list Ebrington was handing out, a compilation of seventy-five words. He glanced down at it — the students were leaving on either side, murmuring Hello, Dr. Passmore, Hi, Dr. Passmore — he loved to hear their voices in greeting — and he saw *objurgate, gerrymander, nacreous, parasang:* what were they, and what did it mean to know their precise definitions? Did the alumni of St. Matthew's who knew such things — did they amount to anything?

"Well, Amanda — which will it be, Hopkins or SAT UP?"

She was walking alone through the foyer and started at his question.

"Well, which?"

"I guess both, Sir. Do we have a choice?"

CHAPTER TWELVE

Vespers. Evening Chapel, and she loved hearing the chaplain's opening phrase: *at the going down of the sun*. This Vespers, the fourth of the term, was recognized as Ingathering, a tradition celebrated at St. Matthew's since the early days of the school. Dr. Passmore remembered and extolled the legacy of all who had gone before, reminding the students that they were but legatees for all Old Matthewsians, and that all were united in comity forever.

Amanda wondered what comity meant. She sat in a state of easy drift, alone in the midst of four hundred students. Chapel induced a trance-like state: the fusty warmth, the gentle slow rhythms of the words and chants, the burnished bronzes and browns of the plaques and walls; the very motion of the choristers as they followed the High Cross during the opening processional.

In *his* sermon, the assistant headmaster, Dr. Carrick, celebrated the virtue of self-sacrifice and its handmaiden, self-discipline, how these would pay dividends later. Self-discipline, he urged, was very largely making yourself do what you didn't want to do, and it could be made a habit, and it was the habit of those who had gone before. Amanda drifted away from him, from his counsel that "worry, anxiety, about *one thing* not be allowed to lap over into the ability to discharge other obligations"; and this is the time of year, he declared, when it began to happen, when confidence could erode. Go quietly among your duties, and execute them calmly. She tuned Dr. Carrick out — to wonder whether she could get her 5K time below 18 minutes. No lower than that, forget about its helping with Dartmouth. The swimming pool runs before breakfast were not destructive, but afterwards it was hard to focus properly in A.P. Bio, or on the second Trinity College essay, which, though not required, was very strongly encouraged. She imagined an admissions person saying "this kid didn't even write her second essay . . ." She sorted through the words she could remember of Tuesday's seventy-five for SAT UP, and she wondered how she would get through Monday safely — her heaviest, and worst schedule of the week, including a practice performance of a Chopin Nocturne — again, unless it is exquisite, using Mrs. Thompson's word, it would be silly to do a video of the performance and send it to Dartmouth. And she remembered that she had not eaten since lunch, the great St. Matthew's staple, Scotch broth, a cup not a bowl.

Carrick's sermon made Amanda wonder whether she could sustain the pace the school imposed. In winters at home she had sometimes run on Tess's treadmill, programming it to make her run faster and faster the longer she stayed on. Negative splits. Eventually, on certain machines, you would break down or get thrown off. But you have youth on your side, Tess said.

"Dartmouth, Williams, Middlebury . . ." Carrick was completing a list. Amanda's agony in April, only six months ago, searing, unmitigable ("So we regret, we truly regret, that we are unable to offer you a place in the freshman class . . . represents no judgement of you as a

67

human being, etc.") still made the back of her throat hurt just remembering it: remembering the *Rejection*.

She thought suddenly of her father, how wonderful he had been. She remembered in particular how angry the rejection had made him. He told her everyone he'd ever met from one of those Ivy League schools was, like, a stiff. Pompous, and all they thought about was themselves. Not only that, Dartmouth was a crude kind of school. That movie *Animal House* had been made about there.

For Tess, the letter became a declaration of war, Amanda's failure to achieve acceptance her own. And in the months between the evil April day and this lush night of a warm October, her mother had worked unceasingly to convince Amanda that she had to remove what was really a stain on her reputation, on her honor, even, one that "can follow you all through life, one that you will never forget . . ."

One weapon in Tess's armory was the piano. She had heard that the really good colleges *build* their freshman classes. Everyone is so smart, they have to look for separators, for special talents — valued-added distinctions. Music was certainly one of them, and St. Matthew's certainly had strong music.

Amanda thought of Mrs. Thompson, the piano master. She was one of twelve of her pupils, all taking weekly lessons, all expected to practice eight or ten hours a week. Only a handful had ever gone on to music colleges. Almost always Mrs. Thompson was teaching students for whom learning to play the classical piano literature was an enriching avocation, and who sensed in their avocations a means of strengthening their credentials — to get into their top college choices. A Mozart sonata might well be the difference between Amanda and another candidate, Tess reiterated, for who is to know that a member of the Admissions Committee at Dartmouth is not herself a lover of Mozart? Proficiency in a musical instrument is no SAT score, it's not a high-class rank, but it has a useful quality to it, no doubt of that. Tess was not alone in her judgement. Others said the same thing.

Amanda did love the piano, and she knew she had a good ear, though not quite perfect pitch. The speaker's voice, Carrick's, was shrill and unmusical. She tuned him out. Mrs. Thompson was a demanding teacher, but her expectations were quietly expressed. "Don't be tentative, Amanda. Be decisive, firm. You make your audience nervous when you're not decisive. Energy, energy — read the instruction to the Intermezzo: *Mit Grobter Energie!* Don't play like a little mouse, a little ladyfinger! Think of Myra Hess, of Wanda Landowska!"

Who are they? she had wondered. Probably great pianists of an earlier time. Mrs. Thompson was in a straight-back chair just behind Amanda on the piano bench.

"Dear, may I say something quite personal to you? You could stop biting your nails if you wanted to. If you thought about it."

Now, alone in her pew, hearing the falling cadences in Carrick's voice, hinting that his sermon was ending, Amanda looked at her nails. She resolved to quit biting them. Carrick stood down from the pulpit and Dr. Passmore took his place. He seemed, she imagined, to be looking right at her.

"Hymn number 125, The School Hymn, All Please Rise!"

CHAPTER THIRTEEN

When Tess had taken Amanda for a physical exam in August, she had gone along in uneasy compliance with her mother's wish and the school's requirement. She sat in Tess's Lexus in a secret terror. Amanda had not had a physical — the very word connoted something viciously invasive and dominating — since she was nine. She dimly connected it with hypodermics, with steel instruments, genital inspections and the smell of anesthesia. All the way to the doctor's she sat mute, Cleopatra in her lap. She could only imagine the shame and horror of the examination: in which she would be discovered to be harboring a lethal but symptomless disease; or, though she was a virgin, one of those STDs with an ugly name and terrible implications.

But Amanda had no reason to worry. Dr. Maine, a social friend of the Bahringers, amiable, passive, and a chatterer, might have been a checkout clerk at Shoney's. He asked cheerily ignorant questions about "boarding school," about where Amanda wanted to go to college ("You ought to go to Tulane — it's right in the middle of that city — what a city"), about her running; and all the while looking into her ears and eyes and exhaling a breath that smelled like Scope.

Maine noted that Amanda was five feet six, that she had had measles, mumps, and an appendectomy when she was seven. The physical was anything but invasive and certainly not thorough. What the doctor saw and appraised was an elegantly well-formed American girl in late adolescence. She was athletic and supple, brimfull of health. Her complexion was creamily golden; she was lean as a thoroughbred, becomingly nervous and composed at the same time. She was proportionately long in the thigh; modestly-hipped; her calves longitudinally well defined, which testified to Amanda's thousands of miles of running: as did her resting pulse, which was fifty-five. Like Tess, she was thin through the chest, with shoulders quite high and pitched, at rest, slightly forward. Her forearms were thin, her fingers long, sinuous, and delicate. Maine noted also that her nails were gnawed to the quick, but what kid's weren't?

They stood together for a moment when it was over. Maine said, "You like to work out, Amanda. I can see that. You're a very fit young lady. What a pulse!"

"Cross-country," she said, "a little cross-country."

"She's actually a champion," the mother interjected, "or very close to it."

"I don't doubt it. Now. Amanda. Your mother mentioned that Dr. Mitchell had you on Xanax for a while, last year. And he had you on the Serax before that. You don't seem to me to be a kid who needs Xanax or anything like it. Xanax is anti-anxiety — but there's a big difference between worry and anxiety. We all worry about things. You worry, and maybe you got a little anxious. But I don't see the pathology there. So, look . . ."

"I had a lot to deal with this past winter. But nothing major. I told Dr. Mitchell it was nothing major and I could deal with it but he goes, well, I want you on this medication, you may have some serious issues, and we should deal with it aggressively. Only a couple of months."

"He give you anything else?"

71

"Inderal. But I hardly ever take it. Only for, like a concert or if I have to give a speech?"

"Well, I'd go easy on that too. You don't need it now. A school like that. Talent like that! Blood pressure of a baby. Look at you!" And to Tess, Maine added: "Look at her, is she the apple of her father's eye, or what?

"But here's a last thing. When you're up there, school maybe becomes a pressure cooker, make time for yourself, because nobody else will. Whatever you do to ease up, do it. Don't apologize for it either. You know what I mean?"

"Yes?"

"Take care of yourself — eat well. Lot of these athletes, they won't eat well." He laid a hand on both daughter's and mother's shoulders. "This young lady's in terrific shape. You like good food, eat it — and don't worry about it. Boys don't like you too thin, they like, hell, all men like a little upholstery. Those magazines you buy, all those models like fugitives from a toothpick box. They sure as hell don't appeal to me. I don't know who they appeal to. Good luck, ladies. You look like sisters. Come see me in December."

Mother and daughter had a light lunch together at the mall and went quickly through Saks, where Tess bought the beautifully cut pants that Amanda, on her mother's advice, had worn her first night at St. Matthew's School.

A movie that had once arrested Amanda's interest was *The Last of the Mohicans*. The leading actor, one of nature's noblemen, tall and commanding, ran through dark forests tracking deer or following elusive enemies; running with a confident, loping gracefulness that seemed almost unimaginable. The floor of the forest was jaggedly undulant, veined and marked by gullies and streams; by rocks slippery with lichen and moss. Yet the runner never looked down. He moved like a panther. He glided; his face betrayed no effort.

Five years later Amanda remembered him with vivid clarity. She was herself running through such a wilderness — a wilderness as silent, as darkly empty as the forest of her memory. At once, she sensed herself running with greater authority and grace: perhaps there was some way you could will yourself to overcome whatever kept you from running the way the man ran. Now, as the path merged with the widening trail that followed along the edge of the Seneca, she found her footfalls lighter, easier; they were almost silent. The green façade of the forest to her left was opaque in its density, a dark wall of trunk, bole, and branch, some strangely fused together in yokings of vine and bramble. This deep Adirondack forest seemed the living heart of another time, its floor still covered by paths worn by hunters and messengers. The river, now only three feet away, lay silent, almost motionless, stilly lapping the scree at the base of the berm.

Amanda had fallen into a habit of staring unfocussed at a moving point three or four feet to her right front, on the ground. She conceived that this drew to it, like a magnet, all sense of effort and of pain. On any solitary run, within minutes, she could make her mind empty itself upon it; could spill out conscious fact, fear, duty, worry, and obsession. She could induce a sense of floating. She could imagine herself a skater gliding over a swept surface of black ice.

St. Matthew's coaches did not encourage undirected solitary running. Junk miles, they called it. Yes, it could be good to run alone occasionally, but according to Coach Kellam you must "stay in touch with your body — the good runners all monitor their pain . . ."

"All right, Amanda. Go for it!" She was ripped out of her reverie by the sound, and by the perfect choreography, silver and garnet oars flashing and hissing, of a St. Matthew's crew — a boys' eight on the river, no more than twenty feet away, virtually abreast at the moment she heard the voice; abreast but moving, shooting forward up the opposite direction. Its thrust was stunning. And, turning, she saw the tiniest inflection of a boy's head at the stern of the racing shell — it might have been Toby's — and eight sucking whirlpools the rising blades left behind with each stroke, stitches on the black water, straight down the middle of the Seneca, deeper and deeper into the forest. And now she saw, no farther away than the boat had been, a girl in a white T-shirt, loping in the same easy stride of Daniel Day Lewis in the movie, running swiftly, silently away from her.

The girl's footfalls seemed weightless, the fluency of her stride suggesting she could run forever. There was an arresting feature: her hair, black and shining, had been threaded through the opening at the back of a white baseball cap, and it bobbed in a gentle syncopation with her stride. Amanda was now thirty feet behind her, the distance between them lengthening irresistibly, even as she sensed the acceleration of her own movements. They began to move in a silent tandem, the air damp and windless; and now, with no gesture or warning, the girl made a quick graceful arc of a turn, ran directly at, then to the side of Amanda, touched her hand as she passed, doubled back again, all in silence, and was suddenly running in perfect step with her, stride for stride. "Hi," the girl said, "Daniella — Daniella Ben. I've seen your name on the door, Amanda. Always working, door's always closed."

"Have to." She wondered, did she say this? But when people take you by surprise, you always blurt out the first thing that's there.

74

"Everyone thinks they have to. They want you to. You have Mr. Carnes for math? He's the champion intimidator."

"How long have you been here?"

"Fourth year, my last year. Four years for books, four years for running, four years for St. Matthew's. Just do it and don't think about it. We won't have these runs much longer. This is all snow by Thanksgiving, snow like you won't believe. It's an icehouse. Everything burrows in."

They ran together in silence, following the path as it turned away from the river, back into the woods, mounting along the ridges in the forest, passing through a bordering stand of trees and across the Far Fields to an old baseball backstop and some benches and a pick-up truck parked next to them. Kellam watched them run, gave a tight little wave — half Nazi salute, half benediction — and resumed talking to several others.

"Thanks for the run." Daniella shook Amanda's hand outside the gymnasium. "We'll be friends."

CHAPTER FOURTEEN

The school moved smartly, quietly, into the settled middle of Fall Term. It was a good term: productive, ordinary, pleasant. Dr. Passmore believed that it had been a *quiet* year as well; and this was his favored adjective when asked, by alumni of the school or parents, what kind of year it was. It was the question they always asked him first — almost as though he were a manager of a baseball team. What kind of a year is it? He had found that to answer it was a *quiet* year always deadened and discouraged response. People didn't know what to do with an answer like that; and in fact he didn't want them probing awkwardly about things that didn't concern them. He certainly didn't ask them how their banks or brokerages were doing. If they pressed him beyond "quiet" he would always say, "quite good." Passmore once thought — so he told Dorothea Rodman — that the school was like one of the old Cunarders his mother had sailed on, years ago: powerful, efficient, handsome. Each year, by mid-October at the latest, all the crew and passengers had quietly become aware that they were now settled in a new if temporary circumstance, and they were far enough both from embarkation and arrival that they were untroubled by thoughts of either. The dreams and anxieties that beginnings engender were forgotten; the anticipatory sadness and worries caused by troubling thoughts of arrivals — these lay in the safe harbors of a distant future. The great ship was safe. St. Matthew's was safe. It was remote from all the wasteful motion, the frenzied activity, the mayhem of life ashore. It might now be assumed that all the school's passengers were comfortable in the circumstances of their passage; and that the few who were not, were nowhere near enough, in their difficulties or their numbers, to deflect the confident energies of the captain and his crew from carrying out their mission with happy efficiency.

By twelve-thirty on this mid-October night, light shone from only one porthole in the whole of Morison Dormitory. All the other passengers were asleep.

Each piano pupil in Class IV was to play one or two compositions at the St. Matthew's Parents Weekend Concert. It was specifically in preparation for this, as well as in the cultivation of a talent that might help with the admissions process at Dartmouth, that Amanda began devoting ever-larger energies to her instruction and practice sessions at the piano. She rushed from her A.P. Biology classes to lessons or to one of the practice rooms. She found, also, that she could do her Czerny warm-ups, almost fifteen minutes' worth, on automatic pilot; that she could mentally prepare for history or something else while practicing. At St. Matthew's you ran to compete. You studied to learn an A.P. syllabus. You played — but no word could be less apt — you *played* the piano for a purpose.

Now the thought of having to perform before an audience of several hundred, particularly such an assembly as this one would be, terrified Amanda. Her palms sweated just thinking about it. In response to this obvious dread, Mrs. Thompson made the suggestion that Amanda's preparations and practices should closely approximate the conditions of the actual recital, "... simply, Amanda, because your imagination is so very vivid. Your fingers tremble even when you play before me, your friend. So, imagine when you play at our lessons that the audience is already before you — what better way to prepare for the real thing? And besides, who could ask for a nicer audience? This is a weekend of celebration and joy in accomplishment. And let me tell you a tiny secret. These people are not professionals. You may drop thirty notes a page and they will not notice. *You* will notice, for you are so very conscientious. I will notice. But they will not. Rubinstein dropped hundreds of notes."

Although Amanda was hardly comforted, she did decide to play the opening composition from Schumann's *Scenes of Childhood*. Mrs. Thompson said it was one of Dr. Passmore's favorites. The music had a wistful, dreamy quality to it; it was fickle, unbearably tender, and brightly happy. Moreover it was well within her technical range. Perhaps she could not play the big bravura pieces, the huge riffs that stirred audiences. But — her self-consciousness and physical frailties notwithstanding — Amanda *could* produce an exquisite reading of certain smaller pieces. Mrs. Thompson, watching her, was struck by the brittleness of her wrists; by how pale and underdeveloped her forearms seemed to be. A baby's hand might encircle them. But what Amanda could play, she could play beautifully. And at the service of her frail talent was a tireless diligence and seriousness of purpose.

Mrs. Thompson was becoming a friend. Her observations were couched in comments both helpful and sympathetic. In their last session before Parents Weekend — Amanda was putting her music away and rising from the piano bench — Mrs. Thompson talked to her pupil for the first time about things other than music and the piano, gently urging her to "Keep up your strength. From where I sit watching you play, I see too much tension. I see a young woman starting to be worn away by obligations and ambitions. And fears. Keep your strength. This," she tapped the keyboard, "is your dearest friend. Sleep easily and dream. Schumann has a little composition, you know it, about a child falling asleep. You cannot dream when you play unless you dream while you sleep. Can you?"

CHAPTER FIFTEEN

A re you all right?"

"Hi, Daddy. I'm fine."

"What's that noise?"

"Mariah Carey."

"Mariah Carey? Is that classical?"

"The last thing you remember is The Grateful Dead. Oh, no, you were in Vietnam — tough guy with short hair. Probably didn't even *have* music."

"You still working out?"

"Oh, yes — of course! Coach runs with us. You ought to hear him. He's like, your max VO Two uptake is a function of interval training, not just mileage, etcetera. He's really into it. He looks like an albino. I just heard the Dartmouth rep will be here tonight."

"They never let up on you, do they? Your mother should have gone there, not high school in Indiana."

"They didn't have girls then." Amanda imagines her father at his desk, placid, amused at something, fiddling with a lighter or a pen while he looks out the window. She pictures him in his starched white shirt with a black tie, brown pants, and black shoes like a priest wears. He calls his pants slacks. Her heart suddenly overflows with love for him, with longing to be with him. The thought of the Dartmouth interview terrifies her.

"Are you taking care of yourself?"

"There's a lot they want you to do. They're very judgmental."

"Judgmental, what's that, another SAT word? I'm impressed."

"You know what I mean. They're always on your case. Daddy?"

"What, Baby?"

"I want you to make as much as Mom does."

"How do you know I don't?"

"That's right, maybe I don't."

"I have to go, I love you."

"I love you, Daddy."

There was an envelope on her Obligations Board, a note from Miss Rodman: "Mr. Carnes concerned about your math situation, so go to him for help. Important." And another note: "Be exactly punctual for Dartmouth rep, Main Library, 5:00 P.M. Good luck — Robert Arnett."

Amanda did not keep all her medications in the pharmacy's issuing bottles. For example, an Excedrin PM receptacle contained almost eighty .25mg Xanax tablets. And she had put some of her Inderal supply from an earlier prescription into an herbal extract bottle labeled Milk Thistle — now it held about thirty, in addition to another forty in a pharmacy bottle properly labeled. She was like a reformed smoker: determined to quit, but not quite ready to throw away earlier stocks.

What the Inderal did was better, more useful, more *reliable* for what you needed, than any medicine Amanda had ever taken. So she believed. The original prescription was almost two years old. Tess had gotten them from Dr. Mitchell, who'd told her mother that he had prescribed for one girl who had to give a poetry reading, and for two concert artists, including a pianist with a recognizable name. The medicine, Tess said, was a Beta block, something like that, and it *totally* cured the jitters, or stage fright, for about three hours, and it was not addictive. You hardly knew you took it, but you could go out there, in front of a hundred people, and make a speech or play a sonata, and be as cool as ice. And knowing the medicine was there was half the answer. The Dartmouth interviewer wouldn't believe her poise.

She undressed and stood on the Harnett scale. 108.10; and now noticed, right next to the scale on the floor, a large brown box that had been left there for her. By Miss Rodman?

Three smaller boxes tumbled out, and with them a pale blue notecard: FOR WORK, FOR TIME, FOR REST. BEST LOVE. MUMMY.

"Mummy" had begun only a month earlier. Until then, for seventeen years, Tess had been "Mom."

The first box yielded four bedsheets and pillow-cases, all in jarringly bright colors: canary yellow and mulberry blue. The second held an alligator filofax notebook. The last, a green box secured with a gros-grain ribbon, produced a Cartier Tank Clock with Roman characters set on a face of blue jasper. Amanda held the thing, beautiful and foolish, noting that it had already been set, and that she now had less than forty minutes until her interview with the representative from Dartmouth — "one of the most important interviews you will ever have at St. Matthew's," — according to Mr. Arnett. Only the fact that the Dartmouth person was en route from the city back to Hanover, and wasn't far from the school, had created the opportunity. The representative could see only two Class IVs on this visit, and Amanda — "your name begins with 'B' " — would be the first. She took two Inderals immediately.

She sat at her desk, trying to compose herself. Her SATs were more than 200 points lower than what Dartmouth even looked at. Her quiz grades so far were all fairly good, except those in algebra, but her Lawrence grades were only moderate, a good word to use, if the issue came up, *moderate*. "Well, my grades there were only moderate, but I hadn't started to focus yet." She had her piano, her running, her cello, though she hadn't even taken the cello out of its case. She was in Dr. Passmore's own seminar. All these things were to the good, but what would she say if the interviewer asked her why she wanted to attend the college? Small class-size? Diversity? What do they want you to say?

What would he ask you? He would be stern, cold and puritan-like, being from northern New England, no friendly questions or idle inquiries. He would already have pretty complete knowledge of your strengths and weaknesses. He would be brusquely businesslike. Remember, Miss Rodman said, asking questions that seem harsh may well be a technique, simply to see how you respond under a certain pressure. Do remember that, Dear. Something like Joey trying to get a rise out of her mother.

The Inderal was working exactly as it had done twice before. She felt as clear as a northern sky on a winter night, and as calm. It was amazing. A young woman, about twenty-five or twenty-six, standing just outside one of the library reading rooms, put out her hand quite suddenly and said, "Hey Amanda — Amanda, too! Amanda Cha!" The woman smiled a radiant smile. "I'm the Dartmouth rep. You're right on time. Let me get my briefcase and we'll go in there," and she pointed at one of the rooms.

When she took Amanda's hand, Miss Cha put her left hand over the clasp, as though she were blessing a union. "I was at Emma Willard," she said. "I thought I'd might as well drive over here. I've always loved this school! God, look at this, it's like a *university* library. Do you kids ever stop to think what you've got here? I mean, don't you ever think, maybe this'll do it? Just go to St. Matthew's, and then blow off college?"

Amanda remembered Mr. Arnett's counsel: what they say isn't exactly what they're thinking. They may just be trying to see how you respond.

"Oh God, no. I mean, I know it has great buildings and stuff, but I'm really here to get to Dartmouth."

"That's what we like to hear."

They sat together on a window box overlooking the main quad, where all the cars had been lined up for opening day. In the first week of standard time the sun was slanted fiercely, making the green of the grass almost scalding to look at. The quad was empty. Miss Cha wondered where all the kids were.

"Most of them are still at sports. I got off because of my interview."

"Now, that's right, Amanda, you're a serious runner, aren't you?"

"Yes."

"I wish I could run. I can't get myself in gear. It won't hurt to let our cross-country coach know you run. He'll be all over us to let you in."

She directed the discussion to Amanda's application for admission at Dartmouth, with the practiced affability of a young professional who'd once been through the mill herself.

"So. Tell me what else you're doing here. Is it tougher than your old high school?"

"Oh, God, yes." Amanda wondered instantly whether she should have said the "Oh, God" like that. What did that make Miss Cha think — like, Oh my

God, you can't believe how hard it is? And then what would she think of me?

But Miss Cha was in a bubbly conversational surge, going on about music at Dartmouth, about nine separate orchestras and students entertaining *themselves,* not being passive. "What attracts you to us?" she suddenly asked.

"Just a great match," Amanda replied. "Plus, I don't want to go to college just to get taught by a graduate student."

It was not smart, Arnett had advised, to be needlessly expansive. Make the point and leave it at that. Lawyers weaken their case when they make more than one point.

"It's a great college, but also a place of what Dr. King called creative tension. A lot going on. A great diversity. Can you see yourself in a culture like that? I mean, how *diverse* is St. Matthew's?"

"I'd be all right. My old high school was diverse, on Long Island."

"You want to talk about your grades and SATs for a moment?"

Joey once told his daughter that if you had to give someone an answer that will disappoint them, you should finesse answering. Don't answer. People like to answer their own questions. Just wait for them. She looked away from Miss Cha, then down at her hands.

"Well, I have most of the data from Mr. Arnett. With an advocate like him, you almost don't need SATs. But I have your grades from your old school."

"I'm doing a lot better here. It's easier to focus in a school like this." Amanda felt a buoying confidence in herself, fortified by Miss Cha's questions. They didn't seem that difficult or searching.

"Well, you know our mean SATs at Dartmouth."

"I know they're real high."

"Close to the mid-1400s — 98, 99 percentiles. Are you a legacy?"

"No."

"Look, Amanda, I can't give you a lot of encouragement, but I can give you some. Your scores are 200 points below what we usually look for. You're not a candidate for aid. You do have St. Matthew's in your favor. We need to see your old grades mutate into As. You know what I'm saying? From Bs to As in A.P.s. We need a big SAT jump. I can't be definitive about cross-country — he'll probably get three or four slots, tops. Problem here is, a lot of runners are smart. That type of person, you know? Have you got questions for me? We are a reach for you, but . . ."

"No. I just want to go there. I'll apply to other places, but I don't want to go to them."

"I know you do. And I wish we could talk all day, but I've got your classmate Blakeley Warburton to interview, and 150 miles after that."

A Class IV boy in coat and tie and shapeless khakis stood next to the door, hovering tensely.

"Thank you for seeing me. I'll get all my stuff in as soon as possible."

"Remember, no great hurry. And good luck, Amanda!"

Again they shook hands. Again there was Miss Cha's special clasp, but it was perhaps insincere this time; it seemed quick and furtive.

One of the things Amanda told herself she could do was, literally, to look up every word she didn't know from now until the retake in November. Learn them all, all the SAT words, anyone could do that: just memorize them and run through them in your mind while you were running. Also, A.P. Bio, that was something you could do by just going after it, not so much by just brains. There were many things you could do.

"Amanda, how'd it go?"

It was Toby, in rowing sweats, running to catch up with her. He was full of the charged exuberance of a schoolboy who has just worked out. He hugged her roughly and danced alongside her like a boxer skipping rope.

"You going to get in?"

"I haven't even mailed in my application, O.K.?"

"So? Will they let you in?"

"How do I know? No, probably not. All she talked about was how great St. Matthew's is and their SATs, and she was nice, but you can't tell."

"It's all terrible bullshit. Nobody cares where you go to college. They'll let you in."

"My mother cares. I have to get my SATs up 200 points."

"You ought to apply to Georgia, U.N.C., schools down there. It's more laid back."

"My mother won't let me."

"Why not?"

"She doesn't like the values down there. She thinks you're all lazy."

CHAPTER SIXTEEN

Tess and Joey have been married almost twenty years, jogging along in loose if not always comfortable harness, devoted in different ways to their only child, and to separate interests and activities that sluice off energies that might fuel and sustain rage and even hatred.

Joey's daily morning cough, the consequence of the previous evening's cigars and cigarettes, has a phlegmy, crepitating texture that revolts Tess, and which, coming from behind the bathroom door, has the sound of muffled bursts of gunfire. The way he gives tongue to his opinions and prejudices — Joey is essentially a silent man — disallows their amendment or any discourse. She abides the most obnoxious of his habits with settled but resigned disdain: he smokes on the toilet, he drinks orange juice from the container, he says "don't" when he means "doesn't," and he does it on purpose. Occasionally he combs his hair in public. He spends hours upon dreary hours gazing stupefied at sports events on T.V. — Yankees, Islanders, Knicks, Mets. And Tess realizes that he's beyond amendment. He is a man of instincts and physique, immobile and silent.

And yet he is also amiable and tender and almost always willing to go along with what she suggests; she can tell that he is proud of her, though he's not very verbal about it.

They eat out often. Joey's menu annoys her. It does not vary: New York strips, medium well; potatoes; beer; cheesecake. He masticates slowly and silently, staring at his plate, pausing only irregularly to ask items of information or to grunt simple affirmatives to her questions.

"Amanda's grades came in this morning. Her first quarter grades."

"Yeah? How'd she do?"

"She got an A-minus, three Bs, and a C-minus. Good but nowhere near what she needs. I might go up to see her when I get back from Boca, even before Parents Weekend."

"Boca" refers to an annual convention of American public relations executives.

"What'd she get the A-minus in?"

"She has a seminar with the headmaster, some kind of poetry course. It's not A.P."

Joey doesn't know what A.P. means. He keeps chewing his food, now looking around. The restaurant is called La Granata, a heavy, ornate, old-fashioned Italian place, everything in it blood-red and muffled. Behind the cash register is a photograph of Frank Sinatra.

"Don't focus on the A-minus. The other courses are the problem."

"I wouldn't worry about it that much. She gets into Dartmouth, she gets in. She doesn't, it's not the end of the world. She can go to three other colleges. She can paralegal."

"Joey!"

"Hey, Tess. No one gives a rat's ass, she gets into Dartmouth or SUNY Albany. We've been through this before. All right?"

Tess picks at her wild mushroom risotto. Through long usage, she sees just ahead the wearisome prospect of an argument that will go nowhere. They've been through this before. She watches him take a long pull at his beer.

"The people that run the world never heard of Dartmouth. Guy that runs Marshall Oil, he never went to college. Bill Gates dropped out. The faculties of these places are all big-time liberal."

Tess reaches down and fishes a cell phone out of a Dooney and Bourke drawstring bag. "I'm going to call her right now."

Tess hears a voice at the other end, not Amanda's.

"'Lo, Morison."

"Hi, this is Mrs. Bahringer, Amanda's mother? Who's speaking?"

"Deirdre Chae."

"Hi, Deirdre, how are you?" Tess has no idea who the girl is, but it registers that she is an Asian.

"Do you want Amanda?"

"Thank you, Deirdre."

"You want a cigar, Tess?" her husband asks.

She stares at him, shakes her head impatiently.

"Hi, Mom."

"Hello, Darling. Are you all right?"

"I'm O.K."

"You sound tired. Are you tired? We just got your first quarter grades."

"Well, are you happy?"

"I know they have a hard grading system up there. I know it's much harder than home." For Tess this is rather graceful, even a handsome communication of disappointment. An A-minus, three Bs, and a C-minus. She senses Amanda's agony and moves on.

"So how's the running going? We'll see you Parents Weekend. Not long. And I could come up before."

"I'm fine, Mother."

"Well, remember, it's aerobic, so you're energized and calm at the same time. And you sleep better. Are you using your sleeping pills or anything? Are you working on your applications? Same deadlines as last year?"

Amanda has a sudden picture of one of her mother's bosses piling questions on Tess. How would she answer them all?

"January. December, I don't know. I'm doing A.P. Latin. Virgil."

"The earlier, the better. We talked about that. Do them before Christmas, and you don't have them hanging over you. Can you write the same essays for all of them?" She points at her wine glass, asking Joey for a refill.

"No, the essays they want are different. It's diabolical."

It registers fleetingly that Amanda has used a word like diabolical, and this gives Tess a frisson of satisfaction.

"Remember last year, Mother? They were all different?"

"Only too well. We don't need that again."

Amanda doesn't answer.

"How's the work going?"

"Fine. I told you."

"Biology?"

"All right. It's not that hard. Just a lot of work. Labs."

"What about your class with the headmaster? Do you like Dr. Passmore? That's a very nice grade he gave you."

"It's fine. We're reading a lot of Housman."

Tess connects Housman with the Lindbergh kidnapping stories and avoids a follow-up. The conversation is typical of their phone talks: Amanda exasperated, Tess persistent but wary. All the while Joey eats and watches his wife. He considers her a control freak; but, he thinks, so what? Dartmouth. Maybe the only way it'll get done, if someone stays on Amanda all the time.

"Can you get the headmaster to write you a recommendation? They must know him at Dartmouth. In the St. Matthew's catalogue they give a list of colleges recent graduates have gone to. Dartmouth has the fifth-largest number. Get him to write you one. That's part of what they pay him for, Amanda. Amanda?"

"Mother, he's *so* not that way. I have to go."

"Go where?"

"Piano practice."

"At nine o'clock at night?"

"I'm doing two pieces at the recital on Parents Weekend."

"No kidding?"

"It's not that big a thing."

"By who?"

"One by Chopin, one by Schumann."

Tess puts her hand over the receiver and whispers this news to Joey.

"That's great! We'll be there."

"Bye, Mother."

"That wasn't bad, Tess." Joey, always worried about Amanda's feelings, has again warned Tess not to come on too strong. "I just want you to cut the kid some slack."

"That's a terrible expression, Joey. What car should we take up there?" Tess is inordinately proud of her new Lexus coupe.

"The Rover."

But this is fine with Tess. It is a slightly different statement, but it's all right, and it's just as comfortable, and it has more room, if the Bahringers have to take some of Amanda's friends out to dinner, or join their parents somewhere for a drink.

Amanda went back to her room, sat at her desk and stared at an A.P. annotated course outline in biology, at a section under the heading *Prokaryotic and Eukaryotic Cells.* "She's a very disciplined young lady," Dorothea Rodman had told Tess; and Amanda could imagine her mother, bridling and bristling at the other end of the line. *Not what I want to hear.* She stood up and opened the hallway door, and sensed a presence, large and shadowy, in the hall, a figure of a certain bulk moving away from her door, already halfway along the hall, and moving with a heavy efficiency towards the far end of the corridor. It was a male figure, and not a boy's. Now the door opened and Amanda thought she saw, lit suddenly like a man passing under a street lamp, Dr. Passmore. She thought — imagined — she heard him say something that ended with the phrase " . . . come in?" The headmaster's voice was singular: he had a kind of accent, like a man doing high-class commercials on T.V.

But all this registered in an instant. Suddenly Dorothea Rodman's voice: "Amanda Bahringer, may I see you?"

Perhaps any Class IV girl but Amanda would have linked Dr. Passmore's visit to the hallmaster's apartment with the persistent gossip of the kind all boarding schools incubate. But no student at St. Matthew's could even *imagine* Dr. Passmore without a jacket and one of his signature regimental neckties; and as for Miss Rodman, well, the mind boggled.

"Come in, Dear, and be seated. The headmaster is here, though he's only happened by, so don't be alarmed." She studied Amanda's jersey for a moment. "Where have you bean?"

"Nowhere. I like to wear this when I study." Her shirt had a silk-screened reproduction of a famous portrait of Schumann, a jokey gift from Tess a couple of years earlier.

The hallmaster was wearing a paisley bathrobe and ancient carpet slippers, her blouse underneath buttoned firmly to the mid-chin. Her fat dog lay at her feet. She had a grade sheet in one hand and reading glasses in another.

"How are you, my dear?" Passmore asked. "I understand you're running with the Ben girl, with Daniella."

"We work out together sometimes. We run cross-country together. She runs faster than everyone else, so it's hard to keep up with her."

"This is what we call raw talent. And a perfectly lovely temperament. I shouldn't even *try* to keep up with her," the headmaster declared. "I doubt she has your gifts of poetry and sensibility, Amanda. All have different gifts: but the portions strike me as fairly equal, take them for all in all. What are those, Dorothea?"

"Amanda's grades."

"Let's have a look."

Passmore glanced at the paper. "There's the A-minus from me. An A-minus is a delightful grade: talent without drudgery. The other little Betas, Latin and, what? Biology, a bit of work will make them A's. Those are not intellectually demanding things — do you see? One can *do* them, whereas perhaps one *cannot* do, say, calculus or Arabic."

"Or algebra?" Miss Rodman pointed at the C-minus.

"I shouldn't frankly place algebra in such a category, either. Surely a bit of effort will bring that grade into line. You do so well with Hopkins, your observations are so acute . . . I sometimes think doing poorly at math is a kind of self-indulgence."

"Whatever else she is, Carlisle, she's not self-indulgent."

"No, no. I certainly don't mean to imply such a thing. Well, Amanda, I am grateful we bumped into each other. I know those laggard marks will improve next quarter. Don't overdo it here, too many of our P.G.s fail to taste the best of St. Matthew's: they work too hard, they do too much . . ."

"Run too far." Miss Rodman concluded. "Don't run too far. You do look a bit thin to me, Dear. Goodnight, now, off you go!"

Back in number 23, Amanda weighed herself: 105.90. Within normal limits for a girl athlete of her height, according to Kellam. It was not weight that mattered, but health, nourishment. She decided to do some history. Later she took her Valerian, and, for her first time at St. Matthew's, a Xanax — but only to get to sleep.

Perhaps she had fallen asleep, perhaps not, but she was certain she heard a knock, and a voice, and a statement, *Another call for you, down the hall.*

"Hi Amanda. It's Mummy."

"Hi."

"After we talked from the restaurant I called Miss Rodman. She had spoken to the headmaster. You know, all these people are working in your behalf, they're professionals who understand your interests and how to work with your potential."

"I don't believe you."

"All right. Why not? Why don't you believe me? I'm prepared to listen."

"Because you think they know what I'm really like, and what I want and what my needs are."

"Your needs? For God's sake, Amanda, haven't we taken care of those needs, every need you or your father or I could think of, since you . . . since none of us can remember? Your needs! Amanda. You have been given everything. And now we have a chance to really give you something more, and you have to trust the wisdom of an adult, this is a great school — do you know what Harriet Cummer said today when I told her you were at St. Matthew's? She said it is the most prestigious school in *North America,* and it can be the making of you. Do not let yourself down, don't wind up in some little jerkwater college no one ever heard of: do you know what that means?"

Amanda hung up on her.

Club Boca
Boca Raton, Florida
October 9, 2000

Dear Amanda,

Here for our trade meetings — you remember, we were here in '97 and '98. I have a couple of hours off, afternoon of the second day, etc.

I'm sorry I got angry with you on the phone Monday night. I know you have a lot to deal with. I know the academic standards there are very high, etc., and that it's much harder than your high school. Your grades other than the algebra are not that bad, and I know you're working hard.

One of the levers you should be pulling is the cross-country. I saw your old coach in Kroger's just before I left. He's says there's no way you won't get into Dartmouth if the coach there sees the progress in your times that you are *capable* of. So keep that in mind.

In our conference guide there're three hundred listed attendees. Two senior VPs and two CEO's are Dartmouth graduates.

Anyway, it's regrettable we had the argument, and it's behind us.

Dad and I will be at St. Matthew's Friday night. We have a room at the Holiday Inn outside Gloversville. It's tacky, but it's the best Marge could do, everything crowded, etc. Good luck especially in your final piano run-ups to the concert.

I love you,

Mummy.

Will try to get you something before leaving Boca.

CHAPTER SEVENTEEN

The prospect from his window: he looks away to the west, towards the dark rising eminences of the Tuscarora Mountains. It is a soft and mellow October morning, a day full of promise that is the rich sustenance of the very young and their masters alike. A bluish silky haze curls gently over the mountains, and between their marbled shoulders and the Far Fields his eye senses a shimmering hint of the Seneca River. The air is mild and sweet, aromatic in a way that baffles the sense: it could be May, it could be autumn. In the middle distance, dewy and virid, the Far Fields stretch evenly away to the edge of the forest. They are marked here and there by hayricks, crumbling smudges of stonewall, disjointed clumps of trees. Immediately before him the campus: the orderly, quirky symmetry of an academic village, cross-sected by walkways of native brick, its grass as green and bright as winter wheat. It is Parents Weekend at St. Matthew's, the fourth Saturday of October, and it is Carlisle Passmore's favorite weekend of the school year. The scene is as ever placid, inspiriting, majestic: it moves him to the premonitory ache he felt the first time he came to the school: the certain knowledge that one day he will have to leave it.

Later this day he will tell the parents that St. Matthew's is unexcelled as a venue for the inspiration and nurture of the young. Here there is still dreaming space. Here is a school that cherishes the old ways even as it makes prudent concessions to the new. Character here will always remain the equal, as a means of judging the young, of intellect. Character!

Passmore stands back from the window and at the edge of the bed. He has been reading Boswell's *Life of Samuel Johnson* and a new *Life* of Lord Curzon, one of his heroes. These and other magazines and books lay scattered on the wide undishevelled expanse of his bed: a bed wide enough for books, dogs, papers; he hates to get up once he has gone to bed.

As he dresses — and with a mild effort to disguise the care with which he clothes himself — he relishes the pictures his memory and imagination set before him. Pictures of the day in prospect, the annual Parents Weekend Saturday, this organized assembly of pilgrims, of shy traffickers to his School. In a way they are pilgrims to a kind of shrine, a place of exalted public stature to which the adjective "exclusive" was always linked: "the exclusive St. Matthew's School," a kind of Homeric epithet that seemed to drive certain parents crazy with a determination to get their children enrolled.

And in prospect for the day: coffee and conferences, the headmaster's greeting, the headmaster's lunch on Buccleuch Common, and the unending ceremonial of The Football Game, The Tea, The Dinner, The Concert — the whole round of activities so settled in the inertia of school tradition that each is preceded by a "the." The Greeting, The Game; The Lesson that he, as headmaster, always reads in Chapel, from St. Paul's first letter to the Church at Corinth. Passmore knows too, and chuckles at the invariable concluding activity: The Serious Talk, dreaded by students and parents alike, but always hovering at the far end of their anticipation. *There are some things, as Mr. Lincoln put it, in regard to which, I am not quite satisfied with you.*

He stands up, threads his cufflinks, walking back to the window. Already an excited cry or two, exclamations of delight or surprise, carries over to Ravenspurgh. He sees younger girls greeting their parents; the first time they have seen each other in six weeks. And his boys — always grave and shy on such occasions: did they still say to their fathers, looking them evenly in the eye like subalterns home from abroad, "How are you, sir?" No, not any longer. The fathers of this generation had themselves been at Woodstock. They had gone to Princeton *after* Princeton went co-ed. Now — he watches it happen — they hugged. He heard a father: "Hey, Tiger, what's up?" The boy and his roommate reminded Passmore of two storks in their tweed coats and khaki shorts and their sockless ankles. How many Saturday mornings had he looked down at such scenes?

Again he stands back from the window, decides on a tie, fills his pockets with his particular things — a Purdey's penknife, a pocket watch, a fold of bills. He flings a duvet over the slept-in side of the bed and strides out of the room as though he were a general leaving a military briefing.

In the twentieth year of his tenure, Carlisle Passmore had long since settled into a routine that almost never varied. Each morning — Saturdays were no different — Mrs. Selfridge gave him breakfast in the sunroom. The *New York Times,* the *Wall Street Journal,* and the Albany papers were laid next to a silver tray with the morning's mail and a single pill, a prophylactic against his only debility: gout. Passmore prided himself both on being fit and in not worrying about being fit. He ate what he pleased, as his father had: chops, hotcakes, eggs, Dover sole, good thick St. Matthew's Scotch broth. He did not "work out," but walked and tramped about the huge school demesne unceasingly, and this seemed to keep his weight and blood pressure (curiously, he could remember his father's blood pressure, but did not know his own) in a reasonable state. The cholesterol thing he viewed as a self-regarding absurdity; he hated liver and kidney, which is where it came from, unless you were born with the tendency. "Mrs. Selfridge, I'm here," he would say, and she would appear with breakfast, and that was that. She would hover momentarily, he might comment on the day's news, giving tongue to his amused and exasperated political opinions — very loosely, those of an old-fashioned American Whig. "It's a pity there's no George Marshall or Chip Bohlen around, these days."

But within a minute or two he was thinking about the day ahead, about School, either a bit apprehensive about having to deal with those naughties, as he called them, who had washed up on the sunless shore of the Disciplinary List, the worst of whom he would have to see himself, and later, with their parents, none of whom behaved well at such times. Harold Macmillan had said that a gentleman is a man who never complains: that simple. But these parents, nowadays, complained all the time. He did believe, with General Lee, that bitterness should be disarmed with kindness, and he schooled himself to the hard habit. Was it not also the message of the Gospel after whose author his school had been named?

If not apprehensive about some unpleasant duty of this kind, Passmore was, quite literally, joyful and grateful for the day in prospect. He was a creature of habit, as such men often are. Of contemporary blather about educational theory, multiple intelligences, tracked secondary paths and all the rest of it, he knew nothing. He was biased against experts of any kind, especially those who tried to excuse weakness of character on medical or psychiatric grounds. A hyperactive boy, for example: could he not be worked out vigorously, and tried or calmed legitimately, in the natural way? And why in the world would an attractive young girl not want to eat what was given her in the dining hall? The food was ever so much better than it had once been.

The Saturday morning of Parents Weekend was, take it for all in all, the best day of Passmore's school year. So he thought; and when he called himself to account for his opinion, he answered himself easily: because now his handiwork, his and the other masters', would be on display — the kind of display that always, reliably, vindicated their vocations and confirmed them in their professions. Adolescent children palpably advance. Their parents come to St. Matthew's in the thrall of an overwhelming prejudice in the School's favor. Its reputation, its fame, its stewardship over the best things in education, its loveliness, its endearing eccentricities, such things made them love the place, if on the weekend only, as much as he did.

He knew his parents and the alumni saw him as a reliable and tested anchor: a steady and weathered connection with what was unchanging, and must not change. He was growing old in St. Matthew's service; it was believed he would announce his retirement in a year or two. He would leave the School at the summit of his authority and reputation, but also full of love for the place and its girls and boys. He could not bear to think of it. He took his pill, buttoned his jacket, summoned his little dog, and left Ravenspurgh to begin his rounds.

CHAPTER EIGHTEEN

Joey Bahringer was indifferent to matters of style and taste, a condition that exasperated his wife. Tess particularly fretted over the impression he was likely to make at Parents Weekend, and she resolved to do something about it. She called the manager of The Regiment, Lawrence's toniest haberdasher, and told him that she would be accompanying Mr. Bahringer on a visit to the store.

But as Joey stood, the Saturday of Parents Weekend at St. Matthew's, at the ten-yard line of the varsity football field, Tess thought that her husband, in his double-breasted mohair-and-silk suit, looked much more like a gangster than a St. Matthew's parent. She made herself concentrate instead on the sweetness of the air, on the silver and garnet pennants floating lazily from the tips of the goal posts. Girls' cross-country, meantime, was soon to begin its five-kilometer race, the event to conclude just as the football teams were returning from halftime.

The time and place were selected to assure something of an audience for the early part of the 5K. Two or three other parents joined the Bahringers near the goal posts, greeting each other a trifle awkwardly with comments about the Glorious Day and the motel. Tess was moved to ask one mother what she did.

"I beg your pardon?"

"What do you do?"

"Oh, I keep busy . . ." came the response, a mischievous, unmistakably snotty inflection undergirding the "I." Tess had never quite bumped into this, this tactic, this amused statement: you work, and I don't have to.

And there she was. Amanda, trotting in dainty circles with six or seven other St. Matthew's girls, all stopping occasionally to bounce a bit on their toes, all the while shaking out their arms like swimmers on starting blocks. Their daughter hadn't seen them yet, but Joey couldn't restrain himself: "Hey, Amanda, Hey, Baby, over here!" — at which Tess grabbed his arm, pinching his flesh just above the elbow so that it really hurt him. "Pipe down," she hissed, "You embarrass her, and you embarrass me. Shea Stadium, this isn't."

But it was too late. She had seen them, and they both saw the quick flash of delight and then her mastering wan smile and faint, waist-high wave — a happy acknowledgement and a nervous admonition both. She joined the other girls from both teams as they lined up along the ten-yard line. A loudspeaker crackled into grainy voice, giving the girls' names and team records. With delicious satisfaction Tess Bahringer heard her own daughter's name pronounced: ". . . Amanda Bahringer, St. Matthew's Class IV, Lawrence, Long Island, New York — the name bracketed between those of girls from Far Hills, New Jersey, and Santa Barbara, California.

Tess watched Amanda lean forward, arms dangling. Amanda looked down at the ground, then over at the starter, and perhaps, Tess could not really tell, at her mother. Just next to Amanda, to her left, Tess noticed another St. Matthew's runner, this one taller, stronger-looking than the others, a girl with shiny raven hair and an olive complexion. She projected a confident attitude, the aura of an easy winner, Tess thought. And when, a moment later, the fifteen runners took off, the girl loped swiftly, effortlessly ahead. By the time the girls had passed under the goalposts at the far end of the football field, running off into the woods to the right, the tall girl already had a ten-yard lead on the next runner — who was, however, Amanda.

"Kid's really something, huh?"

"Probably has a scholarship," Tess answered.

"Amanda looks good."

It is the worst spectator sport of all. One sees the runners for a minute; they disappear; are seen again, hurtling in a foggy distance, their singlet colors suddenly flashing brokenly between stands of trees; then nothing for ten or twelve minutes; finally, in a long, ragged stream, gasping and lunging, heads bobbing on narrow shoulders, they appear again, straining to finish at the original starting line — usually in a desperate and disjointed sprint, each trying to gain a place or two at the finish.

So husband and wife had a few minutes to kill. They walked to the visiting team bleachers on the far side of the field. A thickset man with his back to them was nodding a greeting to two St. Matthew's boys and an adult, the boys both in tweed jackets and ungainly khaki shorts. The man had turned to face them: Dr. Passmore!

He had an expression that made Tess think of pictures of Franklin D. Roosevelt. He walked right over to them, extended his hand: "Hello, hello, awfully nice to *have* you here. Carlisle Passmore."

"Joey Bahringer, Doctor. This is my wife, Tess? Our daughter's one of your P.G.s — Amanda? You may not know her, but she knows *you*."

"She idolizes you."

"How do you do? Thank you. I know Amanda. She has made a wonderful start here. She is in my Hopkins seminar, and I've seen her several times."

"It's wonderful the way you know all the students."

"Well, I can't say I know every one by name, but I've always disliked being in the office; I like to be about."

"She says you make them memorize poetry."

"Yes. That's how to make them learn it. Because after they have it by heart, it comes back to them when they don't expect it to, and they think about it. Are you comfortable in your motel, Mrs. Bahringer?"

"Please call me Tess. We're fine. We're thrilled that Amanda's here."

"Well. She is most industrious. Quite indefatigable in all her enterprises."

Tess had never heard the word pronounced accurately, and it pleased her to hear it in reference to Amanda. She heard Joey say something that sounded like "really great of you to help her, the thing is really working out."

"I'm so glad."

"We thought she hadda have a post-graduate year somewhere," Joey said, his wife wincing at the "hadda." "We wanted to get her into a good college, and it didn't work out at home, at our local school."

"Her dream is to go to Dartmouth College," Tess interjected.

"Very sound school, very sound. Strong history and nicely sized. Rather left-wing of late, of course, but one expects that of the young and of New England generally. Lots of angst and self-absorption."

"She needs to get her grades to where they'll get her in?"

"Yes, yes. They're all obsessed with their grades. Where will the child apply? I've seen her in the SAT UP class."

"You mean besides Dartmouth?"

"Yes."

Tess didn't care for the question or having to answer it: "Colgate College, here in New York."

"Ah, Colgate University. Very decent indeed. I should surely encourage an application to Colgate. Where were you educated, Mr. Bahringer?"

"Joey. At Fordham, down in New York."

"I admire it greatly. There is a school that knows its own mind. A school with conviction. I shouldn't wonder that Amanda might not flourish at her father's own alma mater."

Tess was horrified. Fordham! Did the headmaster imagine they'd sent their daughter to St. Matthew's to have her go to Fordham? She said, "This is a busy day for you."

"Yes, but you know, I love it. I love Octobers — scholars' springtimes, and wonderful new friends."

Tess thought she caught him looking at Joey's suit.

"But I must be off. Another family to meet. What a pleasure seeing both of you. And we will see each other at the concert tonight? And perhaps after Chapel, at Ravenspurgh?"

"Thank you, Dr. Passmore." Reflexively Tess put out her hand, and he took it, not in a handshake, but in a deft quick hold of the fingers, looking directly at her.

"Some kinda guy, no?"

"This is why she's here, Joey."

The 5K ended where it had begun, under the goalposts, the winner the formidable girl who had built a strong lead even before the runners had turned off the field. Her stride, her poise, the easy confidence in her face, seemed no different from when she had started. No other runner was close to her. She crossed the finish line, trotted a few steps, and began walking along the other side of the field. Tess heard the girl's voice, calling out: "Amanda, you've got her, go for it, Amanda!"

And here her daughter came, leading a wobbling cluster of exhausted runners, their heads bobbing like marionettes, faces sallow and arms beating the air. With each desperate lunging stride, Amanda's nearest competitor gained a few inches; until, less than ten yards from the finish, she passed her.

Amanda staggered over the finish line, and — they couldn't really tell — seemed to wave them away. Perhaps it was only a wild, spasmodic gesture of exhaustion and hurt. For a second Amanda threw her head back and seemed to stare straight up, all the while walking in circles with her hands on her hips, gasping. Joey was struck by her color — a kind of unhealthy, creamy pallor.

"It's all right, it's O.K. I went out too fast. We all go out too fast."

She stepped forward towards them, reached at her father and fell into his arms. "Thanks for coming, Daddy, thank you." He made space for his wife and his daughter and they all hugged each other at once.

CHAPTER NINETEEN

Joey and Tess stood in a tight burble of excited parents, all anxious and talkative. The overheated concert hall was mildly intimidating. None of the students they'd seen yelling at the football game seemed to have come to the concert; it appeared that this place was where the parents of the school nerds congregated — but girls were not, couldn't be, nerds. Tess wondered what she would say to another parent, if for example the other parent said anything to her about music; she didn't really trust herself to talk about it, and, as for Joey, he didn't know Schumann from the Grateful Dead. But he remembered Amanda's fondness for him.

He said to Tess, "I remember the one guy's name, Schumann. She likes to play his works."

"He was a manic depressive, there was a thing about him on television Tuesday night. He tried to kill himself by jumping into the Rhine River . . ."

"These composers are all manic, you know?"

"Mr. and Mrs. Bahringer, we meet again!" Dr. Passmore and Miss Rodman were squeezing their way along the wall, trying to get to the entrance to the hall, caught up in the dense press of parents and students shuffling back from the first intermission.

"Quite a crowd," he said. "How was your afternoon? Had dinner somewhere? This concert is the apogee of Parents Weekend."

There was an awkward, half-missed handshake. Passmore took Tess's hand and looked down at it, causing her to think that perhaps he was going to kiss her there. But no. He simply held her hand, beamed out his beneficence, and told her how good she was to have come all the way up to the school for the weekend. "And didn't you tell me that you're out on Long Island? Have they got you in the Holiday Inn? Hostelry is not our strong suit in Fulton County!"

She was transfixed. He seemed to glow. His diction, the way he sounded, his accent . . . she was close enough to notice his Bay Rum — no commercial aftershave, nothing she had ever smelled before — it must be English and his shirt — shirting? — pale yellow and laundered to an immaculate perfection, and there was a tiny Navy device at the edge of the left lapel of his coat. She got a glimpse of an old Cartier Tank watch; it screamed breeding. Even in the dim lighting she could distinguish the unusual curlicues and inverted herringbones in the weave of Passmore's jacket, and the peculiar little devices on his tie, like tiny gold beavers or windmills. Her face was only four or five inches from his shoulder, such was the press of the crowd. She wondered at once what he must make of her, whether he would make allowances for the disheveled state in which he found all the parents by the time they got to Saturday night, whether her scent, an Eau D'Harien of Annick Goutal, was too daylightish. She was still wearing exactly what she wore when she and Joey had arrived late in the morning after their long drive from Lawrence: her Rhinelander wool jacket, her suede vest and beryl ascot. Being put together like this always took the edge off Tess's anxiety, but not much more, because the fabric wrinkled and the colors were lost, and the place made her think she was in a room where everyone had a fever. Her sensible shoes! But perhaps he wouldn't notice them.

Amanda walked out shyly, looking at the audience, or where the audience must be. Focussing only on the Steinway, she walked deliberately to the bench, sat down and placed the tips of her fingers on the keys. The way the stage and the piano had been lit, the dusty lucence of the spotlight slanting down on her, accentuated Amanda's vulnerability. She did not immediately begin to play, and this silence had the effect of quieting the hall utterly, so that, when she did, the audience was rapt. Her playing sounded almost like a harpsichord's, quavering and clear, the rendering of the melody as effortless as falling silk. In truth, no composition she had ever played was closer to her heart than this little piece of Schumann's. Tess looked at Joey with pride and relief. She was amazed at Amanda's poise: she seemed without nervousness or fear. St. Matthew's had done this; she had not played like this before. And the audience had not heard a student play like this before, either, to judge its absorption and, at the end, its applause for her daughter: it sounded both amazed and grateful, and it sounded the same way after she had played her Chopin, too.

Dr. Passmore and Miss Rodman were sitting two rows in front of them, and Tess could see the headmaster's hands, his fingers splayed on either side of his chin, his head shaking from time to time, as if, she imagined, in wonder. At the end of the Chopin, Amanda paused for a moment, her hands motionless over the keyboard, as if bestowing a benediction on the music.

The audience, a third of it students, applauded almost boisterously. There were yawps of Yay, Amanda!

Go, Amanda! And a single All Right! Dr. Passmore turned around and looked directly at Tess, and, rather histrionically, held up both hands to show how vigorously he was applauding her — Tess's — daughter.

They met with two teachers, Amanda's Biology and Latin masters. They heard essentially the same messages from each. Quiet, conscientious, girl. You should be . . . pleased. We are . . . she's a real plugger.

This weary information, which sounded condescending although honest, did not satisfy Tess. It resonated sharply with earlier memories; indeed with the very predicament that had led to Amanda's enrollment at St. Matthew's. These colleges, Dartmouth, wherever, they don't want pluggers. Pluggers! The whole thing now was *not* to be a plugger, but to be brilliant. At the NASDAQ companies, the IPOs, consultants, law schools . . . they wanted . . .

They sat with their daughter in her room — the narrowness of the chamber forced daughter and father to sit next to each other on Amanda's bed — while Tess faced, or rather looked down on them from her perch against the sink, her hand on top of Amanda's computer.

Joey asked whether she was sore from the run.

"No, Daddy. Not really sore. I'm not that happy with my times."

"Are you eating well?" Tess asked. "Is the food good?"

"I think it's all right. It's not a big item, you know?"

"What about sleep? Are you using the Halcion?"

"I think I left it at home, I can't remember. Yes, I'm sleeping enough. I miss Cleopatra, are you taking care of her?"

"She misses you, too. Yes, we're taking perfect care of her."

"Did you talk to Mr. Arnett — the college counselor? Did he give you my performance objectives? What you need to do get into where you want to go?"

"No. What's he say?"

"I'm probably all right at Hamilton and Trinity. Maybe Colgate. It depends on my SATs. He wants me to apply to Emory, it's a school in Atlanta, Georgia."

"What's he say about Dartmouth?"

"The other colleges are eye levels. Dartmouth's still a reach. But I have a shot, I think . . . he thinks."

"That's what I think," Tess said. "Amanda, Sweetie, we put you here to bring out your best. Because I know and you know that your best will get you what we all want. If you bear down and don't let up there will be a pay-off, and we'll have this conversation in ten years, and you will thank your mother. She looked down at a framed photograph on the blotter. "Who's this?"

"Gerard Manley Hopkins. He's a priest? No — he's a great poet who was a priest."

"An Episcopalian priest?" The School seemed so Episcopalian, with all its vestments and rituals.

"No, Catholic. We read his poems in class. I love his poetry and I love him."

"Is the class A.P.?"

"No, remember I told you it's the headmaster's seminar?"

"That's right," Tess said. "I remember. That's a good thing to take. We have to leave. Now, Amanda. Amanda. Now look at me. Give me your hands and look at me. *You can do it.* Maybe go a little lighter on your piano practices and save that time and use it on your algebra. We love you. Don't get too thin. I'm going to send you some care packages. Oh — and watch that girl, what is she, a Native American girl? — watch how *she* runs. Supposedly she's got fabulous grades. What does that tell us about what *this* girl can do?" Tess touched the dimple in Amanda's chin with her forefinger. "This girl?"

PART TWO

CHAPTER TWENTY

The loudspeaker in Savernake blared,

"Victories and Achievements," November 6, 2000, Attention Please: Nigel Hammerbeck, ESU student from Harrow, Class IV, was today notified of his admission to Oxford University, Christ Church College, for October 2001.

Amherst College-Open Scholarship examinations will be held in Gascoigne, Room 200, 8:00 P.M.

There are two systemic departures, both Class III.

SATs to be administered Saturday morning, 12 November, Main Court, Gibbon Gymnasium. Resume."

Obligations Board: YOU DO NOT AND WILL NOT FIT HERE.

Tess would not have revealed the following secret had you threatened her with immersion in boiling oil.

The secret was, that until she was sixteen, she believed that private school was not a category of educational institution, but a place. One night at Girl

Scout camp on the Wabash, she had looked up from the top berth of a double bunk and seen, scratched and darkened in the rough wood planking, ROSE CRANE — 1965 — PRIVATE SCHOOL.

Thereafter she had heard innumerable references, from friends and teachers, to "private school:" how Jill had gone there, how Matthew had been thrown out of there, how going to Private School would straighten out Thomas. She'd even seen a movie about Private School, in which Rex Harrison was the headmaster, in which all the buildings were of greystone, and all the students wore scarves with longitudinal stripes instead of cross-wise ones. Private School had many buildings, not just one; it had grounds, not an asphalt school-yard. It was bewitchingly old, with many fireplaces, libraries, and long black automobiles.

And only a chance overhearing of a conversation, at the same camp to which she had later returned as a counselor, had corrected her misunderstanding. She happened to hear her tent-mate ask the camp director *which* private school the new counselor was from: one of the New England ones, or a private school in Indianapolis?

But a residue remained, even now — an unconscious fixation rooted in Tess's sense of what such a place must be: a privileged academic sanctuary to which one might aspire, a privilege not wholly to be earned, but also to be bestowed, and a privilege now at hand. For her own daughter, Amanda: who — she could now tell colleagues at work and new friends — is at private school (she pronounces the name with an inflection of satisfaction), at St. Matthew's.

The route to St. Matthew's had been circuitous, and not without detours and potholes. Just before Amanda's ninth birthday, Tess's new firm, Warfield Stedman, opened a new office in Garden City, not far from Lawrence. Tess, a partnership in her sights, accepted assignment to the office without complaint, grateful that her long commutes to New York City would be ended — at least for a time. Her focus on her daughter sharpened. Soon she exercised an unflagging surveillance over Amanda's schedule and activities. She attached a daily calendar to the refrigerator first thing each morning, a five-by-seven card with each hourly segment marked off, from 7:00 A.M. until bedtime at 10:00. All lessons, classes, athletic fixtures, dental and medical appointments, piano and cello lessons, counseling sessions, even times allotted to recreation, were set down in Tess's bold hand. The calendar was prepared each night before bedtime, daughter and mother sitting together in an alcove next to the kitchen — Amanda saying nothing, but nodding in docile acceptance. The bumptious little girl that she had been seemed to disappear overnight.

As Amanda's body began to lengthen, undergoing the normal changes of puberty, and presenting a tendency (so it seemed to Tess) to plumpness, it was decided that she was eating too many empty calories. Tess prepared a list of foods and beverages Amanda was not to eat, a list that grew as newly identified dangerous substances came to the public attention. For snacks Amanda was allowed raw carrots, whole grain cereal squares, sliced tomatoes, plums, apples, dried fruits. No junk food was permitted; no gum; no artificial sweeteners. All diet drinks were put out of bounds — their link to hyperactivity disorders having been documented to Tess's satisfaction. White breads, candies, all the vast stock of sugared cereals, coconut — the list, of an ever-expanding inclusiveness as well as eccentricity, became long enough to alphabetize.

Tess insisted that all Amanda's meals be eaten seated, with special attention given the symmetry and arrangement of utensils, napkins, and plate. Meals also became the occasion for administering current affairs tests and questions. It stuck in Tess's mind that the Kennedys, or maybe it was the Bush family, would bombard their children with questions about politics and geography as they sat together at dinner. Tess now did the same. The results did not gratify her. First, because Amanda couldn't answer most of the questions; second, neither could Tess — or Joey. Where was the Strait of Hormuz? What is an ayatollah? Who becomes president if the vice-president dies? May I please be excused?

Still, Amanda had made it to St. Matthew's, and this satisfied her mother, and she thought about the fact of it — Amanda's acceptance and her being there. Each morning Tess strode on the treadmill — Incline, Everest; Speed, Olympic — set up in her large bedroom. *Progress* was what she called Amanda's existence at the school. Not her time there, not her being there: but her *progress* there. "Life is a constant arrival at a departure point." Its corollary is that you look back only to measure how far you have come. Such measurements for Tess were promotions and bonuses, professional recognitions and awards. For Amanda they were grades, and more grades; times and placings in athletic completions; honors; awards; academic recognitions; musical accomplishments. Tess relentlessly calculated advancement and relative standing, assessed and measured the competition that — she was certain — never slept.

For twenty-five minutes precisely she strode out, marched, pounded out the mileage on her treadmill's rubberized road to nowhere. She locomoted in a kind of Gurkha fashion, hands balled into fists, arms swinging high and diagonally across her chest, thumbs actually touching the points of her shoulders with each stride. She stared raptly at stock quotations popping along the bottom of CNBC like little ducks. Each morning she strode along in her bright spandex unitard, waiting for the glow she knew she would feel, a marvelous sense of well-being, capable perhaps — her imagination instructed her — of being willed and transferred to Amanda. What was that silly phrase she had once heard, a long time ago, from her own mother? That the apple never falls far from the tree?

CHAPTER TWENTY-ONE

Among Tess's enterprises of self-advancement was a prodigal purchasing of books. It had become habitual; it was both impulsive and addictive, and its fruits could be seen, stacked about the rooms of the Bahringer home. Little yearnings whispered at Tess as she clicked her mouse, ordering from Amazon.com: yearnings provoked by imagined fragments of conversation that the books might stimulate in guests who saw them. "Oh, Tess, have you read this? I saw her with Brian Lamb. Isn't it wonderful? But she overdoes everything, and what kind of a growing season can they have in Connecticut, anyway?" Piles of books were heaped about in orderly profusion — stacks of generous new biographies; richly-colored volumes or coffee-table, books about the Duchess of Devonshire; about Stanford White; historic Savannah; begonias; the style of the Duke and Duchess of Windsor; David Niven; the Grenadier Guards; Churchill as a Painter; Litchfield County . . . *Selected Sixteen: The Great American Schools.*

Her daughter, now working away up at St. Matthew's, was the constant beneficiary of what Tess was learning from her reading, especially works of autobiography and memoirs, in which a procession of twentieth century leaders had set down the reasons for their success. Tess understood, for example, that Amanda's college essays would be read for what they demonstrated about her *character*, about her fitness to profit from her opportunities — exactly the kinds of things autobiographers liked to say of their own childhoods and adolescence. "Looking back, it is now apparent to me that my refusal to go along with the class's vote to condemn the declaration of war was an arrow that pointed to . . ."

Tess liked to use slightly unexpected verbs of action: I chose, I prepared, I caused. For my trip to Aruba I chose a Norma Kamali. I prepared the meal. I caused my daughter to look into applying to Dartmouth. Her ear delighted to hear herself say, "I caused . . ."; and she prepared the ground carefully for the introduction of completely unexpected words in her daily business discourse. Such words were kept in active reserve, the ground prepared for their utilization, and then the word slipped in as though she used it all the time. The trick was not to do it too often. People might assume that you knew what you were talking about. It was like learning to say *How Are You?* in Russian, and then having someone come back at you with a paragraph of fluent Muscovite. She once told someone that Amanda might "do topology" at her university, and this got her into awful trouble: Tess didn't know topology from a bird bath, and her friend had majored in math at Columbia.

Amanda's own progress at St. Matthew's now provided the staple of what her mother talked about. The school was simply called boarding school — she's at boarding school and they have a cross-country dual meet I have to go up for — the topic introduced to her assistant while Tess was giving dictation — standing up, so as not to crease or wrinkle her skirt, ". . . and they have a three-mile course they run, in girls' cross-country, and the distance is short enough that you can go for it early in the race. That's exactly what she did against Deerfield. Did you know Deerfield has girls now, Natalie? If she gets her times down far enough, it'll get her in anywhere. You know the coaches in these colleges have quotas. Girls' cross-country probably gets five a year at a place like Middlebury. The coach says, I want her, and they let her in. We saw her run during Parents Weekend. Then she played some Chopin . . . we're going up again next weekend."

"Must be beautiful this time of year."

"Yes, so very lovely." But Tess's mind was already vaulting ahead to the next trip, to what she would wear, to whether Joey would watch his accent and keep his cracks to himself, to the other parents she would see, or see again, to seeing how well Amanda was fitting in.

Not only that, but using the occasion to meet, and really get to know, dozens of other parents, so many of whom worked in New York or Los Angeles, and doing things that suggested, not implausibly, possibilities for networking and other professional contacts. Warfield had offices on the West Coast, and in Washington and Chicago as well. Tess immediately visualized herself talking to Chris Mayhew, a Senior Vice President, next Monday: ". . . and we saw Paul Greer and his wife this weekend, up at St. Matthew's. He runs Hammond Publishing now — in the same building with us, in Chicago. Wanted to be remembered to you." And Mayhew would say, "Tess, you know everyone. We did PR for Hammond in '88 and they had two guys pro bono with us in the Bush Campaign in Lake Forest. We ought to talk to them again . . ."

Tess had once read that the head of a vast shipping company began each day by (1) brushing his teeth,

(2) reading the *Wall Street Journal,* and (3) defecating, all at the same time. This is advancement. Money, yes, but, more: advancement, breaking from the pack: *distinction.* Multiple activities should be routinely conjoined. Isotonic facial exercises to tauten and strengthen the muscles under the skin could be performed during morning forced marches on the Treadmill: all the while studying *Forbes,* watching CNN, and planning Amanda's future.

It had worked for Tess: soon-to-be partner of her major multi-national public relations firm. It would work for Amanda. Doing all these things, all at once.

Amanda's study of piano, for example.

Many years ago — Amanda was perhaps seven or eight — Tess and Joey, lying in bed reading the Sunday papers, were surprised — then puzzled, fascinated, and finally astonished — to hear a tentative but accurate piano rendering of a classical piece they both recognized. There was a little Yamaha spinet in the living room, an Indiana inheritance, but hardly anyone had ever played it.

They ran downstairs and watched their little girl, her feet barely reaching the pedals, playing the melody haltingly, tentatively, but without missing notes — and using her left hand, too, they both noticed. She wasn't just picking the tune out.

They ran to her and hugged her.

"Do you want to take lessons?" Tess had asked immediately.

CHAPTER TWENTY-TWO

Amanda's career in grammar school had been unremarkable, her grades almost uniformly in the A-minus range, and her monthly reports studded with commendations for industry, cooperativeness, congeniality, and musical ability. One report had recourse to the time-worn attestation: *she is a lovely girl and a pleasure to have in class.*

Such comments provided Tess Bahringer incomplete satisfaction then and now.

At age seven Amanda wrote the following for a Social Studies requirement:

> Imagine a stream of prairie schooners heading across the Missouri. Put yourself in their place, and think how the rain penetrates the olden canvas and soak all their belongings, plus bears, rattlesnakes. The Indians were friendly until the settlers riled them off, and now treated them unfairly. Imagine the night! The fear of the settlers for a new world and life, that kept them near the fire and near each other. That was all they had, each other.

Miss Hoffman gave her a C.
Tess asked Joey what he thought of it.

Joey read the little essay, written so hard on lined paper he could almost see Amanda's tongue sticking · out as she labored over it. He told Tess it was wonderful. He could actually imagine a Conestoga wagon lit up by bright fire, could envision the worn faces of the Oregon Trail pioneers turned towards the warmth, all listening to stories and singing together. *Imagine the night!* He loved the line and he wondered where she'd gotten the other phrase from, about the Indians being riled off.

"I think we have a little writer here."

"Yes, but look at the grade. Look what Miss Hoffman says. The paper's full of mistakes. We need to get her a tutor."

"A tutor!"

Tutoring and hard work, however, brought Amanda only more A-minuses and B's and a worrisome sprinkling of B-minuses in high school. These grades melded to form *cumes* — cumulative grade-point averages — of 3.1s and 3.2s, not like those of the high flyers in her class, 4.0s or even, absurdly, 4.2s and 4.3s. Tess knew the problem was not that Amanda didn't study. On the contrary: all she seemed to do was study and practice the piano (and now even the cello), write essays for applications, and prepare for PSATs, or run distance. Tess would not let herself think of Amanda as *slow* — a rather cruel adjective, and a word only used rarely by teachers. They relied on such phrases as *perhaps less academically inclined*. She recognized, and was enraged by, its smarmy condescension, its masquerade. Her daughter was disciplined and methodical, but Tess sensed that Amanda was unable, somehow, to improvise, to *convert* things she was learning to some sort of academic usefulness. "You just don't get it, do you?" she thought, but did not, of course, ever say it. Among her three or four good friends with daughters at the high school, only one got grades as low as Amanda's; and none worked as hard, anywhere near as hard, as she did.

Thus Amanda began to fall short of Tess's hopes and expectations. Tess also thought she saw, from time to time, early markers of a possibly rebellious nature, saw them especially in Amanda's silences, in her refusals or unwillingness to answer her questions, or to engage her. Joey was no help. The man she had married and still loved, her industrious, quiet Joey — he absolutely adored Amanda, believed in his bones that a daughter was meant to be loved and sustained, not driven to succeed. Academic recognition — that was fine, if you wanted to be a brain surgeon or a scientist — but beyond that, what was the point? Amanda would marry a good man; they would have children. She could work if she felt like it, and what in the world was wrong with that? It put Tess into high earth orbit to be told to calm down, to give Amanda some space.

Tess became a regular visitor to the high school. She didn't like the teachers or the culture of school. Everything seemed disorderly, tacky, frantic, the teachers uncrisp and badly-clothed. *How much did they make?* They'd be eaten alive in the real world. She clattered down the school hallways right from work, in her Armani suits and Ferragamos, her big black Versace alligator bag flumping at her side. The teachers preferred to see her as a "character," both out of sympathy for Amanda, "a real sweet kid," and because like most teachers they were confrontation-averse. They compounded such tactical errors by caving into Tess's demands: again, out of sympathy for the child rather than any desire to oblige the mother. "This is not a high-maintenance kid," she would remind them; and, sometimes, they would ratchet Amanda's grade up a half-letter or so, promising to look out for her in the future.

In October of Amanda's senior year at Lawrence High School, the whole business overwhelmed her. She was practicing the piano two hours a day. She was fighting to retain a place among the top five girls on Varsity Cross-country. She was desperately worried about the SATs that now loomed only three weeks ahead (for which her miserable performance in the junior PSATs had only stimulated renewed dread); and she was struggling to improve her modest collection of Bs in a course array of five subjects, two of them A.P.s. She was sleeping — and only fitfully — less than four hours a night, keeping awake for late study with a concoction from the Seven-Eleven called HIGH ALERT, a mixture of caffeine, Siberian Ginseng, and citric acid; and by listening to jittery piano music on her Discman, the kind of music that jolts and jerks at you. Dr. Mitchell had prescribed a mild anti-anxiety agent for her, a drug called Serax — "It'll help you relax, and it's a sleep aid as well," — but, though Amanda experimented with it, she was mistrustful of its effects. Tess didn't press the matter. Indeed, by accommodation, her mother had simplified the post-dinner section of the refrigerator cards to read, simply, STUDY. The bedtime hour was no longer noted.

One morning Amanda woke up with a throat so sore she couldn't swallow. The glands under her jaw were achy and swollen. When she got out of bed and tried to stand she literally fell backwards and saw the ceiling spin. "Daddy," she cried — and Tess ran down the hall to her room, almost as though she knew what she would find.

"Mono, Tess. It's a smart disease. Goes right after the bright kids who work like Hell. This is the classic case.

129

Look at her." Dr. Mitchell put his hand on the crown of Amanda's head. "You'll be all right, Honey — vacation time for you whether you like it or not. Ice Cream City."

A couple of nights later, a Saturday, when Tess came in to check on her, Amanda was still so sore and so weak she could barely pronounce her words or move her lips. "How's your dinner party downstairs?"

"It's fine, Darling. I'm using those Medusa plates we bought. They make you want to eat just to see what's under the food."

"Don't make me laugh, Mom. It hurts me too much."

"You take your medications? You can take the Serax while you take the other stuff he gave you."

"Yes."

"I have to go back down. Mr. Mayhew is here with his wife. Her name is Plum. You know him. He was a Dartmouth alumni trustee or something like that. Knows all about you, at least now he does. I think you met him in the office once. Sweet dreams, Angel."

It was almost winter before she recovered. Amanda remembered the episode vividly. Tess had been solicitude itself, had not pushed or pressed her, had brought her CDs of Schumann and Mariah Carey, had brought her books — at least a few of which couldn't conceivably have been useful to any academic purpose. She called her several times a day from the office or her car. During the first miserable week of the illness, when Amanda could barely swallow, Tess spooned her half pints of ice cream, frozen yogurt, chicken soup, at one point, when she and Joey were entertaining downstairs, bringing her both cold vichyssoise and a magnificently crusty crème brulée. "We'll worry about the pudgies later, darling."

The pudgies was Tess's euphemism for little bulges and flabbinesses which show up on Monday mornings after weekends of overindulgence. That quick. Dairy products, Tess sensed, accentuated hippiness. Likewise, weekend slothfulness helps create and build up cellulite. Tess had green plastic hand rubbers, handles really, to which sponges were attached. She applied a formula lotion to the sponges and rubbed them vigorously at the offensive regions — the love handles, bat wings, outer thighs. And if all these rubbings and pummelings, dietings and self-denials were unavailing, there were now plenty of new food supplements, many in pill form, Extra Strength Thera cellulite tablets, full of cider vinegar, lecithin, and potassium.

As Tess considered what to take Amanda on her next visit to St. Matthew's, perhaps something green and white like the Dartmouth colors, a sweater or something, she remembered her daughter on the last day she had stayed home from school with mono: kneading the backs of her hips while walking slowly on the treadmill, determined to follow her mother into a size four.

CHAPTER TWENTY-THREE

Among the weapons in Tess's armory of ambition was a brief business relationship with the CEO of Diehl Brothers, a Minneapolis software firm that made large contributions to United Community Enterprises — which in turn disbursed grants to the Boy Scouts, the American Cancer Society, and other charitable organizations. Tess, assigned by Warfield to advise UCE on a major fundraising effort, found herself on the Diehl corporate plane on a mid-November morning, flying from Teterboro to Minneapolis, and seated next to Coggin Lindsay.

"Went to a little school up in Hanover, New Hampshire," said this new acquaintance, responding to a question. *She's a small college, Sir, but there are those who love her.*

"What?"

Lindsay explained that this was Daniel Webster's famous characterization of Dartmouth. "I went there in the late '50's, and it was the defining experience of my life. I made the best friends I ever had at Dartmouth. God, I loved it. They had great teachers — a great bunch of characters, you know? — and great coaches, and it was remote, up there all by itself. What a place to go to school!"

"Do you keep up with it?"

"Is the Pope Catholic? Three weekends this fall, two telethons in Minneapolis, two home football games. Even interviewed two or three kids."

This conversation occurred only three weeks after Parents Weekend at St. Mathew's. Tess had come away energized — Amanda's disappointing grades notwithstanding. Dr. Passmore's solicitude for her daughter, the fact that he seemed to know so much about her, his enthusiasm for her piano performance — such things in combination had lifted Tess's confidence. The thing was do-able.

"It's a tough college to get into, isn't it?"

"Yeah," Lindsay answered. "It's real hot. Didn't used to be when I went there. The kind of kid getting in now's an Asian with a hot violin. Guys in my generation, we go around saying we couldn't get in today; that's not just talk. I know I couldn't. But they still want my money."

"How hard is it, getting in there?"

"You sound like you got a kid applying."

"Daughter in boarding school. A senior at St. Matthew's. She's just starting to look around."

"No kidding? When I was there, they didn't have girls. She a good kid?"

"Well, I'm her mother, but she's pretty special. Wonderful athlete, musician, grades. Yes, a heck of a kid."

"Good grades and SATs? That's what they go for now."

"Oh, yes."

"Yeah, well, St. Matthew's, it'd have to be — those kids are all real bright, aren't they? Didn't Roosevelt go there, or someone like that? What kind of SATs she have?"

"Around 1300, last time she took them. I think around 1300."

Tess sensed — they were sitting alongside each other in the narrow cabin — that Lindsay was looking her over, perhaps evaluating her in some way, perhaps . . .

"If she applies to Dartmouth, tell you what. Have her write me a letter. List all her courses and grades, any sports stuff if it's unusual. If I can get a sense of what she's like, I can draft a letter for her, and it'll get looked at. No guarantees, but they will look at it. All the kids are above average. You know what I mean?"

"You're great to do something like this." Tess wondered if there'd be a quid pro.

"What schools is she thinking about?"

"Schools like Dartmouth. She's probably on the bubble at Brown."

"I can probably help. They owe me a couple. My wife and I have a scholarship there, a named scholarship. We gave it in honor of her father. The guy *bled* green. I'm not kidding you, he was buried in a green coat and a Dartmouth tie. Played football there in 1936, I think they went to a bowl."

"I mean can you write something that looks like you know her?"

"What's the kid's name?"

"Amanda."

"Certainly. I feel like I already know her mother."

Tess could tell he was coming on to her, but this was nothing. A lot of them did, but a man like Lindsay, an older man, midwestern, somehow it wasn't a concern.

"She sounds like the kind of kid they ought to take. But — no knock on her — they get a lot of kids like that who apply. So a letter from someone they know isn't going to hurt her. I'll write the dean and copy the president. I knew the old president."

"The President of the College?"

"Yeah. That and a buck-fifty'll get you a cup of coffee."

"You're really great to do this."

"Glad to. Where you staying in Minneapolis?"

"Oh, I'm downtown. Not far from our meeting."

"How about dinner?"

"You're sweet to ask. I'm so sorry — I'm going back very early. Commercial. I have to go to a thing here. I'll send you the stuff from Amanda."

"Glad to help."

"You want to talk about UCE for a minute — Coggin? Is twenty-five million realistic? Is local TV on board? I'd love to have your input." Tess looked down at the *Wall Street Journal* in her lap. "I'll probably be back out here next Spring."

"Hi. What're you up to?"

"Hi. Studying. I have a long paper due in Mr. Steele's course. How's Daddy?"

"He's fine. I'm in Minneapolis, in the airport; I got a direct flight home, to Kennedy, so I'll be home in two hours. Now, listen. I have some nice news. Are you listening, Amanda?"

"Yes, Mother."

"Turn that music down — I can hear it. I met a man this morning who's a Dartmouth graduate, Mr. Lindsay. He's one of their most visible graduates in the midwest, and he's going to write their president about you."

"The president of Dartmouth? Mother."

"No, I'm serious. What you have to do, now write this down, I want you to write Mr. Lindsay, give him your record at St. Matthew's and all your extracurriculars, because he can write you a letter, and it's got to have specifics, it can't be, you know, she's a nice young lady sort of thing. He says it's better to have one great letter from an important alumnus than a lot of generalizations from people Dartmouth never heard of. So, here's your chance."

Amanda wrote down Coggin Lindsay's name and a business address. She did so with both excitement and a mild revulsion. This is what you do, she guessed. This man a thousand miles away doesn't know me from Hillary Clinton, etcetera, and he'll write a letter full of specifics to someone maybe neither one of us knows, etcetera, and make it sound like he's writing about his own daughter.

"Thanks."

"You don't sound very enthusiastic."

"No, I am."

"We're so hopeful about your new board scores."

"Yeah, I am, too."

"Amanda. Amanda. It needs to show a sharp improvement. They want a sharp improvement. That will show how far you've come, how the other school wasn't any good. See?"

"I know what it's supposed to do. The whole thing seems, I don't know, fakey, not right. But it's O.K."

The mother heard such things with some exasperation. And not without a nagging twinge of conscience herself . . . perhaps it *was* a pressurized kind of thing. But they were all doing it: you couldn't put your own daughter at a competitive disadvantage. That wouldn't be right, either.

"I hear you. Trust me on this one. Love you, Darling — I have to run."

Two days later Tess read an e-mail in her New York office.

Dear Tess (if I may), Just a note to say how much I enjoyed our talk on the plane, and also that I just received the information on your daughter Amanda that she sent. She sounds *most* impressive. I will do what I can. Though I am no longer active on any of the Dartmouth annual giving committees, I still maintain a couple of friendships in the Admissions Office, and I believe I may be able to help. Like you I would rather have Dartmouth filled with young people like Amanda than a collection of walking computers and deconstructionists (a word I just learned). I will see what I can do. Very best regards and call me the next time you come to town. Coggin.

Tess read the e-mail as though she were squeezing a sponge. On the whole, it satisfied her, but she chafed a little at his casual implication that Amanda was merely a nice young person who was also talented. That was apparently not what they were going for, not at Dartmouth or any of the good ones. If you were a good young kid, you had to be, really, unusually special in some way that would knock them over. Otherwise, they'd rather let in walking computers and inner-city brain kids, etcetera. It was all quite complicated, she was thinking.

CHAPTER TWENTY-FOUR

A high SAT was the Holy Grail. Even if you had only moderate grades it still showed you were smart, even brilliant: *gifted*. But the colleges wanted more: high grades, dazzling extracurriculars, a cultivated vocation that brought visible success — athletic talent or a musical gift. And they also wanted brilliant answers to *Required Essay Questions*.

One of the Essay options was a question that engaged Amanda fully and confidently. Her first draft was her last one; she had never written an answer with greater conviction.

The question was both strange and simple:

> Suppose that through fatal illness your life were to be cut short. What might a friend write about you in an obituary, or say about you in a eulogy? About how you have lived your life, what you have believed, and what achievements you are leaving behind as your legacy?

Amanda had read some obituaries in newspapers and magazines. They focused only on what the man, and they were mostly about men, had done. You never knew whether the man liked to ski or loved dogs, or children; or if he was a drunk, and nothing of what was in his heart. She immediately saw what she should write and went to her computer and began:

First I should state that an obituary and a eulogy have different purposes. The purpose of an obituary is to inform the general public about the events and important features of a dead person's life. A eulogy is given by a friend or relative at the funeral service in a church. Even if the friend is biased and exaggerates, he always tries to remember the good qualities of the person; what they were like, not what they did. Not only are the aims of a eulogy and an obituary different, they seem to be in conflict with each other. In a eulogy the speaker doesn't talk about how well the person did in college or business. Obituaries do that.

This tells us something. People are judged differently by those who knew and loved them, and those who did not know them. Those who did not want the bottom line. What did the deceased accomplish? Those who knew him want to be reminded of what he was like: for that is who will live on in their hearts.

That's how I hope people will judge me. I am only trying to live my life in a way that will make it easy for whoever gives my eulogy to say good things about me as a person. So far, I really have no achievements. I only play the piano, which I love, and run. I give myself credit for hard and continuous work. I do not cheat. If you give me the chance to be admitted to your college, I will make the best of it.

In conclusion, an obituary tells the truth

about those parts of a person's life that are not really important. A eulogy may not always tell the precise truth, but it tries to, and what it says is more important than an obituary. At least I hope it will be for me.

CHAPTER TWENTY-FIVE

And now, a late autumn Saturday morning at St. Matthew's, bleak, cold, and damp — and still, at this hour, perfectly silent. Amanda was slipping from sleep into consciousness as she might have stepped from a summertime beach into a warm lake, the water so tepid she didn't know she was standing in it until she looked down. She had floated, these few minutes before knowing she was awake — drifting in a warm reverie, seeing herself at her grandparents' farm in Indiana. She lay on a blanket spread out on a rich meadow, a soft maize-colored openness bordered by huge sycamores. It must have been late August; the air was unmoving and dense; it seemed precisely the moment when summer was ripest, poised to begin its long deceleration towards fall: towards home, high school, everything that had to be done. Its claims shook her suddenly awake. She was wrenched into her SAT day, November twelfth, and how I do this morning, starting seventy minutes from right now, is *Everything,* my last and only chance at Dartmouth or everywhere else if I really blow it badly, and already my fingers are trembly and I can't hold my hands out straight, and my heart is beating hard enough for me to feel it on both sides of my neck.

*

Seven months earlier, within the space of a week, she had been rejected by Dartmouth and wait-listed by Trinity, Colgate, and Hamilton — Mr. Arnett's nice little schools. It was the first week in April. The wait-listing colleges had contrived letters of explanation and commiseration, each avowing a personal interest in Amanda and sincere remorse for the disappointment, they understood, their letters might cause ". . . Believe me, Amanda, we do not make such decisions without searching analysis and great care; but the huge volume of applications this year . . ." Why didn't they just say, *Amanda, we can't accept you now. If some other kid says he's going somewhere else, we'll let you know. Good luck.*

Her mother took her to meet a Mr. Rogerson, a former Denison University admissions officer who lived in Hunting Acres, and who had set himself up as a consultant to families trying to find the right boarding schools or colleges for their sons and daughters. For a fee plus expenses, Rogerson would guarantee to match the candidate with a suitable institution. He knew the terrain as a good general knows his theater of operations: the colleges, the deans and their staffs, important local alumni, sometimes even trustees. He was particularly admired for his skill in — an advertising flyer stated it impressively — "assembling admissions packages that will maximize the attractiveness of the candidate."

"What about a P.G. year?" he asked the anxious mother and daughter.

"What about it? Could she get into one of those high-class boarding schools? This late?"

"The odd thing is, yes. Even the most prestigious have a few slots. They all have a lot of attrition. Kids get thrown out quite a bit, a lot of juniors get thrown out. I got kids into St. Mark's last year. St. James, Kent, Salisbury . . . we got one into St. Matthew's."

"St. Matthew's!"

"You want to take a shot? They take P.G.s."

He had provided more helpful counsel, advice less troubling when given and heard on a bright May morning than remembered in dark November. In a year of tenacious and determined academic toil at St. Matthew's Amanda could achieve impressive results, not just solid results. (Solid is a kiss of death on any application for any academic appointment anywhere.) She could show what she could do, not only inside the classroom but outside as well. What about your piano? What about your long-distance running? "And *think* about what you could do with the time, between now and then, to raise your SATs! They have a SAT UP program, and before that you'd have a whole summer . . . I had one kid raise her scores 210 points."

A hard year ahead, Rogerson declared, but the payoff could be worth it. And St. Matthew's: *did you know, Mrs. Bahringer, that after Groton it has produced the largest number of cabinet secretaries in this century?* You know the kinds of young people who go there, and you *must* have heard of Carlisle Passmore?

As for Colgate, Hamilton, Trinity — the wait-list people: no problem. "They're nice schools. Can you not do them again?"

Amanda felt a sudden constriction in her throat, and she could taste the Vivarin that had kept her upright at her desk until 2:45 A.M. Going over words. Fractious. Faction. Metaphor. Simile. Selective Response. There were some things that everyone had to do, and they all got through it, but that didn't make them any less terrified and miserable, perhaps even close to losing it. Amanda took a Xanax and an Inderal and drank two glasses of water from the tap.

The SAT was administered on the main basketball court of Gibbon Gymnasium, 240 classroom chairs laid out in rows with much space between each of them. To see the students funneling throug.i Gibbon's dark oak portal, a great, grim, moving huddle of them, bent forward like miners, silent and unsmiling: to see them like this and then to join their movement and be swallowed up in it somehow restored and strengthened her. Everybody was as wretched as she. Everyone looked like someone leaving the hospital after a long stay. Mr. Barber, the clattering man who had been Amanda's first tablemaster, coldly cheerful, shouted out directions and instructions as they made their way to seats. Take any seat!

Amanda slipped into a seat as far from the front entrance as possible, at the very edge of the assembly. All her life, it seemed, people had had expectations for her; she had been raised, groomed, manipulated, derided, and praised — all for doing what some person in authority wanted her to do, and always with the same threat of shame if she did not satisfy what the person wanted or expected. *I will be disappointed in you if . . .*

And here it was, right in front of her on an old portable desk, in this cold gym with 200 other kids; and how she did on the SAT would determine, there was no getting around it, whether she would go to Dartmouth or whether she would go anywhere: because there are cases of kids whose SATs go *down,* and you could get de-wait-listed. And a lot more than that. A whole lifetime's relationship (she thought of it as a relationship, and she called it that) with her mother, fifty years ahead: how she performed on this examination would definitely determine what *that* relationship, that weird but not totally loveless thing between them — what it would become. What everyone else would think of her. *You have to go up a good two hundred points.* One man, a friend of Joey's — that would make him about forty-five or fifty — still announced his SAT scores at parties. Twelve Ninety. Amanda turned to the first question and touched her pencil to the tip of her tongue.

Begin!

PART THREE

CHAPTER TWENTY-SIX

Y ou don't eat a lot, do you?"

On Amanda's plate lay a sallow shell of iceberg lettuce with a single tomato slice on top. Toby stared at it. The P.A. system saved her from answering; the Herald had just begun a lunch recitative of fresh achievements and triumphs: announcements of rankings in the Class II Mathematical Olympiad — almost all the names Asian, university prizes and a few admissions notifications, St. Matthew's victories in field hockey. She concluded with announcements of two systemic departures. "Resume."

"What were they?" Amanda asked.

"One girl stole Ritalin. The other one's a huffing, a Class III."

"A huffing. Wow!"

"It's a cheap high. Real easy to hide. Your father did it with airplane glue."

"Not my father." Joey the altar boy, not likely.

"Class III is very tough. It's the worst year here. They all have to do something to calm their asses down. You missed the worst year of St. Matthew's; our class had fifteen S.D.s the year before you got here. That's why we have all the P.G. spaces. That's why *you're* here. You guys come in, take what you want, polish your resumé, and wham — Yale, Dartmouth,

Stanford. You're getting St. M's lite. You hear what I said about your food?"

"Toby, you eat what you want, I'll eat what I want. If you ever came to breakfast and saw what I ate, you wouldn't worry about it."

"Who's worried? But I notice I got a nice little rise out of you."

"I run in the afternoons, so I don't eat much at lunch, O.K.?"

"I didn't say anything. My theory is, you work out, you can eat anything you want. I'm 6'4" and I weigh 190. It never changes and I eat all I want."

"Rowing isn't cross-country. There's a big difference."

"I said my piece. Suit yourself. The place'll wear you down if you let it. And do me a favor — wave when you run by us? I watch you run by, on the embankment. The expression on your face, it's like you're running from a death camp. Have some fun, will you? That stare! I don't know if anyone's happy here."

"Dr. Passmore's happy."

"He's totally out of it. He's old — he's like your grandfather. He's their face man. The trustees like his accent, that's the only reason they still have him. He doesn't run the school. All these schools, they have a face man like him, and then some shitty, uptight academic guy, he really controls everything. Guy like Passmore, fake English accent, my dear chap, etcetera."

Outside bright buffets of wind swirled around the quadrangle. It was no longer mellow autumn, but cold. Students hurried headlong towards their appointments, a pastiche of incongruous color: skinny Class II girls in J. Crew skirts and clomping boots, boys in sweatshirts and bomber jackets and battered baseball caps. The effect was calculated as carefully as the opening line of an essay written for admission to Princeton.

Amanda could slide by Toby's idle queries about what she ate. But there was no sliding past algebra — modest little Pre-college Algebra and its arrogant ruler, Mr. Carnes. Alone, each was a source of worry; together, of dread. It was funny, there was a controversy going on about whether a Barbie doll, one of the new ones that could talk, should say *I hate math*. On the bulletin board in the Morison Day Room was an editorial going on about how that statement demeaned women. Barbie should be re-programmed: *I adore calculus, give me more!* Yeah, right. Amanda hated math because she was terrible at it, period. Every year was the same. She would buy fresh notebooks and pens and graphing calculators from Manions. She would sit, ardent with attentiveness, in the front row of math class. She maintained earnest eyeball contact with the teacher. She copied furiously. She made her papers incredibly neat. She labored with sustained concentration night after night. She understood nothing.

Now her dread was becoming something close to terror, because she knew Mr. Carnes hated the girls in his class. He made no effort to disguise his contempt for them. He was just old enough to have attended St. Matthew's when it was a boys' school — at a time, now leaking from everyone's memory, of familiar, congenial, athletic challenges, of uncluttered highways to famous universities, and little academic pressure.

No, Amanda didn't get it, and her fear of confiding — to anyone — that she didn't get it was as absolute as her horror of the subject itself. There was only one scenario in her imagination: she would go to

Carnes with a question and he would shoot back: *You Mean To Tell Me That You Still Don't Get It? What Have You Been Doing All Term?*

Another, happier, voice whispered to her: wouldn't Dartmouth maybe go for a girl who was really *brilliant* in, like, poetry, or philosophy, even if she was terrible at math? All those famous geniuses, they were mainly good at only one thing, and awful at everything else. Wasn't Einstein a dyslexic, or something like that?

She gave Toby a courageous little smile and kept walking towards the math building. Toby was funny. He never seemed to be working or even worried about anything. Even when he asked her what she ate, it wasn't as though it was any kind of a big deal to him. He seemed to enjoy getting a rise out of people, but it was all quite gentle. She watched him walk towards the library. He was wearing what looked like his father's overcoat, and he was the only kid not carrying a knapsack full of books.

Later that afternoon she saw Mr. Arnett dead ahead on the walkway, arms folded across his chest and feet planted. "Stop, Amanda: Stop! You owe me at least an e-mail on your Trinity essays. And Hamilton. Are they done? Mailed out?"

"Almost done, Mr. Arnett."

"I know you're being exactly truthful, right? Come on, are you *close?* You need to get them out, *now.* You need any edge you can get . Get them in way before the deadlines, they like that. Fax me copies."

"O.K."

"Remember what I told you. Don't fiddle around with the answers. Make every sentence sting like a hornet. You know what I'm saying? They read ten thousand of those essays. You have to grab them and make them say 'What a great kid this is!'

"I like your sweater. That's a great look. Stress your running. Division III schools like jocks just as much as Penn State does. You all right?"

"I'm fine."

"Got that glow, got that outdoor glow. Algebra O.K.?"

"Better."

"O.K. kiddo. Don't be late for Coach Kellam."

CHAPTER TWENTY-SEVEN

At a week-night Vespers service, a graduate who had been a Rhodes scholar told how he parlayed the Rhodes into a career in international banking, how he had built his home in Telluride, Colorado, and amassed his collection of Native American art. He credited his liberal education at St. Matthew's and Harvard with his success. He concluded by exhorting the students to pay the price now, reap the rewards later.

There was a collection taken up for Rwandan relief, Dr. Passmore segueing into this activity from his formulaic pronouncement of the lines from Matthew VI: "Lay not up for yourselves treasures on earth, where moths and rust doth consume, and thieves break through and steal, but lay up for yourselves treasures in heaven, where neither moths nor rust doth consume and where thieves do not break through and steal: for where your treasure is, there will your heart be also." There were two hymns — "All Loves Excelling," and "America." Amanda sang, buoyed by "Our Father's God to Thee, Author of Liberty . . . freedom's holy light . . . Long may our land be bright." She had a vision, as radiant as fleeting, of an unending line of prairie schooners rolling into the vast western emptiness, with the arms of an angel stretched in welcome before them.

Two letters were pinned to Amanda's Obligations Board. She recognized her mother's stationery and saw that the other was from Mr. Arnett. From Tess: ". . . and there is a new non-prescription food supplement called Pycnogenal. It's an antioxidant. They get it from the French Maritime Pines — Carter mentioned it at work. It's a recovery supplement. You put back in what you've taken out. With great haste, Love, Mummy." And from Arnett: "Heard some good things about you from Mr. Steele — A.P. History can be a major player for you. Best, R. Arnett. Also, think about a piano video."

She undressed, stood on her scale, looked down at the digital number: 104.65. She wrapped herself in a robe and prepared for the evening's work. A.P. Latin, then her essay for Mr. Steele.

Caesar you did not read for A.P. Latin, but Miss Rodman had an interesting observation about him. When they decided to put Amanda into A.P. Latin instead of the less demanding Latin Honors, they went over what she had done at Lawrence High School. "I see they still do Caesar in the public schools," she said. "That's no bad thing. He's politically incorrect, of course. But what I like about him is how organized he always was: how he could move from one thing to another without worrying about what he has just done or wondering about what he has to do next. He focused only on what he was doing. A great skill, my dear. When you have done what you've set out to do, move on to the next challenge. Concentrate completely on what is at hand. It's pure Churchill."

Amanda rigidly allocated her study time, as though she were still controlled by the five-by-seven cards on her refrigerator door. She willed herself into a ferocious absorption in the Tacitus she was translating, working as meticulously as possible. In such work, you did not have to be brilliant; you had to be industrious and meticulous. The tenses were easy and the sentences set down in simple, declarative terms. Absently she tried to imagine the German forests of ancient history, filled with shouting warriors with red beards and spears, all slaughtering one another: did a dark river curl along the forest floor as it did, deep and hidden, in the Seneca Forest — just outside the school gates? Was there leafmeal crushed on the trails?

She stood on her scale again: 105.10 — she was horrified, then remembered her robe. She slipped it off and tossed it onto the bed: 103.89.

She went back to her Latin. She began to pick at some lines from Catullus, a major player (in the teacher's phrase) on the A.P. Latin syllabus. "... *Acme leviter caput reflectens et dulcis pueri ebrios ocellos.*" There was an Acme supermarket in Lawrence, and along one aisle, an aisle so long and so deep you couldn't make out what was at its end, was stacked every imaginable kind of cookie, pie, cake, muffin, cake, pastry, and with a rich sugary smell hanging over it like a fog. Amanda had eaten nothing since breakfast; and then only half a plain bagel, coffee with Equal, a slice of apple. She had skipped lunch. For dinner she had the Iceburg lettuce part of her salad, with lemon squeezed on it, and two breadsticks; and, walking back to her room in the darkness, a Power Bar from her gym bag. Sixty cals for that, no more. She reached with both hands to the tight flesh just above her hips and then to the front, where she was frustrated by the rubbery chunks of hardened fat just over her hipbones. She should not indulge herself. She must not. *Mars quoque deprensus fabrilla vincula sensit . . .*

To control her appetite and to master and train the talent she had been given: one way to get under 18 for the 5K was to slice off three or four more pounds. She vaguely remembered a principle of physics from Lawrence High School. The *impedence,* the drag of an object moving through space is directly proportional to the *square* of the surface presented. Something like that. In other words, each pound, each wider inch, was hugely magnified when you ran. *It really slowed you down.* She thought hard about what it would take to get down to 101. And staying there. Maybe even lower. Below 100. She pinched with both hands — thumb and forefingers — the flesh in the hollows above her hips. *"It's fat you carry around in a race,"* Coach Kellam had said. "You can pay me now, or pay me later. You pay for every pound with five to eight seconds on a three-mile course. I saw Dr. Passmore eating sauce bernaise on his beef, the other night in town. Do you know what that looks like? Skim milk does the same thing for you that whole milk does. Go ahead, pig out on Sundays. Have low-fat with your meuslix. *No,* I repeat, *no, junk food.* Moon pies are for astronauts."

A.P. Latin establishes seriousness of intent — someone said that. She dragged herself back to it.

Morning. She lay on her back without moving, hands at her sides, a white comforter, almost unwrinkled, over her. She always seemed to come awake like this, surprising herself by the way she lay, looking up at the ceiling. Her window faced north, so that she had to judge the day by its early sounds. Amanda began to visualize her day the way Tess used to lay it out for her at home — the note card attached each night to the door of the refrigerator. The narrow gray ceiling perfectly reproduced the shape of the fridge door; she could almost see the card overhead. Her friends had joked about it; it embarrassed her for them to see it. "We'll see who's laughing in ten years," her mother had said.

The note cards and refrigerator door were gone, but the discipline was ingrained and habitual. A memory of Cleopatra flitted through her mind — she missed her more than Joey and Tess put together. She concentrated on her day: first through fourth periods, class; fifth period, piano; lunch; Cross-country at 3:00 — interval repeats on the uphill Seneca stretch. Dinner at 6:00 — and now already dark when you walked over. In-room study hall until 10:30. Each prescribed activity, each to be lined through when completed, right before her as if printed in the kitchen at home, right down to FREE TIME and BED. Amanda's mind churned and fretted like an upset stomach. And she was still horizontal. Still in bed! She reached across to the front edge of the blotter on her desk, clutched at the Inderal bottle, twisted the top off, took out one capsule with the tip of her tongue.

Cross-country runs were a kind of narcotic: they somehow cleared the mind. They were a liberation, even when they were done (like everything at St. Matthew's) for a purpose. Long solitary runs, seven or eight miles, could provide almost everything she had come to crave: silence, solitude, an unclenching of her life and the satisfaction of being able to measure improvement: the shrinkage of times, indeed of flesh. She thought again of getting down to 100, maybe even less. It could help; in so many ways it could help.

That afternoon an alumnus of the school appeared at practice with Coach Kellam. He had his dog with him, a greyhound, a dainty male who watched the activity around him with quiet interest.

"Look at this guy," Kellam exclaimed. "Totally functional. He was made for one purpose. Made to do the one thing perfectly. There's a lesson there."

Amanda noticed the dog's head, the way it was set; his liquid, wary, trusting eye. He was a sweet and quiet animal, bred for the one thing only. Another girl asked Kellam's friend about him, where he came from.

"I saved him," he answered. "When they're three or four, the dog tracks get rid of them. They can't run in competition any more, so that's it for them. They have to be put down."

CHAPTER TWENTY-EIGHT

D_{r.} Passmore's housekeeper came to the door. Amanda could see her expression, the expression of someone interrupted in her work but determined to be obliging.

A reedy, watery voice seemed to be gliding down the stairs. It was a man's voice singing about a foggy day in Londontown. Amanda sat waiting on a shiny settee in the headmaster's study, her hands folded in her lap. Outside it was perfectly still. Sunday mornings at St. Matthew's were the silent times of the week, when the frantic business of work paused — stopped, so it seemed, not because it wanted to, but because it had simply exhausted itself.

Sunlight tumbled into the room; wooden and leather surfaces shone. There was an arrangement of English hunting prints, the flanks of the horses as bright and shimmering as if they had been polished like the floors. There were ranks of framed photographs of St. Matthew's teams; silver trays, bowls and cups; gleaming tables loaded down with mementos and picture frames and vases of flowers. The singing made its way into the study — there was a lilting segue to another song. *From this moment on, you for me, dear, only two for tea, dear . . .*

Dr. Passmore and Miss Rodman called everyone *Dear,* Amanda was thinking . . .

"Amanda, Dear Heart! How are you? Has Mrs. Selfridge brought you some cocoa?"

"She offered me some." The headmaster had taken her hand, touched that she had stood up when he came into the room.

"Sit down, sit down."

He saw her listening to the singer.

"That's Fred Astaire. Sunday mornings I sit here and read the papers and listen to Fred Astaire and Noel Coward."

"You do?"

"If you want to know what someone's like, sneak up on him and listen to the music he plays when he thinks he's alone. Babette — sit!"

The headmaster's trusting-looking, little dog had trotted into the room and nuzzled her master's hand.

"What kind of a dog is that?"

"Babette is a schipperkee — isn't she cunning?"

They were silent, looking at the dog. Fred Astaire was now singing about asking him, if they asked him, he could write a book. It made Amanda suddenly, overwhelmingly, sad, seeing the headmaster like this, with his little dog and this watery old man's music, alone on a Sunday morning. He didn't seem ruddy and robust — not here.

"Are you doing your paper for me on A. E. Housman?"

"Yes. I love his poems. They seem so simple."

"They *are* simple. And that's a good reason to love his poetry. If you get his poems by heart, you'll have them your whole life. They'll touch you a thousand times when you never expect them to."

"Dr. Passmore, thank you for seeing me."

"Of course — certainly, Amanda. Now. What can I do?" He loved their visits, but they never came to him unless they wanted something. It was a cherished part of his life, but also, somehow, heartbreaking. "What can I do?"

"Dr. Passmore, would you please write a recommendation to Dartmouth College, Sir?"

"Of course, my dear, and will you do *me* a small favor? Write down on a little card your grades and the things you think I can emphasize in my letter, things you've done before coming to St. Matthew's, things you've done here. We don't have your new SATs yet, of course, but not to worry. They get *thousands* of these letters. The more specific I can be, the better for you and for them. They don't want to see strings of adjectives slung together. They want to know you. Dartmouth is perfectly splendid, so many splendid young people trying to get in."

"I know," she said. She made her little throat-clearing noise. "Thank you."

"That's a fine college, Amanda." When Passmore had been at Princeton, during the time of Eisenhower's presidency, Dartmouth was thought of as a rough-house kind of school where everyone wore flannel shirts and didn't shave, and drank all the time. Now he understood that it had somehow become terribly political and ill-tempered, always arguing in the papers about something.

"Is the work going well?"

"I'm doing as much as I can."

I'm doing as much as I can. He was leading, he mused about it often — he was running a school where everyone subsisted in a frenzy of work; lived in a ceaseless, enervating welter of labor, work piled up like a tomb, and none of it leading anywhere except to one of those colleges, or the raging despair of parents whose little darlings hadn't gotten in. This lovely young girl . . . "Are you taking care of yourself, Dear?" he found himself saying. Her color was fine, but the skin on her face was taut; there was an unfocussed quality to her gaze. Of course, at that age their hearts were strong, and they could stand it.

"Sure. I run probably thirty-five miles a week."

"I've seen you run. You're a beautiful runner. You and Daniella run like the wind."

"We're getting better. I need to get my 5K times down."

"Yes, we all need to get our times down."

"Have I ever seen Fred Astaire in the movies?"

"Yes — as a matter of fact he made a lot of movies. You've seen him dancing with Ginger Rogers. On the late show. You probably didn't know who he was. He redefined the word elegance. He's the most elegant man I ever saw."

Sitting alone in the study, they could make out the words of another song: *Long ago and far away, I had a dream one day, and now, that dream is here beside me.* After Amanda had left, and he noted that she had a good handshake and had looked him right in the eye, Passmore came back and settled into his deep sofa and listened to messages from another time; a lovelier, better time, long ago and far away.

What could he write Dartmouth about this girl? That she played the piano beautifully? That she was serene and composed? That she was lovely? No one used the word anymore.

And perhaps a reader of the letter in the Dartmouth admissions office might find "lovely" a patronizing term — or, worse, inappropriate.

"Victories and Achievements, 20 November, 2000: The Chancellor's medal at Brown University has been bestowed on Robin Selznick, St. Matthew's, '96, for the most distinguished research project completed by a Brown undergraduate in Academic Year 1998–1999. His work was on viscid lipoproteins and their etiology. Robin graduated second in General Order of Merit from this school and achieved a perfect score of 1600 on the 1996 SAT, one of thirty-seven in the United States to do so. Systemic Departures, two, Class III. Resume."

CHAPTER TWENTY-NINE

Daniella, she can get in anywhere, no problem, just on her running alone. She's been under eighteen four times this year, she'll get offers from Stanford, Michigan, anywhere. She just does it because she likes it. You watch the way she finishes a race, she might as well be finishing putting on a sweater. She's in at Brown, probably won't even run there if she goes."

Coach Kellam was driving a St. Matthew's van back to the hilltop from a dual meet — the Catamounts had won easily — against an upstate parochial school. All the girls were with him in the van, Amanda at his right — designated navigator. As usual she had finished second, twenty-five seconds behind Daniella, who was now asleep in the back.

"You probably need below an eighteen flat, maybe a 17.30, to guarantee a full ride from one of these places. That's the funny thing about St. Matthew's. Nobody wants to go there — except maybe Stanford. You all want to go to Princeton, Dartmouth, etcetera."

It sounded as though he was reading Amanda's mind. "We gotta get you down below eighteen. The guy at Dartmouth has five, maybe six slots, I don't know. If you're on the bubble academically, SATs, etcetera, but otherwise qualified, the athletic piece'll do it for you.

Everything being *equal,* he can probably get you in. They don't like to talk about it, the Ivy League doesn't want the world to think they care about that sports stuff, but they do. Ever look at the Harvard hockey team?"

"Men's hockey?"

"Thank you. Men's hockey. Hell, they look like Moose Jaw, Saskatchewan. Amanda, you've been in the mid-18s. Usually finish second or third. They think, nice kid, good runner. Might take it up a notch if she gets in on her own, walks on, you know, gets it together once she's here. But if you want the guy up there to know about you, we gotta get you down in the seventeen's. You all want to stop? What about it, doughgirls? You wanna eat?

"Let me tell you what I did, 1988. I was still running marathons. I did three marathons in '88, '89. I stayed in the 2.50s, every one. I'd lose it around the twentieth mile. I got home and started training for Boston. I did more intervals, pick-ups, twenty-two, twenty-three mile runs on Sundays, but hills, real windy here. What else did I do? I dropped around ten pounds, on purpose. I did what I had to. A lot of fruit, rice, Scotch broth. You know the drill. All right — you listening? Two hours, thirty-eight minutes — 2.38. I did everything else exactly the same as I did before. That's what eight pounds, negative, that's what it'll do for you in the full distance . . ."

He rattled on and on. He was like Mr. Steele's comment about the young Lincoln; he was a little engine of ambition, but in the closeness of the van and with the coming of dusk Amanda was falling asleep. Kellam made a fist, tapped her on the knee, gave her a little nod — conspiratorial but also, she thought, maybe even affectionate. "So go for it," Kellam said.

CHAPTER THIRTY

Amanda began to dress herself in a way that would make it hard for anyone to tell she had lost weight. It was easier than she knew. Her face, narrowly oval in conformation, framed by brown hair that covered her ears and hid most of her cheeks, kept its golden, almost coppery coloration — its runner's healthy glow — the complexion of a young athlete. Her skin was taut, but not pinched. They had met her young, trim mother; they were impressed with Amanda's quiet poise, her communicated sense of knowing what was good for her. Of being in control.

Except for the wearing of messcoats in Savernake, there was no dress code at St. Matthew's outside Chapel. This helped too. Each morning now, Amanda put on an ordinary T-shirt, a men's small, and over it a baggy men's tubular sweatshirt with DARTMOUTH across the chest. It was an XXL; it hung down to the mid-point of her thighs. Over this she wore a men's Polo Oxford dress shirt — hugely, billowingly, baggy, heavy as canvas, its shirttails hanging down as far as the ribbed waist of the sweatshirt. Ordinary jeans, scoured a greyish-blue, fairly loose; big, thick Doc Martens. These completed the outfit she presented St. Matthew's daily, and there were also days when a North Face jacket covered most of everything else.

Today she was suffused with an eerie exhilaration.

She connected it with the memory of a client of Tess's, a woman who had visited in Lawrence on her return from two weeks at a spa in Bavaria. Amanda remembered the woman talking about how she had been allowed only lemon juice for the first three days, and then only a few slices of a fruit she had never even heard of, for the next week. The woman exulted: "It was heavenly, divine! You're *cleansed*. All that *toxicity* drains from your system." Amanda conceived that the same thing was happening to her, that her bright energy (so it felt) and vivid calm were a consequence of the way she was now eating. The satisfactions of intelligent self-denial were greater, far greater, than those of indulging even the most ravenous of appetites.

Amanda had long since conceived a revulsion towards all meats. The big white serving bowls full of burnt hamburgers and hot dogs that St. Matthew's served on Tuesday and Wednesday nights she could hardly look at without gagging. She had begun to subsist wholly on toast, little sawed-off pieces of apple or banana, and coffee at breakfast, and more fruit, perhaps some lettuce or a cooked vegetable at dinner. In the mornings she would ostentatiously butter two slices of whole-wheat toast, but nibble the third slice, the unbuttered one, while she sipped her coffee. And, she spoke up rather smartly, asking for utensils or condiments, trying to achieve the effect of participating in the meal — *would you hand me the ice water, pass the fruit-plate, etc.* She aimed to seem a full participant in her meals, a presence, even — in her modest, guarded way — an amusing observer of the school's V & A rituals and its little punctilios of dining. "Sink your sails, Laurence!" But she was careful to sit at the other end of the table from Toby, when she could. Once or twice she even forced a "that was great!" after pretending to enjoy her portion of mince pie, another old St. Matthew's delicacy.

CHAPTER THIRTY-ONE

S it down, Dear."

Amanda did so, eyes down, obliging and silent. The quiet economy of the way she moved across the room, just short of prim, the way she sat, folding her hands in her lap, the grave and frank expectancy of her expression, all pleased Miss Rodman. Amanda was always self-possessed; she seemed well-bred. And yet — Miss Rodman had seen a thousand girls at St. Matthew's — this self-possession could be an artifact of effort and contrivance. Sometimes it seemed almost wooden. Was it the consequence of preparing for disappointments, years of family disciplining, of small acts of intimidation?

Amanda wore a dark tartan skirt whose hem was almost at her ankles, and a heather cardigan that might have been cashmere fifty years ago. She was surely a *handsome* child.

"I have your mid-semester grades. Here."

She handed Amanda a narrow green form and waited for her reaction to it. They might have been doctor and patient, facing each other across a low table in the doctor's office and preparing to discuss a bleak medical diagnosis and possible courses of treatment. The document presented Amanda's weighted GPA. Her grades and grade point average: 3.352; fortieth in

a class of 106; and, under these, a single word, SATIS-
FACTORY, next to a heading that said: *Private
Tuition — music (Piano)*.

"You look sad, Dear, are you? Bean sleeping
enough?"

"I don't know. I guess I am. I suppose I could have
done better. Yes, I'm sad." And then she added — the
words just broke free, escaped — "What do you want
me to say?"

"In your case you may say that you have worked
with an application and discipline that are the envy of
all Morison. No one who works as you do should feel
anything but satisfaction. These are the habits that will
sustain you for a lifetime. You seem tired, are you? We
are a bit of a pressure cooker, aren't we, Dear?"

"Yes, I'm tired." Amanda ran her thumbs up and
down the form, as if trying to erase the grades and
numbers.

"Eating enough?"

Amanda looked at the wall behind Miss Rodman.
The plaster was cracked near the molding. A huge colored photograph of a toucan, a bright weird bird,
strange for its setting like everything else in the apartment, hung from the wall.

"Let us start with the bad, shall we? Always best to
face the bad first, *unflinchingly*. If you start the day
with a terrible hangover, the day gets better as you go
along. See? So face it as a wise man should, and train
for ill, and not for good. The ill first. A C in Pre-college
Algebra. He says you haven't a clue. He says failure is
not likely, however, so that's something. You won't get
an F for the term if you continue to work. You can do
that with certain maths — skate hard, just fast enough
to keep from falling through the ice. Do you see what I
mean? So. No F if you work."

"No F if I work!"

She had gotten to her, for the first time. Hadn't really meant to, but had. "No. You remain quite safely in the C range, and never have to do maths after you leave St. Matthew's. In ten years you'll have people do that for you."

"A C will kill me at Dartmouth."

"You don't know that. You don't know what they'll do. Their selections are quite unpredictable."

"I *know*." Amanda was sure she knew. She never should have come here. All these kids her own age, twice as smart as she was, twice as fast, twice as good at something, twice as gifted. The school loved to lob the word around: gifted. And none of them, not even the Asian ones, worked any harder than she did. She had a sudden picture in her mind of Daniella, gliding through the woods, gliding as if sailing on ice; she thought of the boys who did the math answers in their heads and left hour tests after ten minutes.

"Oh, you know, do you? Perhaps you're a clairvoyant. I pass to A.P. Latin. Beta-plus, very creditable, and with smashing comments. He calls you determined and meticulous and he says — I quote — 'The symmetrical precision of her handwriting is a treat in itself.' He says you are reliable and maniacally industrious. The world is run by such people. Your vaunted Housman was a meticulous classicist. No one approached him. Look at Lord Curzon."

"Who?"

"Used to be Viceroy. Dr. Passmore loves him. I am going to smoke."

But Amanda barely heard her. All at once she felt herself drowning, overwhelmed in the thick hopelessness and cruelty of her fate. No matter how hard she ran or studied or played or swam, it was never enough.

It was like a wall of water, a huge wave curling over you and swallowing you up.

"Use this Kleenex. You are far too hard on yourself. Pull yourself together! Let me continue. U.S. History — A.P. An Alpha-minus from our friend Mr. Steele. He gave only two As and two A-minuses. Comment: 'I have always liked this girl. No hyperbole, careful preparations, comments always on point, as reliable as a Swiss clock.' Amanda, Amanda!" — Miss Rodman reached across the coffee table and took one of the girl's hands in her own — "That is rare praise from Mr. Steele. He's a tremendous judge of young people!

"A.P. Biology. B-plus. The same comments. Here is one: 'No one works more systematically, more carefully in the lab.' And for the last, the best, a bright brave flag of Alpha, a straight A from our dear headmaster. He says you are an angel, and that if Housman wrote poems about girls instead of boys, you would have been what he was talking about. Want a sentence? 'I suspect this lovely girl will be a poet. Her understanding of Housman and Hopkins is intuitive and complete. She has a scholar's serenity. She radiates a quiet confidence . . .' You see what your headmaster thinks of you. That's worth every silly SAT score laid end-to-end from here to the moon."

Quiet confidence, Amanda thought.

"Does that make you feel better?"

No, it did not. The poetry course wasn't A.P. No one took it seriously at St. Matthew's or, probably, at Dartmouth . . .

"So a C and two B-pluses, and an A-minus and an A." If your most recent SATs lift you over 1300 then I should have thought Dartmouth would be quite doable." Miss Rodman looked at the door to the study, and Amanda turned to see what she was looking at.

A healthy glowing girl, just shy of stout, her hair in a symmetrical, perfectly-prepared French braid, taffy blonde hair pulled back from her temples with such force that it seemed to make her eyes stretch farther from each other, looked at them brightly.

"Ah, Sumner Buck, come in, come in. Amanda and I were just finishing up. I've good tidings for you, Dear. Good-bye, Amanda. Courage, mon vieux. How are you, Sumner? Sit right over here." The phone rang. "Let me take this, don't mind the smoke . . ."

Closing the door, Amanda could make out two words, both Miss Rodman's: Princeton. Calculus. If she had taken calculus, she would have failed even if she'd stayed up all night for a month. The ice could have been a foot thick, and still she'd have fallen through.

December 2, 2000

Dear Mr. & Mrs. Bahringer,

Just a note or two about Amanda, whom I have gotten to know during the first ten weeks of school. She impressed me as a determined young woman who is a real plugger, and not afraid to pursue her ambition with energy and conviction. I am a young man, and one thing I want to say to you may strike you as unusual. That is this. If I were old enough to have a daughter at St. Matthew's, Amanda is what I hope she would be like. She has a self-containment about her that I do not often see here. She is a self-reliant girl, very independent. She must get it from the two of you. Congratulations!

To the subject at hand:

Our four college choices are Colgate, Dartmouth, Hamilton, and Trinity. We may also do

Kenyon and Emory, down the road, and possibly Mt. Holyoke. Do you know Mt. Holyoke? They have a great *teaching* faculty. Possibly it will not appeal to Amanda because it is a woman's college. I don't know — I haven't raised the possibility. She is, frankly, determined that every imaginable iron be pushed deeply into the Dartmouth fire. She gets uneasy (I see it all the time with all my advisees) when I even *talk* about colleges other than her first choice. She is fixated on Dartmouth.

Maybe we can get her in, but it will be very hard. I have to tell you that her current SATs are more than 200 points below their mean scores. Her Lawrence H.S. grades are good, but not really outstanding, and she does not appear to have any athletic or extracurricular commodities that Dartmouth will want to buy into. (There is a possible exception, according to Coach Robert Kellam, Master of Physics and our girls' running guru, in Amanda's cross-country achievements this Fall. Dartmouth may lower the barrier a bit for athletes of serious accomplishment and promise. In Amanda's case, acc. to Kellam, she would have to do a certain time for the Five Kilometer run, which is the cross-country distance at this level.) I know she is a pianist, but so are a hundred young men and young women who are admitted to colleges like Dartmouth. We can video her performances, but they will help only if she is *really* outstanding. As her parents, you probably think she's a Van Cliburn, and maybe she is; I can't judge that.

She will need to get very high grades here for the fall term, and her SATs will have to rise at least to the mid-1300 range. She has to get the academic piece right. Her algebra mid-term grade is unhelpful. You may have an "in" at the college. Use it if you do.

So this is where we stand. I think she has a somewhat better shot at Colgate and, certainly, at Hamilton and at Trinity College. We do some business with all three and I know them well. I think she would flourish at any one of them. They're good little schools. Ultimately, what kind of person she becomes, and how successful she will be, will have almost nothing to do with whether she goes to Hamilton or Dartmouth. But you know that. Anyone smart enough to send their daughter to St. Matthew's is smart enough to know that. Am I right?

With kind regards. It was good to get a glimpse of you at Parents Weekend.

If I can be of any help, please do not hesitate to call me.

Sincerely,

Robert Arnett

CHAPTER THIRTY-TWO

Tess called Mr. Carnes about Amanda's algebra situation; called him from a seat phone on a United flight from LaGuardia to Denver. She was at her feistiest. These mid-morning flights, she was thinking, were absolutely perfect. They permitted a full work-out in the fitness room at home; time for her hair with her regular girl Marge, in Lawrence; an hour to dress and pack; and a limo, permitted all Warfield partners, from home to the airport. She stretched and purred in 2A; the rest of First Class was sparsely filled, the seat next to her empty, and with her book lying on it: *The Power of Style* — which had a picture of Babe Paley on the back cover. Tess relished the read ahead. She felt deliciously invigorated, that was the word. The day was brisk and fair: the sun beamed at her above a white scurf of cloud — so bright she had to leave her glasses on, big new Fendis with some sort of Roman coin at the temples.

She felt . . . pretty. She remembered a song with that name, Deborah Kerr or Julie Andrews, one of those. Tess always felt this way on trips. Whatever she wore, she liked to honor her curves with soft lines, softer hues — gorsey heathers and teals; even dark sage, a consultant had suggested. There was nothing wrong with bringing in a consultant if you were a principal in a firm like Warfield. Periwinkle also worked for her; and her hair, soft, at chin length, which, according to the consultant, retained some authority, yet helped strike a balance between . . . well, Tess understood. It was like a little retaining grip on a departing guest's hand: a way to be winsome, but not too. She looked down at her left wrist, at a Sobie platinum and gold bracelet that was chunky and airy at once, with intricate latches and punctuating ribbons of a bronzier kind of gold; and her Baume Mercier watch — a serious investment, certainly appropriate.

It might be the fashion to dress down on flights, but Tess didn't buy it. Amanda had no interest in clothes so far as her mother could see, but Tess's turn-out was immaculate: a hunter green pantsuit, the pants wide and with a deep break, but the jacket fitted and with mannish shoulder pads, a retro look; the blouse the thing that made it go — cream silk, summery, no collar, mitigating the possible severity of the effect created. Looking at her right ankle as she made her little circles with her foot, she thought how much she loved her shoes — a perfect black suede and a bit sturdier than a normal pump but not showing the sturdiness.

"Great suit!" A voice intruded. "We're doing a light snack. Anything for you?" Tess said no, nothing, no, wait a minute, grapefruit juice and Perrier. Two of the other three or four passengers in First Class clacked away at their lap-tops, unaware they were about to be treated to one of life's delicious pleasures: watching a *scene* at close range, in perfect safety and innocence.

It took Tess a long time to get Mr. Carnes, Master of Algebra, on the plane phone. These people, she was thinking, are impossible to get hold of. They're always running around to athletic fields or supervising lunch or whatever else they do, and the school's switchboard is run by some scholarship child. And the math ones, the ones that teach math, they're the worst of all. They don't engage the people they talk to. You don't have anything in common with them. The work, the thing they do, is all numerical, the algebra kind of thing. They don't see the gradations of normal human emotions. Not only that, if they were really good, they wouldn't be at St. Matthew's, they'd be at M.I.T. . . . or Dartmouth! Hello, Hello! All right. Well, you tell *me* what Area Code you're in. A bored voice commanded the caller to Hold On, that they were getting Mr. Carnes.

"Hello?"

"Dr. Carnes, this is Amanda's mother, Tess Bahringer. Can you hear me? Do you want to go first, or should I?"

"Go first? I . . ."

"O.K. You have her in your Pre-college Algebra, all right? And you have given her a C and you've written comments on her report, I have it right in front of me, written comments that are unacceptable to her father and me. Can you hear what I'm saying? Amanda's other grades are all excellent. The other comments are all courteous and they appreciate this girl and her effort and the load she's carrying. She is a candidate for Dartmouth. No, no — can you hear me? Look, we're not going to beat around the bush. We know Passmore, the man you work for. Why don't you show *him* the kind of trash you write about a child, eight weeks away from home for the first time in her life? I happen to know you don't have tenure. They don't give it in boarding school. I want you to think hard about that grade and harder about the way you wrote about our daughter — you use the phrase, 'She doesn't have a clue,' like she's on a game show or something — no, no, you listen to me. We have representation at Davis Polk. I know the managing partner there. You tell me, you didn't even know who my daughter was, did you, when you picked up the phone, until I refreshed your memory? You still there? Hello?"

The light clacking had stopped in the compartment. The flight attendant who'd complimented Tess on her suit now stood in perfect silence behind the last seat, her hands on the headrest. There was another click as the phone was returned and seated in its holder; and then — the pleasure it gave was only slightly overborne by her embarrassment — Tess was stunned by an outburst of raucous applauding, clapping, cheering, even a scream or two of *All Right!*; and a finger tapping her left shoulder from behind and a man's voice saying, "I've waited my whole life to hear that done, and I'll bet a million bucks that kid is a perfect reproduction of her mama. God bless you, darlin'! Show 'em who the hell they are!"

CHAPTER THIRTY-THREE

Amanda sat in the waiting room of the infirmary, looking at an advertisement for Virginia Slims. Half the girls on the hall smoked. Miss Rodman smoked, hard. The ad asserted: THERE IS NO SLIMMER WAY TO SMOKE. WHEN YOU SMOKE, THERE'S NONE SLIMMER!

"Come on in, Amanda. You doing all right?"

"I think I'm getting the flu."

"No, no, you're not. That's in February. You're just getting a cold."

"Can you give me anything? I can't get a cold now."

"Oh? Are you singing at the Met? Are you in the space program?"

"I got a race tomorrow. I can't . . ."

"Come over here, young lady. Get up on the scale. Put this thing in your mouth." The doctor noted her temperature and weight, sat her down, and began taking her blood pressure.

"106."

"That's O.K., isn't it? My father's is 130."

"One hundred six is your weight. It's maybe not O.K. Are you eating?"

"Sure?"

"Do you eat your suppers? When do you get in from cross-country? Are you still running cross-country?"

"Oh, plenty of time. I get to dinner when I need to. Class IV doesn't have to if we don't want to."

This tickled Dr. Martin. A girl P.G. reminding him about meal regulations. "So what do you eat, if you skip dinner?"

"I'll get some fruit? I have fruit in my room. Or I heat up some Ramen."

"How much's he have you running?"

"About thirty miles a week."

Dr. Martin looked evenly at Amanda. He studied her record. "You weighed around 112 when you came here — even that's not really enough for your height. So watch it, you know what I mean? You're one of those young ladies, you really don't need to think about weight — all your running, small frame, high metabolism. The reason you're getting a cold is your resistance is down. I'll give you a medical slip for Coach Kellam. You tell him that an athlete does his best times after he's had a couple of days off. It's the truth. He hates to hear it, but it's the truth."

"I have to do my best time."

"You don't have to do *any* time. What *are* you, a horse? This isn't the Marines. This is not the Olympics. You go sleep like a stone, two or three nights in a row. Don't run. Don't skip your meals. Read a novel. Look at the sky!" Dr. Martin jiggled his eyebrows, his way of terminating examinations and interview. "Good luck, all right?"

On the way out, Amanda saw Daniella.

"What'd the doctor say? You all right?"

"He said I was perfect."

Daniella and Amanda had not, really, become good friends. There was no real leisure at St. Matthew's, so friendships were always temporary affiliations or accommodations among students with haphazardly intersecting interests — always provided such interests did not lead to serious competition. Within the bounds of each class, students were like so many locomotives racing alongside each other on endless parallel tracks, their engineers totally absorbed in their duties, far too absorbed to do anything more than glance over at their rivals. Systemic departees were simply engines that had worn out or careened off the tracks. Such attrition was constant. This, too, was an efficient prophylactic against the formation of friendships.

If Toby — indolent young leopard — was ambling imperturbably through his father's boarding school, Daniella had made her way and her reputation by applied will, by fierce tenacity of purpose. Self-possessed, as silent as Amanda, she united to such endowments an analytical mind and the physique of a natural athlete. "Just kept coming back for more, when they handed out talents," was Coach Kellam's judgment. As a little girl growing up on an upstate reservation she had seen Olympic marathoners train; had been captured by their determination to master the full distance. She made that determination her own.

By the time Daniella was a junior, the colleges were seeking *her*. Her WISC scores, measured in 1995 — generalized I.Q. — aggregated 152. Her SATs, 1560. In general order of academic merit (posted at the end of each term in the Savernake Common Room), she ranked second in a class of 110. She was a National Merit Finalist; had strong pretensions to becoming an all-American in cross-country; and was bombarded, there is no other word for it, with letters advertising a wild range of merit scholarships — many from schools of which she had never heard. She wanted to be a doctor.

182

Amanda noticed that, although Daniella rarely talked, the responses she made to questions put to her by adults, by masters and coaches, by Dr. Passmore were so wise, so acute in their understanding, that her questioners often responded with little ironic nods of incredulity. It wasn't a question of academic smarts; it was a precocious wisdom — the kind that both amazed and silenced.

They did their van time together, travelling to cross-country meets all over upstate New York in a smelly school mini-bus, both of them silent, listening to the anxious conversations of the other girls. "He's like this preppy little hockey player from Westport, Connecticut, who went on NOLES and now he thinks he's Leo diCaprio . . ." And Kellam's voice cutting through always with his spiel about *Leaving It,* leaving all of it, on the course, he didn't care what course it was. "Don't you ever, *ever,* let me see you sprint the last hundred of a 5K. All that says to me is you didn't leave it out there, where it belongs. Hey, fun couple," he addressed Amanda and Daniella, "at least one of you left it out there today — how about it, Michelin Lady?" Daniella was big for a runner, strong and shouldery, two or three inches taller than the others. Her running was of a piece with everything else she did. She trained, aimed, and executed.

Amanda's final chance at peeling a minute off her best time fell on the first Wednesday after Thanksgiving break. It was St. Matthew's last dual meet of the season, a competition with a girls' school near Albany, St. Anne's. She had a goal, a time of 17.50 or better for 5K — a time, she calculated, so flashy, so persuasive, that the Dartmouth coach would simply have to give her a slot. Her mathematical estimates of how she might achieve such a time (based on complicated calculations involving lost pounds, average training times and distances covered) would have amazed Mr. Carnes. By now she was feeding on various vitamin formulations, bee pollen pastes, Power Bars, restricting her fluid intake to athletic drinks or water. She had almost doubled her mileage, some of it in her early morning sessions in harness, in the Gibbon pool. She was wired for the race.

In longer races it was hard to tell how you might do in the great distances that stretched ahead — marathons and 50Ks — but the 5K, the regulation girls' high school cross-country distance, was altogether different. It was an extended sprint. You could tell at once, right from the start, whether you had it that day: something about how your body responded to its first physical insult, the suddenness of the urgent demand for wind, for oxygen, right at the start. If it was going to be a good run, Amanda always felt a potent surge — as she thought of it — a surge of air, linked in her mind to a sense of easy bounding, almost of gliding. Her running felt effortless. And no place accommodated the sense better than the Seneca Forest.

The afternoon was ideal. The sky, the color of uncleaned pewter, was a runner's sky; the air was chilled, but barely so, and windless: not a shiver of branch, not a whisper or crackling of a leaf scratched the silence. Even her footfalls were silent.

As usual, Amanda fell in directly behind Daniella, running easily and maintaining a distance of ten or twelve yards behind her. She sensed at once that this would be the best race she had ever run. She bounded along in an easy lope for the first quarter-mile or so, the distance carrying the pack to the edge of the forest and then down, down into the woods for the switchbacks and blind curves of the Seneca Trail. Right from the start Amanda was able to maintain her pace, Daniella's pace, with an ease that, the longer she ran, seemed less — not more — taxing.

Whiskery stems brushed her face. She shot past the ragged forest façade on either side, feeling herself *flung* off the Far Fields into the woods. Off, off forth on swing! She was a Windhover! The forest was silent as a listener; it embraced her. She felt stronger with each stride. For the first time, the distance between Daniella and Amanda was actually shrinking; she was, yes, closing the gap, and without laboring or forcing the pace. She thought suddenly of Coach Kellam, standing and cheering at the finish, grabbing her off her feet in a wild hug, yelling *Look What You Did, You Did It! Amanda!* And how it would lift her life off her back — totally, completely *guarantee* Dartmouth, put her mother on the moon. With 17.30, they didn't care *what* your math SAT was!

The forest swept by, and she no longer saw it as bare branches, only as a buffered opaqueness until finally, polished and gleaming, the Seneca lay before her and she made her left-hand turn up onto the embankment, five-eighths of a mile now ahead of her, maybe three minutes, all straight and flat. There was Daniella, perhaps fifteen yards ahead, both girls running silently, so that Daniella did not, had not, had never, looked back; her own movement sustained effortless gliding as always. And then, as if time had been drugged and their motion conjointly slowed somehow, Daniella seemed to pitch forward, tumbling aslant, soundlessly propelled off the embankment trail by her own momentum, arrested in the soft scree on the flank of the embankment only an inch or two from the yellow scrim at the edge of the river itself. She had — there was no telling how — tripped somehow, somersaulted, her motion arrested several feet below the trail: she lay silent but in an agony that not even her self-control could hide. Amanda was on her in an instant, hands under her arms, pulling her away from the water. Daniella moaned deeply.

"Where is it? Where're you hurt? Daniella!"

The girl somehow got onto an elbow, reaching down towards her right ankle. From Amanda's vantage it already seemed violently swollen and angry, purplish, a terrible sprain or worse. She thought of getting Daniella to thrust it into the water, cried: "Daniella? Can you drag yourself up onto the bank?" Somehow together they managed it, up onto the rough margin of the trail on the forest side. Now, a runner in Navy and white shot by, a skinny little runner, and then another, very fast. "I'm all right . . . Go on, Amanda, go on! They can't get here any faster — they can't get anyone here until you finish." And she whispered: "It's your day!" She hugged her.

Amanda jerked herself up and began sprinting up the embankment, soon making her turn back into the forest and onto the steep uphill Kellam loved to train them on, more than half-mile back towards the Far Fields, and now so far behind the two runners that she could neither hear nor see them. It was new to her now: running alone and as hard as she could, but no one in front to pull her along. She wondered how much time she had lost — thirty seconds? A minute? More? The incline had begun almost at once — a cruel, cruel hill. She clambered raggedly forward, each stride a painful effort.

She came to the end of the forest trail. She felt renewed, she exploded back onto the brown plain of the athletic fields. Now, not fifty feet ahead, running in a careless tandem that showed total unconcern at even the possibility of being overtaken, were the two St. Anne's runners who had passed them on the embankment — had passed, she remembered, without so much as a question, *you O.K.?* or even a look back. They seemed drained, wobbling, from the effort of the forest uphill, their hands flapping at their sides, their legs without lift. Amanda began reeling them in, in that happiest of runner's phrases, recapturing the buoying confidence that had fueled her at the start. She was consumed by the sudden thought of *leaving it,* only two hundred yards to go, perhaps; the little cluster of spectators and timers gathering at the finish, and Amanda already close enough to hear a shout, a wild yell of encouragement. "The last time I will ever have to do this here," she remembered. Suffused by a new kind of fuel, one that said *Victory,* not *good job,* but flat-out *Victory!,* she ran faster than she had ever run in her life.

She reeled in her rivals, passed them, seeing at a flash the disbelief on their faces and now in her final sprint she charged into the funnel of spectators and coaches, kept running past them, crossing the finish line and circling back, scarcely winded, towards Coach Kellam.

"Get someone down there for Daniella, she fell! Right by the river!"

"Why didn't you stay with her?"

"Ran here as hard as I could."

"O.K. 18.25. Not a bad effort. I'll go get her."

5 December 2000

Dean of Admission
Dartmouth College
Hanover, New Hampshire 03755

Dear Sir,

Amanda Bahringer, a Class IV girl at St. Matthew's and a candidate for admission at Dartmouth, has asked me to write in her behalf. I do so with pleasure.

If you wish to populate your freshman class with girls and boys whose principal qualification for admission is sheer brain-power, particularly of the kind that glitters on the examinations contrived by the Scholastic Examination Test preparers, I urge you to decline her application.

If you wish to leaven the lump, so-to-speak, with young people of certain rare qualities of character and mind, of the kind that academic evaluations typically misconstrue (or are baffled by), then I hope you will grant a tender solicitude to her claims.

She has the soul and the heart of a poet, of a young Willa Cather; she has the serenity of the guileless and good. She *intuits* things about literature and people that the rest of us labor to discern, and then often miss. "What heart heard of, ghost guessed . . ." Her beauty of character, her talents in the making of music and in the understanding of poetry, her simplicity, and the goodness which "puts ambition out of countenance," these things surely entitle her a place at your table.

Believe me to be,

Yours most sincerely,

Carlisle Passmore
headmaster

CHAPTER THIRTY-FOUR

1866. For Lent. No pudding on Sundays. No tea except if to keep awake and then without sugar. Meat only once a day. No verses in Passion Week or on Fridays. No lunch or meat on Fridays. Not to sit in armchair except can work in no other way. Ash Wednesday and Good Friday bread and water. ,

Dr. Passmore asked his seminar to read through a collection of entries from the journals of Gerard Manley Hopkins. "See where the poetry comes from." He believed, most sincerely, that adolescent students yearned for voices of authentic corroboration, for the writings of sages and poets, which seemed to affirm what their own instincts told them to believe. Passmore himself had fallen in love with Thomas Wolfe, the first time he read *Look Homeward Angel,* just as he had done with John Masefield's poetry.

He cherished Hopkins, but no one else seemed to. The rest of the seminar thought him weird. Passmore would read a line or a stanza out loud, and Amanda would watch the three boys in the group cringe in revulsion: *what is this guy, like, a freak? Give us a break!*

She listened to Passmore rapt, staring at the mountains that glowed hazily in the early morning distance.

She heard him: "... he considered every humiliation to be something willed by God. In a strange way he relished his pains, his deprivations, his mortifications. Can you see?" He read a sentence or two from a journal: "This life here though it is hard is God's will for me, as I most intimately know ... which is more than violets knee-deep ... I have asked for six months' custody of the eyes ..."

"What is 'custody of the eyes?'"

No one answered.

"Toby, what is custody of the eyes? Amanda?"

"It's when you deliberately look down at the ground. You don't allow yourself to look around."

"Yes, Amanda. And what would be the purpose of such a practice?"

"To deprive yourself of what gives you pleasure."

"Exactly. Hopkins seemed determined to mortify himself, his body. What do we mean, Toby, by 'mortify?'"

"It means reminding yourself that you are a physical body, and must die. You do it by inflicting deprivation or pain."

"Excellent. Who else liked to mortify himself? Let us be ghoulish for a moment. Someone Hopkins would surely have admired. The moral equivalent of Marcus Aurelius. Who was Marcus Aurelius?"

"Don't know, Sir."

"Amanda?"

"He was this emperor?"

"Yes. Forget him for the moment. The Englishman. Who was that?"

"Thomas More."

"Daniella — how do you know these things?"

"My mother took me to New York, and I saw his portrait. Also — we're reading *Utopia* in an A.P."

"How would he mortify himself?"

"Hair shirt."

"Do him any good?"

"Kept him warm."

"So why was he in prison — in the Tower?"

"Because he would not deny his faith. He wouldn't agree that the king was the head of the church."

"The idea of the shirt was discomfort, not warmth." Passmore drew a handkerchief from the sleeve of his own lavender-colored shirt, and Amanda noticed his cufflinks. He passed the handkerchief across his forehead, something he did habitually — a peculiar gesture, a tic.

"Who else used mortifications?"

"Virginia Woolf."

"Virginia Woolf? Really? How would you know this, Amanda?"

"I've read some Virginia Woolf on my own. She never ate anything. She had a fascination with excrement."

"What?"

"She was very strange. She killed herself by filling her pockets with rocks and jumping into a river."

They had these strange little lodes of information, little clumps of facts that floated around in their minds, waiting for places to land. The headmaster was always *enchanted* that they would know such things.

"But getting back to Hopkins. What do these things tell us — not about him, but about his poems?"

"You can't separate them like that."

"Yes?"

"Because," Amanda answered, "because you can't understand what he writes unless you understand *him* . . ."

"He was a manic depressive, plus he was gay."

"Thank you, Toby. That will do. You have obviously read the introduction to your text. As a matter of fact, there isn't a shred of evidence that he was actively homosexual. He may have been mildly depressed, but nothing more than that."

"If they'd had him on Prozac he wouldn't have written this weird stuff. Prozac'd calm his ass down."

"You talk like this before your headmaster? How must you talk in front of your friends on the river! Watch your mouth, young man."

Toby laughed. It was his conceit that the Head loved all oarsmen, and would forgive them their language and their sins. "We make it to Henley this year, you won't care what we say in the boathouse."

The headmaster bestowed a look of tender exasperation. "Yes, Father Hopkins may have been a bit depressed. Many great poets and artists are — many have full bipolar disease: periods of florescence and manic activity, then times of self-hatred and depression. Virginia Woolf is a good example. So is Amanda's adored Robert Schumann. It's interesting, *he* threw himself into the Rhine, three or four years before he died. No, Hopkins couldn't have written his poetry if he hadn't been upset in some terrible way . . ."

"He had to be an ascetic. He had to deny himself what he wanted."

"Yes, Amanda?" he urged.

"He needed this discipline he imposed on himself. He needed to deny himself. That's why his poetry is so great and so strange."

"Thank you. That is all for today. Toby Carrington, you are a cheeky lad. Will you go St. A. at Charlottesville?"

"No, Sir. Phi Kapp. My father was."

"Are they all right?"

"Yes, Dr. Passmore, perfectly suitable."

"Good-bye, Toby."

"Your boy Hopkins — he's plainly light in his loafers."

Where had he learned this phrase? Passmore hadn't heard it since Princeton.

"Amanda, stay for a moment."

She turned to face him, laying her book-bag on the sofa.

"You're quite taken with Father Hopkins."

"Oh, yes, Sir. This is the first poet I ever thought I understood. I understand him completely. I don't know how, but I do. I can tell what he's trying to do, all the time. I love him."

"You are knee-deep in violets."

"Thank you, Dr. Passmore."

Amanda hurried back to her room, as she always did after Dr. Passmore's seminar. She'd begun using the free period to study Latin. You could wear Latin down, she now believed. Organized work, enough of it, could actually wear it down. It was that kind of a subject.

Her way was blocked in the corridor. Four girls, one of them Sumner Buck, were pushing or dragging heavy suitcases and bags full of clothes down the hall, towards the landing.

"Hi. What's happening?"

"Nothing that concerns you, Amanda." It was the girl who'd asked where she was from in Long Island.

"Sumner got S.D.'d."

"Oh my God. What'd she do?"

"She had an affair with a Class III. If you did anything but work and think about yourself, you'd know about it."

Back in her room, Amanda looked down at the lot. The same girls were loading Sumner's things into a Mercedes sedan. Sumner's mother stood watching. Amanda thought of running down to hug Sumner good-bye, but she decided she'd better not. All she could think of was Sumner having to deal with her father.

CHAPTER THIRTY-FIVE

About five weeks normally separate the administration of the SAT from the receipt of results. Amanda learned her latest scores from her mother, who had had them read out to her by the housekeeper in Lawrence. Tess was at a convention in Tucson and had phoned in.

It was odd, listening to the housekeeper reading out the information — the numbers — and with no greater comprehension of what she was reading and saying than a boy soprano's comprehension of the *Magnificat*. But Tess heard the bottom line clearly enough: SAT — V: 730; SAT — M: 610. She did the math in her head, fast: 1340.

1340!

It was a number both gratifying and satisfying. The SAT UP course, the counseling, the vocabulary lists, all the encouragement and hard work, seem to have worked. St. Matthew's had been the right thing to do. *1340 was a fine number!* It had a creditable heft, a cachet. "She's in the mid-1300s." Higher, the kids were frequently nerdy, even manic — like pumped-up weightlifters on steroids. University admissions officers wouldn't be fooled by them. In Amanda's case, now, the whole package was coming together, and it was impressive. At a poolside tête-à-tête with a colleague, Tess twice contrived directed conversations that permitted her to say "the mid-1300s." A good, *a great,* number.

And it was better, much better, than Amanda herself had allowed herself to expect. Coming out of the SAT, she'd bleakly fantasized going below a thousand, wondering whether she'd even be allowed home at Thanksgiving. You could never tell how well you were doing on the SAT when you were taking it: two of the four answers were so close, and they'd been designed that way, just to trip you up or to expose kids who might be too smart for their own good, kids looking for hidden meanings, deeper values. She attributed her success to Mr. Ebrington and to the SAT UP manuals — and to the mastery of nervousness that SAT UP inculcated.

"Well done, dear child, well done!" Miss Rodman handed Amanda the faxed report a day later, Daniella standing next to the hallmaster in front of her apartment.

"What'd you get, Amanda?"

"1340."

Daniella nodded in her grave and thoughtful way. The nod communicated a message that perhaps only Amanda could understand. It seemed to say: I admire you. You did what you had to do, you did it alone, you made the best of what you are. For a moment Amanda saw fierceness in Daniella's expression. It gave her joy.

"V & A, 13 December, 2000. *Let me have your attention.*"

Another batch of early decision and early-action triumphs.

This group comprised not only the small fry of the industry, colleges whose names sounded like places from the Sunday *New York Times* football list, but also the formidable fortresses of the business: Penn, Harvard, Brown, M.I.T., Yale, Virginia.

"Virginia. Carrington, T.F."
Mr. Barber winked at Toby and moved his lips in a stage whisper — "Big surprise." Toby groped clumsily for Amanda's hand. Found it and winked at her. "A great shock to all of us," she said to him.

"Continuation. Mark Mathew's, St. M's Class of 1995, has been awarded the Pitt Scholarship for study in an English university. At our school he was graduated as Scholar of the First Rank and Captain of Varsity Lacrosse. At Harvard College he was editor-in-chief of the Crimson, a Phi Beta Kappa as a junior. Resume!"

"Well, Toby, your worries are over."
"I never let myself have worries. And neither should you."

"V & A, 16 December 2000. *Let me have your attention.*"

Silence. It might have been the silence that followed the last word in a sermon.

"The following constitute further early-decision results communicated to College Counseling and Dr. Passmore's office as of this morning. These results are incomplete. Acceptances: Amherst College, Santa Maria, R.; Bates College, Barra, R., Mathews, K.; W. B. Davidson College, Beck, T.; Dartmouth College, Gordon J. P., Linstom, R. A., Bonifors, T. H.; Georgetown University . . ."

The voice droned, plummily accentuating the vowels as though the herald was in training to be an anchorperson. All early-decision results had been mailed to members of Class IV; most would have found the letters in their mailboxes that morning. But now all *knew.* Everyone at St. Matthew's knew. Early-decision and early-action successes were no longer conveniences: they were battle trophies, the combat decorations of a fevered little garrison of ambition. Together, also, they gave the first signs of what kind of a year it was going to be for St. Matthew's. It was like hearing the first election returns from Indiana or Connecticut.

Amanda could listen in wonder and simple curiosity. She herself was a candidate for Regular Decision.

"... *Yale University, Ramirez, B. A., Lawton, R., Jr. ... Announcements concluded. Resume.*"

Applause, self-satisfied, decorously robust, swelled up, shaking — so it seemed — the very pennants and banners that hung from the rafters above.

CHAPTER THIRTY-SIX

Isn't that the girl we saw during Parents Weekend, the Indian girl?"

Amanda and Tess were together in the car, in a line of vehicles leaving St. Matthew's for Christmas. It was snowing lightly; and on the broad esplanade in front of the Chapel, groups and pairs of students hugged each other, shouting happy farewells. Tess felt a twinge of nostalgia, remembering the joyous beginnings of her own girlhood holidays. The student she recognized was indeed Daniella. She stood, alone, immobile, a bright yellow duffel at her feet.

Amanda rolled down the window. "Hey — going our way? Want a lift? Where you headed?"

"Hi, Amanda. Michigan. Ann Arbor, Michigan. They're flying me out to a scholarship interview." Daniella leaned forward a bit, nodding an awkward greeting at Amanda's mother.

"You're all set at Brown though, right?"

"Yes. That's all set. But . . ."

"Have a great Christmas. Your ankle's OK, isn't it?"

"All healed. Take care, Amanda. See you in January."

Daniella wore her usual expression: composed, guarded, a bit wistful. She waved a gentle good-bye.

"I do remember her," Tess said. "Another reason St. Matthew's has been good for you. The diversity. You'd never meet anyone like that at home."

CHAPTER THIRTY-SEVEN

At the end of the long Christmas vacation, well into bleak January, Tess returned her daughter to St. Matthew's. They drove up in the Land Rover, traversing a landscape that seemed featureless, almost polar, that swallowed them up as soon as they crossed the Hudson and turned north. The family vehicle, its British Army green usually polished to dazzling iridescence, now wore the battle-dress of a grim northeastern winter — streaky grime that told of long suburban drives, that marked the car as functional, not merely ornamental.

Mother and daughter fought. The pre-St. Matthew's daughter had been prim, obliging, and demure, and her mother almost prissy with displays of solicitude — perfect models of family grace and harmony. But no longer. When they walked together through the shiny mall concourses, fulfilling Christmas rituals of shopping, holiday lunch tête-à-têtes, visits to beauty salons, fixtures with friends, the daughter skittered ever-so-slightly away from her parent, like a leashed dog that cannot bear to be too close to its master. Mother's and daughter's eyes did not engage when they sat opposite each other in restaurants: Amanda's head constantly shifting to the menu, to the edge of the table, to the faces of other patrons being led to their tables, to her meager pile of bean sprouts and penne.

On the trip north they slid hopelessly into little abraded disagreements about trivial things. The disagreements escalated with a speed and fury that stunned them both, rocketing forward in shouting, outraged insults, these followed by earnest re-arming silences: the two sides in truces collecting their wounded and contriving fresh forays, new tactics. And if the arguments were provoked by trifles, the fighting, re-ignited, was sustained by deep, vicious forays and counter-attacks aimed ultimately at breaking the very wills and souls of the combatants.

"A-Man-Da," Tess pronounced, as if shushing an exasperating child. "A-Man-Da."

"You called me stupid! Call me anything, but don't call me that!"

"I'm sorry, Darling. I am sorry. You are anything but stupid. We both know what your abilities are, and you're anything but that. Do you want to stop? We can stop in two or three miles. Did you read any of this during the break?" Tess pointed to a book on the seat titled *Roman Poets of the Silver Age.*

"Yes, let's stop."

Each side moved her forces back from the crests of facing hills. There was a sheepish, palpable relaxation of tension. Each realized she had not behaved well, but there was enough scarring, enough scar tissue, to protect both parties.

The car turned off the interstate — it was the same restaurant where Joey and Tess had stopped in September after dropping Amanda at St. Matthew's. The cold, Tess thought, was perfectly outrageous. "How can people live up here?"

"Guess I'm about to find out."

They resumed the drive.

"What's the other paperback?"

"Poetry."

"By?"

"Hopkins."

"Oh, yeah, you told me. The headmaster's seminar. And who's the other one he teaches?"

"A.E. Housman?"

"So how's that going?"

"It's not a 'how's it going' type of thing. That's not how a poetic sensibility operates."

"Don't be crabby, Amanda. Don't be snotty with me."

"O.K. On the first day of class, this girl, Testy, asks him why we should read it? And he goes, it will make your life fresh and sweet. You just won't run around making money? You know what I mean?"

"Don't obsess on this stuff, Amanda."

"I'm reading Anne Sexton, too."

"This time next year, we won't be on this Interstate. We'll be on I-93, whatever, the one going to Hanover, New Hampshire. Hold that thought."

Just below Albany they turned west for the last hour of the trip, the sun shining directly in their faces. The snow lay crusted, violent in its brightness.

"Did you get your Colgate application mailed in? You could have done it on your computer, on *Macapply or Collegelink.*"

"I'm amazed you asked me that. You have one goal. I have one goal. It's in Hanover, New Hampshire."

"All right!" A bit self-consciously, Tess used her husband's athletic phrase: *the Knicks won, all right!* She reached over again, patting Amanda on the knee. "When do you hear from all of them?"

"Around the end of March, first of April. Hamilton a little earlier. Sometimes Mr. Arnett knows before then. He'll give you a hint if he wants to, but he's not supposed to. So I could find out about Dartmouth late in March. They mail the letter to the house, not the school. He wants me to add Emory to my list?"

"Where is that?"

"Atlanta, Georgia."

"Atlanta?"

"What's wrong with that?"

"You just said it yourself — let's not lose sight of the object of the exercise. Your shot at Dartmouth is better than ever. Look what you've done with your SATs! You're in the mid-1300s."

"That's still low for them."

"Your mid-terms were good. Maybe not great, but good, and improving. If a kid applied to my college with an A.P. Latin, *I'd* let her in."

"It all depends on my finals."

"When do they start?"

"January 29. We're the only school that still has them after Christmas."

"What's Mr. Arnett say? The academic piece is the main thing, right?"

"He doesn't say anything, really. He's very careful."

"It's funny, I don't worry about it any more. I feel good about it. He can spin what you've got, he can package you just right for them."

"Package me?"

"Are you feeling O.K.? Daddy said he heard you being sick to your stomach a couple of nights ago. That little bathroom, the way the house is laid out, you can hear everything. It sounded like you were throwing up. Do you have your medications? Did you get refills?"

"Something I ate."

"You look a little thin."

"Not that thin, I'm fine."

"No, not that thin. You can stand on your head for two and a half weeks, Amanda. Stephen Crane wrote *The Red Badge of Courage* in eleven days. We're doing a campaign for the Crane Writers' Memorial. So you can do what you have to do for a couple of weeks. There's no way you're going to get turned down if you do what you have to do. They all like you."

"All but Mr. Carnes."

"Forget him. He's a peasant. Here — take one of these zinc lozenges. Keep you from getting a cold. How was your visit with Dr. Mitchell?"

"O.K. I like him."

"Meaning?"

"Everything's O.K."

"He didn't give you anything?"

"Mother."

"No. Tell me, Amanda. I'll call him myself when I get home."

"Celexa. It's, like, Paxil. It's more of an all-purpose medication, they can use it for anti-anxiety, it's not that big a thing. It has a low side-effect profile. If you're stressed."

Tess looked straight ahead. They weren't far from the interstate turn-off. She understood that this was not a good time to get into the discussion that the new medication invited. It was not comfortable. She was more-or-less certain Amanda knew that *she* had been on Paxil and other things during her own troubles. It was just not something she felt comfortable pressing Amanda about.

"There're times at school when I just need . . . "

"I understand, sweetie. You're no different from anyone else. My only advice is, minimum use consistent with need. And this is only short-term."

"Daddy seemed fine. His work is going well."

"Fine."

They arrived at 2:00. St. Matthew's seemed desolate, empty. It was as though they had driven out onto the surface of a frozen lake. The cold billowed around them in angry buffets. Amanda thought of a little girl in the movie *Schindler's List*. The child had been separated from her mother; she ran — terrified but full of resource and courage — amid a great throng that had stampeded from a Nazi patrol searching buildings. The movie showed her finding a place to hide herself; but a few minutes later it showed the girl's body in a mound of the dressed dead.

Tess parked next to the only other car on the service lot, a battered old Pontiac with New Hampshire plates and a bumper sticker that said MY KID'S NO HONOR STUDENT HE DON'T EVEN KNOW WHERE HE'S AT. A scrabble of sleek black crows patrolled about the empty lot, pecking at the packed snow. Mother and daughter paused, standing side by side, their arms folded across their chests, watching them.

"Are you O.K.?"

"I'm fine. All Christmas breaks have to end."

"I know they do, I know they do. It's a sad time, but you'll have your friends back. Got enough money?"

They waddled stiffly along the unsanded walkway, carrying Amanda's things up to her room. When they got to number 23, Tess excused herself to see Miss Rodman, and came back a few minutes later.

"We conferred." She stood in the doorway of Amanda's room. "She says you don't seem to like to interact with members of your peer group. She wants you to try to do a little more of it."

"What else did she say?" Amanda couldn't conceive of Miss Rodman using such language.

"Not a lot else. She plainly cares for you. You can see that." Tess surveyed the taut little chamber, musty but in perfect order. "Bedspread looks O.K. Ought to get you one made out of this." She held out her arms, modeling her shearling coat, Joey's Christmas gift. "Walk me out to the car."

It appeared Amanda was the only student back from vacation, and Tess made a show of reluctance at having to abandon her daughter to her work, to her duties. She took her arm in comradely fashion as they walked down the corridor. The long drive loomed ahead, all the way back to Lawrence and with only a single pit stop. Two hundred miles. From another dormitory they could hear a pianist plunking out "Heart and Soul,"and with the same hesitancies and mistakes Tess remembered from I.U. almost twenty-five years earlier. The feeble song, the sound, the emptiness of the school, the cold — their awareness of what lay between them — made them both wish for the leave-taking to end quickly. Three of the spaces where student names had been affixed on Opening Day were now covered with masking tape. Systemic departees. As far as St. M's was concerned, they might as well have dropped off the face of the earth. She had never known them. It was like Stalin, or Bosnia, or something.

"And so, you ready?"

Amanda turned to face her mother directly, lifting her chin in a little gesture of confident assertion. "I'm fine."

"Good. Amanda." Tess took both her hands in her own. "You can stand on your head for three weeks. Miss Rodman said you were struggling with your algebra. I told her, and I told her nicely, look, struggle is the South Bronx. Let's remember who we are and keep our proportion. *Struggle*, my God, after the Christmas you've had, and here you are at this school, and you

207

have everything you want. Plus, this period, she says, there's no mandatory anything between now and exams, just review periods, nothing new in your classes, just filling you up for the exams. It doesn't have to be a problem. Your father agrees with me *completely* on this."

"He's a sweet man. He adores you, Mother."

But Tess received such intrusions silently, without acknowledgement: not a nod, not the tiniest hint of sympathy or agreement.

"It's true, Mother. It's better to be a good man than some smart Wall Street guy . . ."

"Amanda. I have to go, sweetie. I love you. Memorize what you have to. Miss Rodman says you can get As or A-minuses in almost all your courses. Biology, you can get that grade up — it doesn't have any math, she told me, it's all the inside of cells, etcetera, so you shouldn't have your anxiety about that. And focus on your algebra — sit down and make yourself do it when you don't want to. That's what you have to do. Lot of times, that's what I do every day. Everyone does!

"Give me a hug, hug your mother. No, not an air hug! Look, walk over to the car with me — I've got something in there for you. Open it after I leave. Have some fun with it. Use it every day. It's ideal for *you*."

Tess jerked herself up on to the driver's seat of the Land Rover and handed Amanda the package; it was the size of a small photo album.

"Kiss me again."

And she was off.

A minute or two later, just before turning onto the school drive leading out towards the Interstate, Tess looked into her rear view mirror. Amanda stood, perfectly framed in it, tiny and unmoving. Tess couldn't make out her face, but she thought she saw the stiff lifting of an arm, a sad little wave.

Ten thousand other kids were probably doing the same thing, waving good-bye. Christmas holidays always ended. Amanda had a pile of work to do; once she got back into her routine, she would feel much better. And the other kids, her friends, would be there later in the day.

The phone rang in the landing, and it was her father.

"You made it back O.K. How was the trip up?"

"It was fine. We only stopped once. Mom gave me another present, a beautiful journal, almost like a nineteenth–century journal? It's so cold here, you can't believe it. It's like the Arctic."

"You the first one back in your dorm?"

"It's funny. I think I am. You don't have to be back until 10:00 P.M."

"How was Mom on the way up?"

"Fine. We had an argument on the Tappan Zee Bridge. She's so hyper! Otherwise she was fine. Can I ask you something?"

"Can you ask me something? What am I, General MacArthur?"

"Is she on anything? I saw Paxil pills and a lot of other stuff in her medicine chest. More than a bottle or two. Green and beige capsules."

"What can I tell you?"

"I don't care if she is, I really don't."

"What're you gonna do, right now?"

"Go work out. Work the trip out of my system. Write in my new journal. I know just what I want to write on the first page."

"What?"

"It's a quote, from Hopkins?"

"Go."

"*These things, these things were here, and but the beholder wanting.*"

209

"Explain that to me."

"Everything that's important or beautiful needs someone to see it that way. Otherwise it's wasted."

"I'm very proud of you, baby."

"Thanks, Daddy."

"Don't overdo the working out. You looked thin to me when you were home — I thought maybe something was bothering you." Her father stopped right there. Amanda imagined him thinking, *I have to be real careful with her, it'll set her off or something and she will get one of those eating disorders.* The thing she loved about him was that she could tell what he was thinking, but that what he was thinking was always something nice about her.

"I won't. Just want to get the taste out of my mouth."

"Sweetheart, I can be up there in four hours, you need me for anything. Call me."

"I have my exams in three weeks. I know what I have to do. I can stand on my head for three weeks. I love you, Daddy."

"Love you, baby."

AMANDA'S JOURNAL

January 18

The Tundra of Russia.

"THESE THINGS, THESE THINGS WERE HERE, AND BUT THE BEHOLDER WANTING"

Me only cruel immortality consumes. Me meaning with barely nothing. 103.00 lbs.

This heavy beautiful journal, her last Christmas gift to me — large and dark green with heavy lined pages. GM Hopkins must have written in a journal like this. The scrape of ink. If it works out I will hold this same journal in my hands in September in Hanover, NH., another dark green place. Then I will look down at this page and remember where I was and what I was doing when I wrote it. Empty here, and hardly anyone back. Only one master, passed him coming into Morison and he said, quote, "That's the stuff." What? Clanking radiator and wind. On the way up she acc. me of being selfish, etc. Asked abt. Dr. Mitchell.

Write in this book observations and thoughts, as acc to Dr. Passmore, Hopkins did. Mixture of exquisite things and thoughts. Write in a journal as though it will be read in 100 years by a great-grand-daughter.

Perfect iambic pentameter line:
I hate to see the evening sun go down.

I am here to burrow in and lose myself totally in what I have to do. "You can stand on your head for three weeks." Everything here glancing off everything else — slanted sun glancing off the ice, glancing relationships, friendships, people greeting but always thinking of something or someone else. No one looks at you by the time you finish your answer to their question.

Celexa to replace comb Xanax/Inderal. But I made an inventory of what I do still have, incl mother's leftovers with elapsed labels — Fiorinal, Paxil, Klonapin, Luvox. En route to Gibbon, trmill.

CHAPTER THIRTY-EIGHT

Amanda woke up feeling washed-out, jittery. She had studied until 2:20 A.M. for late morning tests, one in A.P. Biology, the other in A.P. Latin — the second described as the last major run-up to the exam. At 9:30 she'd had two Caff-Alerts, at 1:30 two Valerian tablets and an Inderal. With the exception of a trip down the hall to the bathroom, she had left her desk only once or twice to stretch and do sit-ups. She had the impression, studying, that what she was doing was force-feeding herself, quite literally cramming and stuffing in information; but without any confidence that she understood what she was taking in. Musical empathies and quicksilver intuitions — such abilities, if she could call them that, were useless to this kind of work.

She had labored away, conscious of an alertness that was quite satisfying. She wrote down everything she wanted to get into her memory, writing in the perfect cursive that gave her pleasure — abandoning the Latin at 2:00 A.M. to write in her journal. When she had finally lain down under her coverlet with her Walkman she realized at once that she would never get to sleep — not with the one Inderal, not with what she had taken in, not with what she had to do. She turned on the light to look at Tess's clock: 2:58. She found the Halcion bottle and swallowed a single pill, without water; before getting back into bed, she took another one, held it in her hand as she lay there — and then took that, too.

Class IV students could skip breakfast. When Amanda woke — the sun hideously bright in her room — it was 9:50. The first of her classes was at ten, the second at eleven. She made them both somehow, wrote her test answers, and walked by herself to lunch. Her hands trembled so much she couldn't manage her soupspoon. Did anyone notice? Toby was at the other end of the table; since Christmas he'd said almost nothing to her. The space next to her was empty. So she picked up the bowl with both hands and drank from it like a child in a high-chair — to the wonder of half the table and the shouted exhortation of Mr. Barber: "Go for it, Amanda! Here's a girl who loves her Scotch broth!"

The P.A. system broke through the noontime din, terminating in a stout cheer at the news that a St. Matthew's woman, Class IV, already early at M.I.T., had just been announced as a Westinghouse Talent Finalist in New York, for her work on enzymes. Hadn't they had enzymes in A.P. Biology? She couldn't remember. At the command *Resume!* she looked down at Toby and saw he had been staring straight at her.

Lunch ended. In his journal Father Hopkins wrote of giving himself custody of the eyes, looking down and disallowing your eyes to feast on God's glories. She did this often at St. Matthew's — and now felt a pressure on the small of her back, Toby's hand, and his quiet easy southern voice asking whether she was all right. "Yes, fine." Everyone at St. Matthew's asked you that, "All right?"

"I'm worried about you. What'd you do, stay up all night? Don't you go outside any more? You eat anything beside that soup?"

"Don't worry about it, will you?"

Mid-year examinations began January 30. The four days beforehand were designated a reading period. Immediately after the exams there was a long weekend, observed as mid-year break. This was followed by the beginning of spring semester, a cruel misnomer for upstate New York.

For post-graduate members of St. Matthew's Class IV, January was the cruelest month of the year. For most, in a phrase they heard over and over again, "it's everything." They were all at school to demonstrate compelling progress: specifically in grades and SATs. Often the colleges that had denied them the preceding year had coyly implied that they would accept them *this* year, provided certain criteria, never made exactly plain, were met. For Amanda, the last grades Dartmouth would see would be those of these exams and the final term grades they would dictate. An easy conventional wisdom, purveyed by Mr. Arnett and others at St. Matthew's, was that a B or a B-plus in an A.P. course was the equivalent of a straight A in a regular one. Amanda didn't believe it. Neither did her mother. Her goals were two As, two A-minuses or B-pluses (at the worst) and a B-minus, conceivably a C, in Pre-college Algebra.

An A in Dr. Passmore's course seemed likely, the only danger being the headmaster's peculiar attitude towards grades. Hadn't he once said that an A-minus was a delightful grade, and something about an A being "too obviously the product of vulgar effort?" It did seem slightly sick to talk about acing Hopkins, as Mr. Arnett urged, but Amanda wasn't concerned about that, compared to the stakes involved. But after this, things got much less predictable. She supposed an A was just barely possible from Mr. Steele, in history, but only if she wrote a brilliant exam. In her heart, however, Amanda understood that "brilliant" was an adjective to be applied to certain other pupils, but not to her. "Brilliant" meant a shining, glittering, exalting performance. Something like that. It implied a conjunction of detailed knowledge, of conveyed understanding of that knowledge, and an understanding that depended partly on intuitions and inspiration: what Mr. Steele had once called wit. It sometimes depressed her to hear other students in history make easy allusions to other periods of history, to other cultures of which she knew nothing. Another Steele pupil might compare the Mexican War to the Athenian adventure in Sicily, for example; or Henry Clay to Benjamin Disraeli. Huh? No. Such brilliance could not be counterfeited. Only the kinds of parallels, references, comparisons of which she was incapable could produce work Mr. Steele might call "brilliant." Still, Amanda remembered his declaration at the opening of school: that first-rate work might be the product of a mind that was not brilliant. Certain minds proceeded methodically, patiently. They could anticipate likely exam questions; store up tons of facts, memorize the arguments of others, use psychology on the exam. "Here's a technique," said Toby. "Begin your answer like this: 'The trouble with this question is that it fails to examine the central issues raised in the course . . .'" No, too risky.

Under A.P. Latin and A.P. Biology — courses taken to establish seriousness of intent, Amanda wrote B-plus — if she worked hard enough. The sight translations would come from Ovid or Catullus, passages already assigned. Sheer effort could take her a long way here — given her work in Latin in Lawrence. And she felt a cold confidence in her biology preparation. Her grades in the course were good. It was irritating to hear her mother say biology was nothing but the inside of cells, etcetera, it's not a math thing: but she was partly right. Cellular analysis, hereditary and evolutionary biology, you could study and learn those things. The section was small, and Miss Cushing *liked* pluggers.

That left Pre-college Algebra. She remained miserably overmatched in the course. Even walking by Carnes' classroom at night was scary. She felt as though she were passing in front of a neighbor's house with a doberman locked in the front yard. She could hear his snarl fifty feet away.

She knew three or four things in algebra. Nothing more. Again: perhaps this one bad grade would somehow accentuate her . . . brilliance . . . in what? On the other hand, her math SAT had gone up; it was High Average. Would Dartmouth think . . . ? What would they think?

Mr. Arnett had mentioned that a showier, more bravura piano performance on video might make a strong impression on the Dartmouth Admissions Committee, and Amanda took it not only as an order to be obeyed but as an inspired suggestion.

Chopin's G-Minor Ballade, Op. 23, a long, gorgeously melodic and difficult composition. It would take, she estimated, about twelve hours a week to do it right — between now and mid-February. Doing it on video would make the performance easier but not much. She didn't think she'd need the Inderal to do it that way, as she had needed it for playing in public. Done right, maybe the Ballade could blow them away . . .

The school lurched into the resumed fall term, a tense community absorbed in its academic work. Two Class II boys were found sharing a bottle of Cinnamon Schnapps their second night back. They were S.D.'d two days later. Another was caught stealing a book on Joyce from the library: he confessed his purpose had been to copy a long passage and then destroy the book. An atmosphere of unrelieved gloom descended upon them all, its chief quality a powerless compliance with unceasing expectations, and an absence of any activity to delight or refresh the spirit. All now was work; all in a landscape bare of the bright domesticating features of winter warmth in happier places. The only escape from work lay in activities undertaken only to prepare for new periods of work.

Many of Amanda's classmates spent January afternoons in the Catamount Room of Gibbon, the boys hoisting huge rolls of free weights, grunting and screaming, cinched up in their belts, popping pecs and triceps in front of dark walls of mirrors. Not far along another wall, a line of treadmills and Stairmasters faced a blank expanse of sheet rock. All who trod or ran on these engines of therapy were girls. It was as hot as an old cellar with a furnace. Music, tired heavy metal, rasped out of two battered speakers hung from a low rafter, while boys in breaks between sets of reps strode around the grim chamber like women in labor walking the halls of maternity wards.

Amanda had begun running on the treadmills a week after cross-country ended, not so much to stay thin as to — in the phrase she used to herself — *stay down*.

Dr. Mitchell had indeed looked her over, between Christmas and New Year's, and had shown a mild concern both over Amanda's general physical state and her *affect*. "There's a lot of pressure there. On me. I just need to control it, and to, like, relax and not think about it when I don't have to, you know?"

Yes, he knew. Dr. Mitchell gave counsel as to easing up, making time for herself, eating right, and starting with a new drug protocol, a medication called Celexa, an anti-anxiety agent that also had slightly different potencies not all of which, in Amanda's case, would really be needed. It was an up-date from the Xanax he had given her two years earlier and some of the other things they had tried. "You told me you were symp-tomless during cross-country season; you need to relieve that excess tension and energy, and this'll help, and you can run indoors. You're not using anything else now, are you, dear?"

"Inderal, once in a while."

"I'll start you out on this, right now, and you should let me know before you go back to school if you've had any disagreeable symptoms. I've given you a prescription, but here's enough to get you started. But *you're* the major player, Amanda, not the drug. You've got to want to ease up . . ."

Now, in the January afternoon dark of St. Matthew's, at a time in her life that imposed more relentless demands on her than any she had known, the treadmill seemed a kind of lifeline. She came to crave it as an alcoholic craves a drink: not for pleasure; for need.

The machines were obliging. Like Tess's equipment at home, each one featured an array of digital read-outs that let runners measure progress: energy and calories expended, mileage, angles of elevation. Each thing could be measured in precise terms. Amanda might run, for example, 5.5 miles. The machine might be set for a pace of 7.1 miles per hours and the hill ele-vated to an incline of 4.5 percent. The Elapsed Calorie screen flashed each calorie obliterated: four-and-one-half double paces, at such a pace, meant one calorie. And so on. Amanda knew that after thirty minutes at such a pace she could glide into a state in which all her worries and pressures could be made to subside. The digital read-outs, noted and memorized, were the first things recorded in each entry in her new journal: 6.3mi/51.22/596 cals.

Such a work-out left Amanda both invigorated and "down:" mellow enough, alert enough, that she could work productively until 1:30 or 2:00 A.M., rigidly keeping to her schedule, and with only an occasional need for medications, other than the Celexa or occasional supplements of Inderal. But not really much more than these. Once in a while, she took Halcion, but it often caused, at least seemed to cause, a scary dream, and left her washed out the next morning — and so that argued against using it any more than was absolutely necessary.

AMANDA'S JOURNAL

January 20   *22 Degrees.*

Cleopatra, slinking and sleek, curled before the fire, staring at Mother, expressionless.
   96.50
   Reduce Spongy Cellulite, firm to sleek. Passepartout, Inc. Box 75, Dept. F2, Glenville, Conn. Body Firming and Moisturizing Gel, $18.00. an 800 #. Hippiness.

January 22   *–6 Degrees.*

They may have heard me at home. When Daddy knows anything about me that he knows will hurt me — if I find out that he knows — he won't say anything. But I can tell if he knows something. Phone. He wonders if I was sick at home.

The frigidness here. Hopkins' cell, in the monastery in Wales, in deep winter, skim of ice in his bowl acc. to Journal.

*96.80   Treadmill.   28.00/342
        cals/4.3 mi. Incline at 4.
        ExBike: 14.25 mins.*

Six systemic departures announced, total — three did not come back from Xmas break.

Mr. Steele said that Harrell Wilson, Prime Minister of England, studied an average of 14 hours a day for three years straight at Oxford Univ, so none of us should feel the least bit sorry for themselves. If you can, you must: Housman. If you know yourself to be capable of a Thing, you have an obligation to do it fully, if it is right. If you are (1) told to and (2) not a problem of morality. Doctrine of Self-reliance, Emerson, cont of Abraham Lincoln. If you do not give all effort, you will look back, and hate yourself. Your own self let yourself have pity on.

And what else is there to do in this school in Jan? Exams in less than 3 wks, total make-or-break for Dartmouth.

Chopin Ballade.

January 24   Silverback Sky, Black clouds. 20.

So icy, so dark that it made me ache just over the roof of my mouth as though I had eaten huge scoops of Häagan-Daas, as if the water that had frozen was black ink, not water.

*96.20.   Treadmill only   35.00/390
        cals/4.9 mi.
        100 sit-ups, diagn.*

Thighs, gross from any angle I look at them,
incl adductor muscles, which even running, etc.,
cannot do anything to. Parts that no matter
what you do, do not benefit.
Lettuce, 1 full head. 70 cals.
Prozac: green and beige. Another med. tried
last year, Klonapin, instant sudden mellow, too
heavy. Someone said her father took it before a
speech and got up and fell down. Inderal, any
public-type obligation. The most intricate rapid
passages in Chopin — Inderal doesn't interfere.
Today Dr. Passmore talked to us in his study.
The expression of his eyes, when they look at
you, as though a father wrapping a blanket
around his children. A long talk about Gerard
Manley Hopkins and the freedom his order and
discipline gave him. *Everything regulated for*
him. The Certitude of his belief and his convic-
tion. Duns Scotus, Medieval philosopher who
agreed with Hopkins on God's glory. Shewing,
Hopkins says. *The tangible world of loveliness*
can be cherished despite hard Faith and denying
of all other Wish/Impulse/Desire. Hopkins was
prob homosex but So What Not the Slightest
Shred of Evidence he did anything about it.
Jesuits went overboard on Vietnam, acc to Dr.
Passmore — long way from Ingatius Loyola,
actually a soldier.
Today rec'd letter from Colgate, all creden-
tials have been sent in and rec'd waiting only
for first semester grades. Personal note on bot-
tom of last para — looked like a personal note
from a motel manager.
AP Bio, 2 hrs/25 minutes. AP Latin, Catullus,
1 hr/30 minutes.

PART FOUR

CHAPTER THIRTY-NINE

Amanda, get your fat ass out of the way!"

There is a long underground passageway in old Gibbon Gymnasium, a dingy corridor smelling of liniment and leading from the basement locker rooms, themselves clustered around communal lavatories and showers, to a service entrance at the rear of the building. From this entrance St. Matthew's teams emerge into the bright sunlight of spring and fall afternoons — emerge, huddle together, grasp hands, and break with a rough *Catamount!* Yell, and jog together towards their playing fields. In all seasons the corridor echoes with the hollow clicks of cleats, flat explosions of bounced basketballs, dragging sounds of the implements of games — bats, hockey and lacrosse sticks, and so on. There are sharp outbursts of laughter at shouted punch lines; shrieks, taunts, angry grouses.

Along the passageway, next to the showers, sit long stacked rows of old-fashioned metal lockers with birdcage doors and combination locks, assigned to postgraduate and new girls. So narrow and congested is the hallway that if you are getting something from a locker anyone walking by is likely to bump into you.

"Amanda. Get your fat ass out of the way!"

She felt herself fill up with horror and shame. She turned to see who had said the words, but already two or three clumps of boys had muscled past her, some with hockey sticks, one or two with basketballs, their heads backlit starkly in the brightness at the far entrance.

She had no more recognized the voice than she might recognize the make of a bullet that had penetrated her heart.

For a second after she looked around she felt somehow anchored in the fresh paint of the floor, unable to move. But now she was running, pushing along the wall of the corridor, bounding out over the sanded ice of the exit ramp, running as fast as she had ever run, unable almost even to breathe, running up the stairwell of Morison towards her room, fumbling wildly at her shoelaces for her key, tearing the door open.

It slammed behind her. Already she had reached with both hands over her shoulders to pull off her sweatshirt, and her T-shirt. She slid out of her sweatpants and running shorts and opened the closet door to stare, in a thirsty frenzy, at what she saw, to stare at what the boy had seen and to see it as he had seen it. "Gross" was a word she almost never used. Now she said it to herself, and then said it out loud.

Five minutes later, she was still standing in front of the mirror, grasping with the fingers of both her hands taut flanges of flesh about the hips. The flesh she kneaded was so insubstantial that she had to clutch at it, clutch and re-grasp it, the meagerness if it dissolving, slipping from the press of her fingers. The thin folds of flesh seemed to her like welts of fat, deposits of slackness, physical proofs of a life indulged and uncontrolled. Her flesh seemed spongy and inelastic at once, a painful sharp redness where she pinched, blanching to

CHAPTER FORTY-ONE

H er heart does not pound. No Halcion last night, or anything. She lies on her coverlet, her eyes looking at the ceiling but seeing only the reflection of a meadow lustrously green and silver, speckled with the wildflowers of early summer, long Indiana grasses, ruffled by tiny breaths of wind. Now she finds herself standing, a hand on the window frame, looking beyond the limit of a January morning at the empty brown hills that roll away motionless towards Canada. She feels . . . serene, and this feeling is what she has heard about. After a one-day fast, the feeling that follows sleep is the feeling of a flowing serenity, of an easy, dreamy, calm.

Now Amanda has half of an oatmeal cookie (40 cals, 2 grams of fat) and a bottle of Evian. She dresses and leaves her room. From 8:45 to 10 A.M., piano and Mrs. Thompson — thirty minutes for Mrs. Thompson, the rest for practice. The video she is doing for Dartmouth has to go out in ten days, and she is still far from mastering the Chopin G-minor. The key is repetition of each phrase in each hand, twenty, twenty-five times — but the stretches are too much for her; her fingers are unsupple and disobedient; her hands too compact and too fragile. Mrs. Thompson is still with her: a human metronome. "And again, yes, and again, no.

No, look! Do you see? Again." She is uncharacteristically abrupt with Amanda, but she is gone by 9:30 and now Amanda slides into her little Schumann melodies: they fit her fingers and her soul.

Back in her room by 10:05. Amanda undresses completely, weighs herself, standing as usual before the closet mirror: 96.10. She presses, drums her fingers against the upper part of her belly — it is taut, pulled tight: it must be hard fat just underneath the epidermis, still so thick and so resistant. And just under the hip-bone sockets her thighs flare out, perhaps half an inch: not muscle, not tendon. What? She clasps her hands together over her head like a child playing *this is the steeple,* leans as hard and as far as she can, first to the right, then to the left, stretching, flattening out the love-handles on either side. She hears a soft shuffle, a bare bump, puts on her robe, opens the door and removes an Obligations Board message just pressed there. *Reminder that all U. S. History term papers are due NLT noon 28 January:* that is all right, she has done it, it's been printed. Abraham Lincoln communicated *compassion,* Mr. Steele said, "like a weary, tender father." *She has to have an A-minus from Steele.*

"You sit next to me today, young lady!" Mr. Barber, tapping her on the wrist, pointing to the high-backed chair. She takes her messcoat from her own chair and puts it on. Fat up! For lunch today it's hot dogs, chili, buns, iceberg lettuce, Scotch broth, junket. Junket, she thinks, looks like plaque. Mr. Barber cranes his neck, leans back, hanging an arm from his armrest, talking to another master at the head of another table; Amanda breaks the bun in half and chews at half of the half. The fool turns back to her: "Any more? You want another hot dog? How's the history going? Good.

Steele taught me when I was here. All the masters were like Steele, all the students were like Toby. What're you doing, Toby; the river's frozen over, rowing in the tanks? Keep those washboard abs?"

"Mr. Barber, I was so happy the first time I saw this place, I was miserable knowing I'd have to leave it."

This unusual answer does not interest Barber, who turns back to his friend. Toby wonders, aloud, "Amanda, things going better for you?"

"Better than what?"

He's hurt by this, just barely, she can tell, this *Better than what?*, and she feels again a peculiar disengagement from her surroundings.

"I'm looking out for you. You get your moods, and then a look of total preoccupation, a cut-off, I don't know what it is. But don't let St. M's get at you, that's all, you don't have to answer me, I have to leave . . ." Toby pats her on her wrist, takes off his messcoat and leaves.

All the while, Amanda has made a bustle stirring her soup, has taken in two spoonsful. She doesn't know why, but she likes him, but not *that* way. The Herald announces a Morehead nominee for the University of North Carolina and one S.D.

Exams begin in four days. *At this time, four days from now, I will be in my first exam, A.P. Latin.* Mr. Gregory, Master of Latin, puts a one hour translation from an unannounced and maybe unknown historian or poet at the beginning of the exam. Get your motor turning over. The last two hours are Virgil, Catullus, and Ovid. Pretty serious business. She imagines the anonymous writer will be Tacitus. *Atque ubi solitudinem faciut, pacem appellant.* And when they had made a desert, they called it peace. And A-minus here, no an A, is

essential. A.P. Latin "establishes seriousness of intent."
Who told her that? Amanda lifts her head to her framed
picture of Hopkins, a great classical scholar. And so was
Housman — Housman, according to Dr. Passmore,
spent his life translating and studying Latin poets of
lesser quality than himself. She must make herself focus
on the one thing, the Latin exam: then a break, all Saturday afternoon and Sunday, until Pre-college Algebra.
These are the last grades Dartmouth will ever see. So:
direct focussed study from 1:15 P.M. until 4:10 only A.P.
Latin, only Book II of Virgil, which she is now confident
she can translate perfectly, and some of those really
weird words she looks up anyway, even though they
may give them to you. By writing a word down, and
staring at it as hard as you can while you chisel it onto
the page. Takes a Xanax, one of the bigger .5mg ones
and swallows it without water, changes, weighs herself,
the meal did almost nothing, gets dressed and walks
toward Gibbon and Catamount Room. There is a water
cooler at the entrance and she leans down and drinks
from it for a long time, and sees several people see her
drinking. Latin, she thinks, is such a private thing; nothing you can talk to anyone about; you control the
whole thing yourself; it bends to your effort.

The problem with lean muscle mass is that once
you get down to it, it's harder to melt and scrape off
what you want off. Amanda fastens her Walkman
tightly onto her head, mounts the treadmill, which is
number four in a line of seven, six of them in use, all
Class III or Class IV girls, five with Walkmen. She
prides herself on always running negative splits on the
machine — each half mile increment, that is, to be run
faster than the one before. Sometimes she covers the
calorie dial with a towel, so as not to watch the green
digital numbers as they change — until, say, four min-

utes later, then there's an increase in the number: 37 or 38 burnt off. She wonders how accurate that is?

It is pitch black at 5:10; there is no required dinner tonight because they are using Savernake for some special dinner of rich alumni and parents. By 5:45 she is at her desk again — her new robe, a sweatshirt. She has weighed herself, made a journal entry, taken a .25mg Xanax, and she imagines Miss Rodman looking in on her: *How are you, Dear? Good. Tucked up for the evening?*

19 January 2000

Dean of Admissions
Dartmouth College
Hanover, New Hampshire 03755

Dear Sir,

It is with pleasure that I commend to you Amanda Bahringer, a senior young woman at St. Matthew's School in New York State. I believe she is the kind of young woman who would be right at home at Dartmouth. She is not only an excellent student with SATs in the 1300's area, but with excellent grades and the extracurricular activities that indicate a well-rounded young person. These include accomplishments at the piano and outstanding cross-country running attainments.

In my own years at Dartmouth I recall that the academic requirements were to be fleshed out with a strong life outside of class, especially in sports and comradeship. Amanda Bahringer's record at St. Matthew's, one of our best schools, shows clearly this potential.

I give her my unqualified support and stand ready to furnish additional information should you require it.

Please give my best to the President of the College.

Yours very sincerely

/s/ Coggin Lindsay
Chairman and Chief Executive Officer

At the bottom, a note: "Darling — here's a copy of Mr. Lindsay's letter in your behalf. He's the Minnesota alum who is a major donor to the college. This will help. Best love, Mummy."

AMANDA'S JOURNAL

3 February 17 degrees.   92.90

*Old, old women in black, their skins like parch-
ment walking like crows up and down the aisles
of Shop Rite. Darting down like waterbirds
make their grab of cookies, etc., angry scrutiny
of each box. Throw the box into their cart. At
eighty they have reverted to what they were told
they couldn't eat when they were ten.* Still disobedient to what they were told by their mother.
   *Sick in sink this night
   Housman iambic pentameter line:*
   Was cut in little pieces by the train.
   *Body Traps, J. Rodin
   1-800-924-JENNY
   Echinacea Herb
   No contact of the body.*

Celexa 2, at 9:00am/Xanax, 1 at 5:00. All right.

"V & A, 31 January, Attention please: Men's hockey has won its last four games by a combined margin of 26–3. Robert Proxmore, St. Matthew's Class IV, has been awarded the Pitt Scholarship at Cambridge University. Linda Furihashi has won a Caseby Scholarship at Amherst College. There are three Systemic Departures, all Class III. Resume please."

CHAPTER FORTY-TWO

A.P. Latin was scheduled for Monday — the first exam. Amanda returned to her room from Savernake, conscious that perhaps she had not eaten enough — part of a salad, some bread, a piece of cold chicken, and lemon wedges. She had taken an apple from the bowl set out at her table — she always took a piece of fruit with her. She settled into her desk chair and looked at the priest. She had done too much on the treadmill. Eighty-six minutes starting at 3:30, mostly at a 7.6 mph pace, average incline 3 per cent: 1185 calories. She faithfully recorded the data in her journal. Last night, she had spent four hours, forty-five minutes on Latin and algebra. She weighed herself before the mirror: 91.88. She put on a running sweatsuit and a T-shirt, took a Celexa and two Vivarins — they had them at the convenience store in town: *No Mo Slo Mo,* the display said.

The Latin text lay open. She wondered what would be on the Pre-college Algebra exam. She noticed algebra ended in bra. She thought of her mother's reaction if she did badly: rage disguised as a broken heart, but soon she'd be out of control, hysterical, shooting at anything that moved, railing against the scummy bastards, blaming Joey, blaming the school, then going after her. It was ridiculous to send Dartmouth the piano video; they got a thousand of them. The big

Chopin Ballade was . . . too big: too big for her fingers, she couldn't manage a convincing velocity when it was needed . . . she had no control over anything she had to do. A.P. . . . her Trinity essay . . . she felt suddenly very hot, stood up, opened the closet door and saw in the mirror that she was flushed, red as the passion red on the chaplain's sleeves, red from her collarbone up to her jaw, and, standing there, she felt her heart, suddenly, flop! — it seemed like a goldfish flopping around, the flopping accelerating, now her heart beating so fast it was like a painless whirr, almost, a pounding whirr . . . she put her hands to her temples, felt the room twisting under her, the floor careening away.

Somehow, somehow, she got her overcoat off the hook on the back of the hallway door and forced the door open; then, pressing her way along the walls of the empty corridor, she lurched down the hall, down the stairs, out into the frigid night — which, she hoped wildly, would stop her nausea and revive her. Get her to the infirmary.

"Let me have a listen again,"
The nurse practitioner pressed the stethoscope against Amanda's breastbone. She listened raptly — a scary act in itself, so intent was her listening — all the while holding up her left hand, right in front of Amanda's face, silencing any attempt at conversation: a sudden irritated outstretch of palm: I'm tired, you've probably made yourself sick, just don't say anything.

"All right, and you said you weren't on anything besides the Vivarin you took, right?"

"Yes. Right. I had some coffee, too."

"No medication from us, none from home? Are we keeping and dispensing for you? Any Ritalin, any antidepressants? You don't self-medicate, do you?"

"No?"

"Were you on anything before?"

"Yeah, Inderal, and maybe a, I don't remember, maybe something else. I can't really remember. Something with a X."

"Xanax?"

"I can't remember, I've been off it for awhile."

"Who put you on that?"

"The doctor in Lawrence, he thought I was stressed out and couldn't stop worrying. It was like, anti-anxiety?"

"Are you eating? Did you have a good dinner?"

"Oh, sure. That's not a problem."

The nurse stared into Amanda's eyes at close range.

"I had pasta and tomato sauce. Salad. A glass of milk. Fruit."

"Anything else unusual?"

"No, I have four exams, I had to take my SATs again."

"Do you know how much you weigh, Amanda?"

"Not exactly. I think about 107 or something. I'm small-boned."

"Mind getting up on the scale?"

The nurse took a long time, listening to her heart again, this time with the instrument all over her upper back, fiddling with the old-fashioned scale weights, fitting a blood pressure cuff on her.

"You're not an eating problem, are you? Let me see your teeth."

Again the nurse practitioner — her terse conscientiousness would have pleased Tess — again she looked, searching and grave, her tongue depressor cambering about in the back of Amanda's mouth, the nurse seeming to consider the color of her tongue, the backs of her front teeth.

"I'm not going to keep you in. I want you to go right back to the dormitory, back to your room, get right into bed, drink two or three glasses of water, forget your exams. Let your mind go blank. Sleep. Do not take these caffeine preparations again. They don't help anyone, and that's what caused your rapid heartbeat and made you sick. Did you work out a long time today?"

"Ran on the treadmill?"

"For a long time?"

"No, maybe fifteen minutes, something like that."

"Well, you may have dehydration anyway. If you have replacement fluids in your room, take them instead of water. Check in with your hallmaster when you get back to the room — who is it, Rodman? I'm going to call her and tell her you're on your way back. O.K.? Any questions?"

"Yes, Here's a question. What evidence do we have that Mr. Lincoln, if he had lived, would have enforced a generous peace on the South?"

"Wow, where'd you read that?"

"Question on the A.P. History final last year."

"Someone as smart as you, you might as well stay in bed until the exam."

It was just like the Dartmouth interview, just like the recital. The Inderal cut in about thirty minutes after you took it. Amanda's heart no longer pounded; she was steady as a church, no nausea, no worry — only a fierce and demanding tiredness that made her want, really want, to sleep.

"Amanda, Dear Heart, are you all right? We're terribly concerned. The nurse prack called to say you'd be stopping by."

"She told me to." She stood before Miss Rodman and the headmaster, Dr. Passmore folded heavily into a corner of the sofa, the fire crackling directly in front of him, the dog Gretchen at his feet and the hallmaster at her desk. Seeing them stare at her, perhaps solicitously, though you could never truly tell what they were thinking, she brought her hands together, left hand clasping two fingers of her right. "She said I should check in with you, you know? Hi, Dr. Passmore."

"My dear."

"She told me, here's a young lady who's simply worn down, trying to do too much. She said you were dehydrated, maybe."

"That's right, maybe I am."

"Well, your great admirer is as vexed about these things as I am,"

It appeared that Miss Rodman had a drink, some kind of cocktail, on the desk in front of her. It was a clear tan liquid, and there was a cherry at the bottom.

"I'm sorry you're vexed." Amanda imagined the word meant they were worried about her. "I'll be O.K."

"Forgive me, Dear Child, but how does one get dehydrated in January? Winter is icumen in, but one is merely baked in the central heat. Do you study hard enough to sweat, Dear?"

"Oh, Carlisle."

"No. Work out. Run."

"Not outside, surely."

"No, in Gibbon, in the Catamount Room. They have fifteen apparatus, including ten treadmills."

Passmore, for whom the word treadmill existed only as a metaphor for exhausting but pointless activity, nodded and beamed. Every time you gave him information new to him, he beamed. "Mustn't overdo it," he managed. "I should have thought you'd sail through the examinations. You already know more Hopkins than I do. She's a wizard, this child, Dorothea . . ."

"Golly, I'll say. Well, Amanda, you are plainly restored and your own best place right now is in number 23 Morison, tucked up in your own room, your own bed, snug as a bug in a rug, sleeping for ten hours and then eating a big breakfast. No windmills to tilt at and no treadmills to run on. What made you go to the nurse in the first place?"

"My heart was like, fluttery?"

"And what'd she say?"

"Worn down and dehydrated?"

"Right, then, off you go, Dear."

Passmore looked at Amanda in his stolid, kindly way. He was always struck by how meager, how spare, their speech was: even though they wrote, some of them, like angels. Amanda had written some very nice things for him, very nice indeed. Lovely things. But when you asked them something, all they did was tap it back to you, a weak lob that barely kept the ball in play. *My heart was like, fluttery?* Yet she did seem peaky and exhausted. Maybe that was why. He said. "I think Amanda looks wonderful. Had I been the nurse I should have denied her admission myself. And isn't that a handsome coat? Is it a Christmas coat?" "It's most attractive," Miss Rodman agreed.

Actually, Amanda had hurried into the infirmary in a bizarre outfit, one that reflected her panic — Timberlands, a Patagonia sweatsuit with an Absolut T-shirt over it and a Navy overcoat Tess had given her for Christmas two years ago, a fitted Searle coat, cashmere and wool, with vertical parallel rows of heavy brass buttons and deep raked pockets. And a black velvet collar. The first time she had put it on, right out of the box, Tess said to her, "I'm putting you back in maryjanes. I could eat you up with a spoon!"

"Yes, it's a Christmas coat."

"Well, it's very good-looking, a good-looking coat. You always have an excellent turn-out Amanda, God love you."

This from the headmaster. Amanda noticed a glass on the coffee table in front of him, too. She waited to see that they were finished with her, made her little throat-clearing sound, and simply left.

Dorothea and Carlisle Passmore had been in the hallmaster's apartment for an hour, having returned from Fells College, over in Aitken, where they heard the Moroni Quartet. They had had a wary and difficult progress on a tattered ribbon of icy roadway; and they had learned, as soon as they arrived at the concert hall, that a Schubert Quintet had for some reason been cancelled and that the ensemble would be playing one of the late Beethoven quartets.

"The audience didn't like that, Dorothea. You don't think they liked it, do you?"

"Oh, yes — they liked it. Professors love that kind of music. The later the quartet, the better."

"I suppose you're right. He was deaf when he wrote it. You can tell by the music, all that abrupt scraping, all that unmelody. The thing didn't have any melody at all. I wonder whether you can develop a taste for that kind of music?"

Himself, Passmore liked positive, ebullient music, preferably played by the full orchestra, not a spindly quartet. He delighted in his memories of being taken by his mother to the Academy of Music in Philadelphia to hear Stowkowski and Rachmaninoff. Brahms. The Tschaikovsky Fifth Symphony. He loved the big luminous exhalations and powerful resolutions of large-scale symphonies and piano concertos. They ended like arguments or wars won.

"I suppose you could. Just keep listening to them. Not my cup of tea. But you probably could, Carlisle. Listen to them while you shave."

"I use an electric."

"Carlisle!"

But Passmore disbelieved her. He was not a simple man, and he had had two whiskeys, but his tastes were quite simple. They ran to bright, primary, affirming colors, melodies, shapes: bracing happy things that lifted you up — writers like Macaulay or Thackeray, composers like Mendelssohn and Dvorâk: bracing things that uplifted and celebrated. Why should you leave the concert hall cast down by the muddled, inharmonic ravings of some angry modernist? Everyone was tired at that hour, to begin with. He hadn't liked the seats in the recital hall at Fells College, either. What they did to his spine. And the cloakroom was a mile from the hall. That college was probably in trouble.

"I'll be going. What's this?"

The headmaster stood up, holding a shiny crystal apple in his right hand, an apple with some sort of design on top.

"It is what is called a corporate gift. Your lovely Amanda's mother sent it to me for Christmas. She has a list, I imagine, of people to receive corporate gifts. I'm on the list."

"Well, lock up your grade sheets."

"How does she seem to you?"

"Amanda? I teach her, so I see her three days a week. Very run down, tired. They all are. We're running an anthill."

"Ants never run down."

"You're such a clever girl, Dorothea. Don't *you* run down."

"People who live with large dogs don't run down." She nudged the sleeping Gretchen with her toe.

"Is that a fact?"

"Yes. The child will be fine. We have to praise her, Carlisle, lift her up a bit."

"I have to go. What about the Macklin girl?"

"She's fine. Good-night, Carlisle." She tilted her cheekbone at him slightly and he blew her a kiss from at least eight feet away.

Amanda heard what she imagined to be the heavy tread of the headmaster's footsteps, advancing towards the stairwell. She was fine now, with a Klonapin and some Valerian. She had tried the Klonapin only one or two times, but now it seemed to take her down easily and gently, though perhaps that was because of the Inderal still in her system. But her heart no longer fluttered and she had done what the nurse prack had instructed, had taken in a lot of fluid.

Now she concentrated on making her mind go blank. And she found, at the very moment she hung on the edge of her sleep, a warm sleep that seemed to welcome and cradle her as if she were a little girl who had slipped into her parents' bed — she found that she really could think of nothing at all.

CHAPTER FORTY-THREE

For history, "and you need an A-minus from him, at least," there'd have to be a major essay question on Lincoln. Mr. Steele loved him. He talked often in class about how in the President's writing and life his genius mixed the homely and the profound, the pure and the political. Steele once read the class a letter Lincoln wrote a general, in which he said that ambition, *within reasonable bounds,* was fine. Some ambition was all right. The phrase stayed in Amanda's mind. What she had to do, was maintain all the pressures and demands and forces that assaulted her *within reasonable bounds:* each had to be answered excellently and fully, each had to be controlled. Her weight and her work now fully demonstrated she could control what she needed to, if she wanted to. She wanted to and she had to. Reassurances abounded: the perfect order of the room; the abundant arrayed supply of medicines and nostrums; the hidden stuffs and symmetrical piles of clothes; the cordoned chunks of time that she could impose on the long solitary times St. Matthew's allowed all Class IVs during pre-exams. There was only one daily-required meal attendance; no mandatory athletics or college counseling, no music lessons; above all, she was quite sure, no one noticed anything unusual about her. Why should they?

She had two old bottles of Serax. One with twenty-eight tablets left, the other with twelve, both leftovers from a year ago — a reassuring reserve, though the drug, she inferred, was out-of-date. She had sixty-eight .25 mg Xanaxes and thirty .50 mg Xanaxes, and if she kept to an average of no more than four a day, including three from the first category, she would be fine. There was a whole unopened bottle of Luvox, from Tess's medicine chest — the Medical Presentation Sheet said it did about the same, she understood, as the Paxil — and that bottle was still almost full. Thirty-two Celaxas. Twenty-six Inderals, easily enough for the exams, and she would take one exactly forty-five minutes before going into each one — it had done the trick to perfection during the Parents Weekend concert. Sixty Halcion — reliable, and combined with the Valerian brought a heavy blanket of sleep. Two bottles of Benadryl; one of Fiorinal, an old migraine drug for headaches that gave a weird sparkle along with the relief, a sparkle of gold dust. In an Aleve bottle she had sixteen Prozacs. Thirty Klonapins. And of course all the anti-inflammatories, but you didn't need them in the winter.

The important point, she considered, was that her need and her dosages did not seem to be growing. They could be kept within reasonable bounds.

There was a phone call for her — a new girl who'd filled the systemic departee's room across the corridor knocked on her door. It was, Amanda noticed, a quiet, respectful knock: she was no longer a new girl; another one was. "Amanda?"

She picked up the receiver.

"Hi, It's Dad. Real quick, I'm on the car phone."

"Hi, Dad." It was strange, calling him Dad.

"There's a property in Albany we may have to look at next week or the week after, so we could be in your location at that time. Still a maybe."

"Who's we, you and your tapeworm?"

"Good line, where'd you hear that? You doin' O.K.?"

"Oh, God, you have no idea."

"Exams, yeah, I know."

"How's Mom."

"Fine. Better. She feels good about you. She ran into her buddy Coggin Lindsay, that guy that went to Dartmouth. She's doing a deal with him, a P.R. . . .

"I'm going under a tunnel . . ."

It was 11:52. Her study card allowed for a fifteen minute break between A.P. Bio Prep and History; she looked at a magazine, *Self*, the whole thing was about new regimes to prepare for summer season, to slice off the remaining pounds and be firm everywhere, how to achieve a better butt and beyond . . . "Once you're on the beach, there's nowhere to hide anything" . . . she had a new Sunday *Times, Fashions of the Times*, FedExed from Warfield, with an article highlighted by Tess, full of words like trims, nipped-ins, hugs, clings, clamps . . .

Molecular Genetics. RNA and DNA structure and function. Gene regulation; viral structure and replication; nucleic acid technology . . .

She pushed the newspaper away. It was 12:18. Nothing she read in her history sourcebook at this hour could stay in her brain. Dr. Passmore gave five points extra credit on his exam for every twenty-eight lines (i.e., two sonnets) of Hopkins or Housman. She sat, palm supporting her cheekbones, staring at another poem, a thing called "Pied Beauty," the kind of poem that would have driven Tess crazy, a poem about loving and tolerating unusual, weird things . . . loving and cherishing them. Supposing, Amanda wondered, supposing she told her mother she had decided to go to Bard or Antioch, some really freaky place, where half the students had nose-studs and navel-rings and wanted to live in an ashram. *All things counter original, spare, strange. Whatever is fickle, freckled, who knows how?*

Her exam was at 8:30, A.P. Latin. She set one alarm and then turned up the volume on her clock radio as high as it would go. She set the radio on no station at all — set them both for 7:35 exactly.

Ten days later, Amanda wasn't certain how she'd made it through the exams, but she'd survived to write the last sentence of the last of them, A.P. History. "No man or woman of Washington's, Jefferson's, etc., abilities would put himself through what politicians are today going through — media, ridicule, sheer exhaustion . . ."

The exams finished, she listened to Toby and his friends talk about having pulled all-nighters for a week, as though they were describing an athletic triumph earned by being tough. She had a sudden conviction that she had nothing to say to these people. She walked directly to the Music Building, and began working on the Chopin Ballade. She had arrived at what Mr. Steele called a broad sunlit upland, a place of exhausted satisfaction, a certain pride and the ease granted the truly deserving.

AMANDA'S JOURNAL

February 5th   *35°sleet.*

Bran muffin, coffee w. Equal — Bkfst. Breadsticks/Powerbar lunch. 1 ½ herb tea. Four oat-

meal cookies p.m. in room. "A bright sunset lines the clouds so that their brims look like gold, brass, bronze, or steel . . . but it is also lusterless." GMH, Journal, December 1883. Trmill, 4 mi, 29.15. I finish writing this and look over to my left, without getting up, at the long mirror on the back of the closed door. I stand up and see . . . I cannot see what someone else sees. E-mail, mother: study for exam you least want to study for, with alleged quotation, Huxly, Education is making yourself learn to do things that are necessary but that you don't want . . .

Passmore's gentleness but one master said in Savernake, he's totally out of it and the deans run everything.

CHAPTER FORTY-FOUR

On Wenlock Edge the wood's in trouble;
His forest fleece the Wrekin heaves;
The gale, it plies the saplings double;
And thick on Severn snow the leaves.

Looking out from her narrow window, Amanda saw through a steamy dusk the dense stands of trees at the limit of the Far Fields, all gathered and shaken together in the storm. Behind them, eerily etched against a pallid sunset, lay the Tuscaroras. There had been a sustained thaw; the air around the school had turned warm and blowsy. She looked down at the poem. "Read it, soak in it, the language has a taste to it."

It was one of those conjunctions of a life lived and a life recorded: Amanda was watching something exactly like what she was reading. The poem described the brutal pummeling of a forest in Shropshire, and the harsh soughing of a wind though forest was exactly what she was hearing: from far down the hallway in Morison came the sound of a wailing singer; and the hills seemed to shudder in dismal syncopation, the rain pelting against Amanda's windows and the forest shaking its fleece: just as she shed her sweater, nudged it into her closet with her foot, reached into the bottom drawer of her desk, a deep drawer directly under a picture of Father Hopkins, reaching for what had sat there for two weeks at least: pastries, chocolates, thick packages of Vienna Fingers, Oreos, chewy granolas, Tollhouse cookies, boxes of Swissair chocolates. Housman's Collected Poems slid off her lap and she tore open the last of the packages, laid the cookies onto the bed behind her, scooped and gathered them in a cradle she made with her arm and T-shirt, and began eating, eating desperately, as though the act of filling her mouth as completely, as heavily as she could, — was the door locked? Amanda. Are you sure? As though getting as much in and down at once was the only means of appeasing this terrible compulsion. She took three or four Vienna Fingers at once, heard footfalls in the hallway, shuffling toward the door, retreating away towards Miss Rodman's apartment. The hills heaved and wrinkled in the gray hefts of wind; in the murky reflection in the window she could make out the outlines of her own ribs. She ate as richly and heavily as her mouth allowed. She thought, shuddering, of a huge snake, a constrictor able to swallow huge things, and that the swallowing had nothing to do with nourishing, only the wild, wild need, only the frenzy of eating.

She had less than fifteen minutes to deal with it. After that it would be absorbed. The payment had to be offered the moment the frenzy subsided. Amanda used the rubber pick at the end of her toothbrush. She threw herself over the sink, water running, and it took her less than a minute to get rid of it, and she knew how to do it as quietly as a lover knows how to muffle a sob of joy. And the remainder of the ritual: cranking the window as wide as it would go, room freshener, mouthwash, flapping heavy towels like a child trying to get smoke out of a room, driving all the traces and remnants and evidences out towards the heaving hills;

253

all papers and packages grabbed and stuffed into suitcases under the bed, all evidences gone. At this time of year, hardly anyone ever knocked on your door at St. Matthew's. The wind, obliging and satisfied, collapsed. It was perfectly silent in the narrow room and all along the hallway and outside Morison. "The gale, it plies the saplings double. It blows so hard, 'twill soon be gone." It was gone, had never happened. It was 5:45 precisely, and there was an A.P. Bio preparation to be started precisely at that time, almost as though the refrigerator card was insisting on it. Cell Mitosis, and there would certainly be a quiz in the morning. She was wholly, fully, relaxed and restored. No one was in the hall, and there wasn't a sound in the building.

CHAPTER FORTY-FIVE

On February 17, two weeks after her nighttime trip to the infirmary, Amanda returned. One of the nurses, or maybe it was the school doctor himself, had asked Miss Rodman to remind her to come by every couple of weeks. Just check in with them. Nothing to worry about, but — Miss Rodman added — "you've been under a strain, Dear. All of us are under a strain from time to time."

Amanda didn't think they'd ask her to undress, but they might weigh her. They might check her blood pressure and listen to her heart and check the enamel on the backs of her front teeth. She knew what they did.

She went over from Morison at 10:00 A.M. precisely, her best time of day. She had skipped breakfast, eating only a Power Bar in her room, but drinking Orangina and five glasses of tap water. Her calculation was that the weight gain the liquids provided was at least four pounds. And she wore her baggy painter's jeans, the ones with lengthwise side pockets at the level of her lower thighs, each pocket with two rolls of quarters. She wore her heavy boots, waxy combat boots laced high up on her shins; everyone wore them in the snow up here. And on top: two T-shirts; her Dartmouth XXL sweatshirt — not too billowy when it was tucked under her overalls . . . ready.

The nurse was seeing people; there were four students ahead of her and a master who had had chest pains and who was being sent to Gloversville for a closer look. It was a quiet morning. The flu had not yet struck. The receptionist told her to have a chair.

Amanda went into the restroom and took an Inderal, more for the psychology of it than anything else. She had a couple of more cups of water. She began reading an old *Cosmopolitan*.

"Amanda! Come on in. How are we today?"

We. "We're just fine. I'm fine. The other night, the night I got sick? Two weeks ago? They asked me to check in with the infirmary in two weeks. So . . ."

"So, all right. How do you feel?"

She'd heard Joey say *Never Better* all her life, so she said, "Never better."

"Don't you like this winter weather? It's a winter wonderland, isn't it? Makes the cheeks pink and lifts the soul."

"Oh, yeah, I really love it. It's great to be outside."

"What'd they have you in for?"

"My heart was like, fluttering? They said it was caffeine pills and dehydration from working out. Plus it was close to finals."

"You do all right on them?"

"Oh, yes, fine."

"Are you on any medication now?"

"Oh, no, no medication now."

"And you're not an eating disorder, not with that complexion."

"Oh, God, no, just the opposite."

"Well, let me take your vital signs anyway."

The nurse practitioner moved quickly through her routine — probably her idiot card or something told her

what the night people suspected about Amanda —
with an air of bright complicity, which is to say, that
she was just doing these things because, you know, you
have to do it with everyone, otherwise why are they
paying twenty-five grand a year, or whatever it is?
"Wonderful pulse, are you an athlete? Nice B.P. 105
over 70. 101 — what'd you weight when you came to
St. M's this fall?"

"Around 108 or so. I'm down a little. We're all
wound down."

"No problem. Nice clear lungs, ears clear . . .
brain. Your brain clear? You're outta here, kiddo,
thanks for coming over, I love your shoes. Christmas?"

"No. Pretty quiet day for you?"

"Oh, yeah, real quiet. We had a kid full of Zoloft,
his father was on it. We had a girl, an amennorhea, kid
with a serious eating disorder, taller than you, weighed
in the low 90s. They got her back there now. I still
don't understand why she won't eat anything. If you let
her out, she'll run around *her own room* all night. Nice
kid. Hair growing on her forearms, the body trying to
keep itself warm?"

"God."

"O.K., hon. Good luck."

AMANDA'S JOURNAL

18th February   9:35 p.m.   —4 degrees

92.65
Girl in newspaper: I have, like, negative
charisma.
    I have lack of affect. Heard that.
    Influence on cals burned off by incline
adjustment on treadmill?

*Music, for run. Kriesleriana, Op 16. Pavane
for a Dead Infanta. Chopin G-Minor.*
*Ceramide Time Comples Capsule. Arden
2 Xanax. 1 Halcion. ? Kava. Celexa.*
*Now 2 a.m. River like obsidian, black
molten carmel. Black adirondack winter like
photo of child Pasternak at Tolstoi death. (Dr.
Passmore)*

CHAPTER FORTY-SIX

Among the venerable traditions of St. Matthew's is an end-of-term ritual called Grade Sessions. It is held a week or two after the term ends. Students stand in line, in Chapel dress, arrayed by academic class and in alphabetical order. When their names are called out they mount the stairs of Gascoigne Hall's narrow stage, pause before the assistant headmaster, and receive their end-of-term and examination grades, which are printed on a simple gray card. Each student now shifts a pace or two to the left, receives some personal greeting from the headmaster, shakes his hand, and then walks to the other side of the stage. He walks down the stairs, down the aisle, and out into a crowd of students, excited and voluble, who have preceded him.

Perhaps, once upon a time, the atmosphere had been pleasant: when all the boys seemed to have done rather well, and when the headmaster, in shaking their hands, would inquire as to the health of their fathers. But now the tension at the ceremony was palpable, almost unbearable. From his place on stage, searching his students' faces, Carlisle Passmore saw dread, fearfulness, resignation, occasional bravado and resentment. They stood uneasily in their wavering lines, one or two with their heads in their hands — an unusual posture for people standing, he thought. One by one,

at intervals of thirty seconds, they clambered grace-
lessly up the stairs, centered themselves before the
assistant head, received their grades, looked down, and
moved over for his handshake. All was silence; except
that, each half-minute, a thin sibilance might, just
barely, be heard by those waiting their turn: a sound
not unlike the words of a priest bestowing communion
at the rail. *So good to see you, Jeremy. A ste; ling effort,
Courtney. Marvelous, dear boy . . .*

"Bahringer, A., Class IV."

She was early in line and had taken courage from
the brisk and frequent smiles and nods she could see
being exchanged between the assistant head and her
classmates. Perhaps it was a good year. At the same
time, desperately self-conscious in such a setting,
exhausted and weak, with the Inderal and Xanax both
at work in her, she was fearful that she would slip
going up the stairs, would somehow disgrace herself
even before seeing her marks. But she did not. Dr. Fitz-
maurice handed her the report. He looked directly at
her forehead as he put it into her hand. She looked
down at once:

Bahringer, A.	Class IV	
	Term	*Exam*
A.P. Latin	B+	(B-)
A.P. History	A-	(A-)
A.P. Biology	B+	(B)
Seminar/Poets	A	(A)
Algebra II	C-	(F)
Weighted G. P. A.	3.20	

An F on the algebra exam! She thought at once of
Miss Rodman's grim warning two months ago. "He says

you haven't got a clue." No, she didn't have a clue. Neither did her mother, who bragged about her ugly phone call to Mr. Carnes. Word of that had gotten around.

She stumbled to her left, towards Dr. Passmore, her eyes so full of tears she could barely see him, her lips pursed in a fierce effort to keep composure. She heard as if in a dream, *Dear child what a lovely effort you gave in the examination,* and felt herself gently propelled by his handshake off to the other side of the stage. She had a wild thought of Housman, what the headmaster had said, how he tried to harmonize the sadness of the universe . . . what a lovely effort. She descended down the stairs, up the long, long aisle, out in the terrible sunlight and whipping cold and a shouting throng of navy blue suits: Whadja Get? Whadja Get? Howja Do? Hey Toby, Hey Ashley. Already they were spinning the results like tops, certain masters identified as living bastards or geeks, bad grades as personal vengeances. *That prick will work for me some day. Hey Amanda, let me see — are we looking at Hanover, N. H., or what?*

But she could not speak. All she could do was show Toby the report card.

"All right," he declared. "Number one, the bastard failed half that section. Number two, Steele gave only two A-minuses in the whole course and you got one of them. Number three, the whole thing is total bullshit. Number four, you'll get in anyway. All right?"

"Oh, Toby," she sobbed, "I don't know what my mother will do."

"Amanda. Come on, will you? You had one bad grade. Look at all your other grades!"

She sensed he wanted to put his arm around her, comfort her. But she wanted no one's comfort.

She wanted to be away from him and from all these shouting avid people, all these . . . they were like

Japanese commuters trying to get onto a subway, she thought. She had to be away from all of them; she had to be alone in her narrow room, with her priest, and her pills, and with the time and solitude to think what she should do.

February 19

Dear Amanda,

You're the one who prefers letters to the phone or even e-mail, so now here's a letter from a very disappointed mother, one who forced herself not to call you back or write anything rash or immediate, but to sleep on the information you gave me on the phone, and what I found in the mail. I find that thinking about the results on the exams does nothing to change how I feel.

We have paid, counting your expenses, almost thirty thousand dollars for your education this year. We got you into St. Matthew's. We have worked with you, encouraged you, focussed all our emotional energies and hopes on you. Not only that. I know what your scores are, on your aptitude tests, the tests that measure innate ability. No one with scores like those has any business failing anything, especially not a public high school-level course in so-called Pre-college Algebra. Even if Dartmouth only sees the C-minus and not your exam grade, how in the world can they admit a girl with a grade like that? I still don't know how it could have happened.

I am not going to call your algebra teacher again. I did it last time and it didn't do any good, and your part of the bargain was to make the effort that would have shown him what you are capable of when you put your mind to it. Unfortunately you spent your time up there running and playing the piano. You knew that if you did not get the academic piece right, the whole thing wouldn't work.

You are my daughter and I still love you. I ask you, Amanda, to re-think your priorities and what is important to you.

Love from

Mummy

"And hold it," Tess told her secretary. "Here's another dictation. Coggin Lindsey, we have his address in Minnesota."

Dear Coggin, Just an update on Amanda, because you were very kind in offering to put in a plug for her at Dartmouth. With one not very significant exception her First Term grades are just about off the charts, so this is one kid whose application you can bird-dog with a clear conscience. You are very sweet to help me on this, and I'm grateful.

"Finish up, Felicity, and put in something about the convention."

CHAPTER FORTY-SEVEN

Amanda burrowed in. She turned away even from the casual greetings of other students. Her heart in hiding rebuffed Toby's exasperated efforts to engage her, to comfort her, to . . . perhaps something more. She neither knew nor cared. Her isolation now became her manna. Her grooming, once so deliberate and meticulous — and so obviously, to anyone who knew her, the result of painstaking effort — became slipshod, negligent. She dressed only for warmth and concealment — concealment by uniformity and by bulk. Her hair became lusterless, lank — what an earlier, even crueler generation called mousey. Teachers who stopped to talk, themselves harried and preoccupied, rarely noticed, and when they did, they remembered, after the fact, *hey, the Bahringer kid looks real tired.* But who isn't, this time of year? For it was a time of winter duties, a slog, a time to be endured and survived. Upstate New York is not Currier and Ives wintertime, not Sugarbush or Budweiser Clydesdales and hearths. It is merely gray, frigid and cheerless.

She now took two .5 mg Xanaxes before leaving Number 23 for morning classes. Once in a while, because it seemed to do the same thing, only harder and faster, a single Ativan, sometimes with Benadryl. She made exceptions only for mornings of supervised piano or lessons in the music building. For only the music there was the Inderal, which by itself still worked amazingly; it kept you crisp and let you play accurately. There were only four days now until the mailing deadline for supporting credentials, for the filming of the video and mailing it off — the Chopin Ballade, the one that would supposedly knock them over, make them gasp at the end. She was right at the edge of full memorization; but the thing about the video was, you could stop if you forgot your notes, and patch it back . . . but that was not optimal.

The familiar anxieties that pounded Amanda whenever she remembered something else someone expected her to do, these did not abandon her in the music building. For even as she pressed out the opening stately section of the G-minor Ballade, not a bit challenging technically, even then her mind was racing ahead to the terrible passages that lay in wait, the fiendishly demanding coda, *presto con fuoco* (as fast and hard as you can possibly do it), and the jubilant harmonics of the resolution, the parts that made listeners gasp, the ones that made the Admissions Committee — made them what? Forget her math SAT and her algebra grade and her class rank? Who knows?

She warmed up with Hanon exercises, fairly complicated scales, thirds, double thirds, complex arpeggios. The door to the little practice chamber began opening slowly, so slowly Amanda wondered whether it was being pushed open or if there was a snaky draft loose in the building. She looked towards the doorway and there now appeared a girl, small and frail, Asian, perhaps twelve or thirteen years old. Amanda stopped playing and looked at her. Now, following her into the room, was another, older woman, perhaps her mother, and behind them both, Mrs. Thompson.

265

The girl pointed at a reproduction on the wall over the piano. She smiled, nodded vigorously to her mother, said, triumphantly, "Brahms."

"Amanda — good morning! This is Sylvia Chae. She is from Seoul, Korea, and she's a candidate for admission to St. Matthew's: Here *you* are, a candidate to attend Dartmouth, and here is Sylvia, a candidate to follow in your footsteps here! She will do piano with me if she comes here."

Amanda stood up awkwardly, wedged between the bench and the keyboard. She put out her hand, "Hi, Sylvia. Welcome."

"Want her to play something?" the mother asked, nodding an indifferent greeting at Amanda, but addressing Mrs. Thompson. "We have twenty minutes until the interview in the admissions office. She's got the jet lag, so I am hoping that you will make allowance."

"Oh, thank you. That would be lovely. Amanda?"

Amanda slid aside. The girl replaced her, her hands down on the front edge of the piano bench, as if to stretch her fingers, then reached towards Amanda's sheet music — the Chopin piece. Amanda noticed how narrow and frail her wrists and fingers were.

"Shall I attempt this? I have done it once before." Sylvia spoke in a stilted British English.

"That'd be lovely. Amanda's working on the same composition. The odyssey of Chopin's soul."

Amanda had heard the story about Toscanini and Horowitz — how Toscanini, hearing the young Horowitz play the first chord of the Tschaikovsky Concerto, had run from the podium to stare at the pianist's hands: to look at them and at the young man who had drawn such a sound from the instrument. And so potent was the authority Sylvia Chae brought to the first annunciation of the opening theme of the Ballade,

that Mrs. Thompson and Amanda, had they been con-
ductors, might have done the same. They were aware
instantly that the girl held in her heart the unity of the
whole work, that she commanded not only the technical but also the emotional resources to translate the
composer's ideas in authoritative ways. She had the
piece down cold.

Having explored the opening motif, the girl gathered her energies for the first strong restatements of the
theme; and now began literally to rip into and through
its demands with an almost miraculous facility. In the
coda she threw off fiery descending octaves, effortlessly, with wicked velocity and a radiant clarity.

All the while, Amanda was watching the girl's
mother, who was studying her daughter with a look of
admiration, but also, perhaps, judgment. Where had
she seen that look?

The girl finished, looked reverently down, folded
her hands in her lap, turned to Mrs. Thompson, and
bowed:

"Thank you for the opportunity to play for you. I
will aspire to train with you if I am admitted to the
school. And I thank you, too," she said, regarding
Amanda with evident gratitude. "And give good
wishes for your work at Dartmouth. The Chopin is
great."

"Be back in a minute," Mrs. Thompson winked at
Amanda. "I have to see them off."

But she did not come back.

Amanda resumed practicing, reverting to some
Schumann that she loved: only to see, again, the door
opening slowly towards her, this time to the best visitor
she could possibly have hoped for.

"Daddy!"

"Hi, baby."

"What're you doing here?"

"Looking at a building in Albany — just came over to say 'Hi,' see how you were doing. What's going on?"

"Practicing. You know, Schumann, the composer you like."

She looked so frail, so thin, Joey thought. This is what the exams up here do to these kids. God, she must be exhausted. And so he said, "Well, all that exam stuff doesn't look as though it did you any harm. Keeps you inside, I guess."

"You know what it is, up here? Like, ten degrees, maybe five. You can't go out. So all I do is study and work out indoors."

Amanda knew what she must look like to her father. She loved him for his ignorance of what kids do in boarding school; and she was not afraid to use that ignorance to convince him that it was absolutely normal at St. Matthew's to be very pale and tired and thin this time of year.

They sat in the snack bar and Amanda ordered an egg salad sandwich and a cup of coffee.

"Any games going on?"

"The whole school is a game."

"You did fine on your exams. I mean, what more could a university want. The Latin grade gave me a kick. I just about flunked altar boy Latin. Now my kid's got a B-plus in — what? — fourth year Latin, school like St. Matthew's."

She loved him, knew exactly what he was saying: that he couldn't have cared less about algebra.

"Guess I won't wind up teaching math at M.I.T."

"Got that from me. I can't even calculate commissions. Don't worry about it. Something we all might do, I was thinking about it coming over, is go down to the Islands over Easter. Don't you get out for that? Easter's late this year."

"Yes. Mid-April. I'd love that, Daddy."

"Bring a friend if you want to."

"No, I'd rather be with just you and Mom."

"So, who you seeing? You see Dr. Passmore? Your mother has a crush on him. Thinks he's cool."

"I see him two or three times a week. He still teaches, but he's totally out of touch. The school's completely out of touch with him, I mean, they treat him like he's an old mascot. Everything he says he believes, the school doesn't. I get so sad? And I'll see him, and he has this angelic way he looks at you, as though he'd got all the time in the world, and we love this poet together, Gerard Manley Hopkins? I asked him, what're you going to do when you retire, everyone knows he's going to retire, go to Florida and live in the sun or go see where Hopkins wrote all his poems."

"He's a very intellectual man, isn't he?"

"Yeah. I don't know. He's not like grades n'stuff. He doesn't care about that."

"I won't tell your mother. You got the one bad grade, so what? You want to *be* in a place that turns you down because you got one bad grade? What kind of place is that? When did you start drinking coffee?"

"Oh, you know. Years ago."

"You getting enough sleep?"

"Sure. You?"

"Season the Rangers are having, I sleep on the couch. I don't want you to let any of this stuff get you down. You're not down, are you?"

"No. No problem."

Joey looked at his daughter. That face, so beautiful, he thought. And it hid everything, just like a priest's. And she probably practiced hiding everything, just like a priest did.

"That sweatshirt looks like it was made for King Kong."

"Everyone wears an XXL. It's the style."

"Want to order anything else?"

"No. I had a big breakfast before my music lesson."

Joey asked — because he hardly knew what questions to ask — "How's the girl doing that we met on opening day with her parents, I think her name was Sumner, remember her? Her dad was pretty full of himself."

"Oh, Sumner, she got S.D.'d."

"What's that mean?"

"Systemic departure. You get let go for some reason. You're not supposed to talk about them after they've gone."

"That happen often?"

"Yeah. Fairly. I don't know, maybe three or four times a month. The Herald announces it. There's a fair amount of turnover."

"That's worse casualties than my unit had in Vietnam."

"Yeah. Well, they push you hard. It's not exactly a game here."

"And what do they expect to get out of it?"

"Get me into Dartmouth. Make Mom happy."

"What's supposed to happen to you then?"

"Daddy!" She reached over the table and slapped him on the forearm.

"No, what?"

"You just keep going."

"What a way for a kid to talk. Keep pushing, keep going. What're you, like the Iditerod?"

"What do you want me to say? You put me here."

Later they walked together along the icy walkway that led to the lot, past the entrance to Morison.

"Want to come up?"

"No, I have to leave." Joey studied a large dark plaque on the side of the building. "Let me see that thing."

"The dorm used to be for boys. They decided not to take it down."

The plaque, dated 1911, said: BE STRONG AND SHOW YOURSELF A MAN / FULFILL YOUR DUTY TO THE LORD YOUR GOD. 1 Kings 2:1.

"O.K. You better go fulfill your duty. Jesus, out of the blue, *Fulfill Your Duty!* I can't get over this school."

"Oh, they have them all over the place. It was this guy's theory, an old headmaster, have plaques everywhere, for inspiration. There's one on the other side of Morison, it says *he that sheds his blood with me today shall be my brother.* They were supposed to rub their hands on it before every football game."

"Baby, I have to go. Will you make me a promise? Take care of yourself? Get outside more, get more sleep? I don't care what you get, Algebra, Latin, you know? You do what you can, hey, honest day's pay, honest day's labor, play some music, pack it in. You're outta here, what? June 5th? There's three thousand colleges in this country. You O.K. for money, anything you need?"

"No, I'm fine."

Joey took Amanda in his arms and held her to him, his cheek against his daughter's hair. He slid onto the seat of his rental car. He always cried a little when he left Amanda and he didn't want her to see it.

"I love you, Daddy. Thanks for coming to see me."

That afternoon, leaving the cardio room in Gibbon, Amanda bumped into Coach Kellam. She hadn't seen him in a month. He had his darting, gloomy look — always for something to be improved. She had almost forgotten it.

"Long time, no see. You fit?"

"Oh, sure. Just been in there."

"What, treadmill?"

Amanda nodded. She was thinking, he's a male version of my mother. Gets it right on, no preliminaries.

"You can do all kinds of things on it, Amanda. I know people that run marathons on treadmills. You know those rowing ergs — those ergometers? Same deal, they set up a thousand of them in a room in Boston, wired to a computer. They race on them."

"I don't run that far."

"How far'd you go?"

"About four, maybe four-and-a-half-miles."

"That's all right. You *maintain*, that's all you need to do now. *Maintain*. Remember, the calorie dial doesn't work for *you*. Not on those machines. They're old."

"What?"

"See, you weigh, what, a hundred and five, and the thing's set for a 150-pound guy. To get the same burn you gotta run an extra fifty per cent. See? If you calculate 300 calories for three miles, forget it. You, it's probably only 200. Because of your weight. Hear anything from Dartmouth?"

"Not really. No."

"Whaddyou mean, not really?"

"No, I didn't hear anything."

"Hey. You hang in there. Girl in San Diego went under sixteen in a 5K last week. You believe that? Kid's a sophomore."

February 20   *13 Degrees*
92.10
4.7mi/565 cal

My heart in hiding.
Should be absolutely clinical.
Yesterday, 3 classes. Long afternoon with
Daniella in her room. Sometimes she talks like
a computer on the Weather Channel. She said
Dartmouth would not admit me, just said it
based on 5K times, which I already knew, and
also I am just an average Caucasian Catholic
girl, and Cath is no longer unusual in the Ivy
League. 1340 SAT only average for them,
maybe lower. Conceivably could happen if I
had a political connection, i.e. Mother's air-
plane acquaintance. Daniella in at Brown, early
med program, waiting to hear about Michigan.
1560 SAT. Do not obsess. Left her and worked
out again. 31min/38 cals, fruit, coffee Saver-
nake — oranges and salad.
*   7:50 p.m. — 11:45 Latin only. Horace.*
Could not focus and drifted and jerked back
again and again. Xx, 2. Vivarin. Midnight. 1
Ritalin from C1 III girl Lamindari who goes off
them two days a week a/c to Dr. Mitchell, at
least Amanda doesn't take Ritalin, she's the
opposite way — she, me's, too revved-up.
*   W/in 25 minutes my heart started to flutter*
like a bird, like a butterfly dusting the inside of
my chest. Like last episode: No regular beat
and I started to sweat in streams, hands like an
earthquake measuring needle. I stood up and

*almost passed out. Looked up, got my coat,
kissed GMH and outside the air like black crystal. Infirmary and back by 1 a.m. with class
excuse. Spent morning here in the room. Miss
Rodman, how am I, Dear, etc. Said: this happened on acc you have been under a strain.
Infirmary basically made me sit there again.
Took bloodpressure, what weight are my
clothes, etc? I had plenty of water before going
over there, rolls of quarters, pants, etc. so I was
all right. The nurse said it was all dehydration,
and I was practically bursting. Last time I saw
Dr. Passmore and Miss Rodman when I got
back, in her apt, they looked like people in an
old black and white movie. He stands up when
I come in, "My dear," etc., and loves Tess's
Xmas coat.*

Took Inderal and slept fast . . .

*February 22   St Matthew's, 6 Degrees
92.30*

*WLH Moon: silent and hasteless river; black
liquid between white rimes of ice, the Seneca in
mid-winter. No "soft inland murmur."*

*In Chapel tonight they began with an organ
arrangement of the Walton Crown Imperial, that
sounded like a Star Wars re-run. Everything in
Chapel done for hype, the Episcopal idea of
squeeze the heart if they cannot persuade your
brain — all heavy, blood-red banners stream
afar, etc. This could not have been Fr. Hopkins'
church. Not pure and clear sound, not like clear
icy water of the river or sound of boy soprano.*

Sermon by an Episcopal priest, graduate of St.
Matthew's who used to be an executive. St.
Paul's letter to Colossians? "Seek the things that
are above, where Christ is, not the things that are
on earth." Then the concluding hymn as lovely
and pure as any might be. Perfect in every way, a
hymn GMH must have known as it was written
in England 340 years before his birth.

> *O may my soul on thee repose,*
> *And may sweet sleep my eyelids close.*
> *Sleep that shall me more vigorous make*
> *To serve my God when I awake.*

I am alone, so alone now.
Celexa 4.
1 Fiorinal.
Sick in sink.

February 28   *11 Degrees*
92.10

"One of his primary reasons for choosing the
discipline of the Society of Jesus years later was
that it demanded absolute obedience of the sort
he knew he could have and was deeply aware
he could never achieve unaided: the most diffi-
cult course always seemed the natural one to
him." R.B. Martin Hopkins.
When he was in St. Matthew's-like sch.
refused all liquids, incl. water for ?three weeks
to demonstrate total self-control. Stoicism, even
though his tongue turned black. Human ability
to control and endure.

Great taste never looked so good.
Exhausted.
Ellotrim caffeine-free diet aids.
4937 Woodville Road
Northwood, Ohio 43619
SVGS. Skim/reg. 65/cup

CHAPTER FORTY-EIGHT

In the rear of the classroom listening to Mr. Steele, Amanda could not remember how she got here. But here she was. He had shot forward in the A.P. syllabus, was what it sounded like, and now he was talking about the Vietnam War that her father had fought in (when she heard *fought* she thought of her father fist-fighting against dirty men with curved swords) and that had begun, Mr. Steele was saying, as a gorilla war. All continued fighting in this war, despite the bombing of the B-52s, and even if the war was unjust, the infiltration of these gorillas was continuing during the period we are now discussing.

A grainy scruff of snow slid off the canted roof of the Haney building. Watching it tipple and float away, Amanda wondered how the enemy had made gorillas fight for them, how they trained them. It was possible. She had seen it done, something like that, on the Discovery Channel, about communication with gorillas, or perhaps it was with chimpanzees, and how they had learned more than 300 symbols and gestures. A young woman, very thin, very blond, and with an English accent and a kind of tropical suit like a Ralph Lauren *Safari* ad — this young woman lived with the gorillas and communicated with them. They would threaten her, then suddenly withdraw. There was something about her that they respected. So they must have been smart enough to have fought for the enemy, in the early years of the Vietnam War, which was a gorilla war. She had had the two Celexas and two Xanaxes and they might get her onto some other drug protocol if she asked for it, but the Xanaxes and the Inderal together had cut in so hard: she wondered whether *bleary* could mean how your throat felt. Her eyes were barely open, the lids fluttering shut, and she felt herself drooling on her palm, where she had her cheekbone. *The gorilla war was only in the countryside, in the jungle-paddies of the country at large, and so the cities would be continually bombed, until the Communist factions would be* something, and within them a number of students *your own age,* please keep that in mind — *they were no older than some of you.* The gorilla war could not by itself be successful. The Kennedy advisors had not been enough. War is not susceptible, Steele argued, to *rational* management. That is the most foolish illusion of all. Kennedy and his son are now dead. But the President's high ideals were needed to block the further Communist advances of the gorilla war. *Are you having trouble concentrating today, Miss Bahringer? JFK was surely no Andrew Jackson. Toby, wake your friend up and escort her back to her room, if her next period's a free one, which I most sincerely hope it is.*

March 3   *12 Degrees, Snow*
92.0   6pm

   They hated him, no, maybe did not hate him,
but couldn't deal with him or with it — what
he did. The whole inevitable slope he went
down, first Catholic, then priest, then Jesuit,
each step that he had to take, took him farther,
farther from all family, to Ireland finally and
totally remote, full of sickness, despair, etc. Dr.
Passmore said, they thought a convert priest a
stuck-up English snob and would be even more
suspicious of him than they were of an out-and-
out Protestant. He did what his heart heard of.
I do what they make me and expect of me,
what SHE expects of me. What I must do. As
for Dartmouth, it's got to be all over but the
shouting. I should come to grips with it, Miss
Rodman says; it doesn't mean that much. Com-
plete aloneness, solitude of ice, ice cold, my
heart in hiding rebuffed the big wind. Last para
of letter from Mother. "We sent you there, you
know the purpose why, and now if the purpose
is attained it will not be through any effort of
yours but like everything else attained by you, it
will be done by our intervention. Nevertheless,
we will support you — Daddy does too." I am
as alone as GMH in Dublin. Passmore:
Owen — eyes like a Devil's sick of sin.
   Bkfst: Power Bar. L: coffee, Scotch broth,
lettuce.
   PM: Treadmill, new counting 6.7 mi x 66
cals — 442 cals.

Xanax: 6 during day. Halcion last night Ind. Before lunch.

A perfect iambic pentameter line:

If I should die think only this of me. *(Passmore war poet.)*

CHAPTER FORTY-NINE

This time Mr. Arnett began by holding up his hand, palm outward, shushing the reaction he anticipated. He said, "Got a preliminary read from Colgate — here, Amanda, have a seat. Cold out, no? You all right? You look a little peaked."

She had curled around the entrance to his office and slid into a chair, book bag between her knees, her eyes already on him. Like a puppy's, he thought.

"It's not good, all right?" Palm up again, warding off outrage. "Just listen to me, all right? They've had a hell of a year. It happens. College'll jump fifteen, twenty per cent in apps in one year. Gets hot. Look at Vanderbilt. Look at Wellesley. Look at Tufts — like trying to get into Ft. Knox. You got caught in the gears. They had a big year. You didn't get your letter, did you? Because they're not supposed to mail until Monday."

"No."

"All right. You got wait-listed again. They denied four, wait-listed five. We got only two accepts. Neither one of them wants to go, either."

"I don't know what she'll do. She won't believe this. *Colgate!*"

"Your mother?"

"I mean, last year they wait-listed me. What am I doing here? What does this mean for Dartmouth?"

"Doesn't mean anything. I'll probably hear something from them in a week or ten days — you'll get your letter a week or so after that. I'll have a pretty good idea. But no, it doesn't mean anything. I know a kid got turned down by Berkeley and got into Amherst. These places are funny. So don't lose any sleep over it."

But she had lost it. She sobbed noiselessly, face in her hands, her head bent down, almost in her lap. Arnett wanted to touch her shoulder, to hug her, some little gesture of consolation, but you can't mess with that stuff these days. You had to let them work through it. A guy at Sweet Briar told him, when girls lose it, put a LifeSaver right there on their tongue — you can't sob with something on your tongue. She'll rationalize it in an hour, tops.

"See, look, Amanda, they probably sensed they weren't your top choice, all right? They can't deal with that. Not only that, it's much more of a judgment on St. Matthew's than on you."

"A judgment on St. Matthew's! Then why am I even here?" Amanda cried out — loud enough for Arnett's secretary to pop her head around the door.

"They want to show they're not impressed by the school. Colleges do it all the time. They're sending a message. Amanda." He reached out and tapped the back of her hand — "you can't tell me you wanted to go there anyway. So what's it mean? I mean, analyze it for a minute — someone tells you you can't have something you didn't want anyway, see?"

But she was already on her feet, looking down at him, her hands on the straps of her book bag, lifting it up. She seemed weary, emaciated. She was strung out. But how else do you tell them? They have to work through it.

"Hey," he said. "It's not that big a thing, you know? Look where I went to school: UC Santa Barbara. No one here ever heard of it. Did that hurt me?

282

Why don't you go lie down? You want to be in a place that doesn't want you?"

"Bobby," Arnett's secretary called him. "Paul Hart from Stanford, on line one. Must be 6:00 A.M. out there."

"I'll take the call." Again, the hand extended. "Don't let it get to you, all right? I'll be back to you. Work it out. Go work it out, whatever you do, try to forget about it."

She went right down to Gibbon. There were ten new ergocycles lined up in a row, bolted to the floor. No adornments, no computerized videos; just dials for calories and distance. The arms of the machines looked like beetles' legs, skinny long black arms that you gripped at the ends. After six or seven minutes you were at seventy RPM's, twelve calories a minute, and you could burn off three hundred calories in not more than half an hour. Two big muscle groups recruited at once. You could wipe yourself out on these things, have your Xanaxes and whatever, empty everything out. And Mr. Arnett had a point.

Colgate!

AMANDA'S JOURNAL

March 19   *Warmer. Showery.*
91.0

*I had to have "tea" with Miss Rodman and
Daniella and two other girls. Miss Rodman had
bacon and avocado sandwiches but only one got
eaten. She asked Daniella if D liked to bathe in
the sea. D stared at her in her fashion, a long
time, I know she was thinking, no I bathe in a
bath tub and swim in the ocean. Miss Rodman
said to me that I looked better, complexion*

283

higher and my face looks fuller, *but I look as if I
don't brush my hair anymore, which is true. I
put icewater on my face before I come into her
apartment. The peculiar nice woman.*

*Did not go to Savernake, ate in room
Assigned a Housman poem:*

*Into my heart an air that kills
From yon far country blows:
What are those blue remembered hills,
What spires, what farms, are those?*

*That is the land of lost content,
I see it shining plain.
The happy highways where I went
And cannot come again.*

Dr. Passmore asked that we look up into the sky.
Acts of the Apostles. *Try to remember a time and
place, a scene of childhood, that we now understand is
completely lost to us forever. He says it as two words:
for ever. And then knowing that our hearts were broken by such a thought. I never had one.*
Celexa/Xanax(4)/Inderal/Halcion, sleep.
*Also (Passmore) more of the great poets and writ-
ers never even* went *to any* college. *Colleges are for students to learn what writers, artists, etc., create. Colgate
turn-down is meaningless. My* Dear *Child.*

Obligations Board, 27 March: Your e-mail
down? I talked to the guy at Dartmouth this
morning. I need to see you.   R. Arnett.

Her body felt like all of it spasmed at once. She
stood alone in the corridor of Morison, outside her

284

room. If the news was going to be good, he would have given a little hint. It wouldn't have sounded like: "I need to see you . . ."

And, well, what? People lost children to cancer. Struggle! Struggle is the South Bronx, after the Christmas you've had! The pain will be bitter if you let it be bitter. And it was coming on her, so bitter it hurt her on both sides of her throat, and also because everyone knew what an obsession it had been, that it was the only reason she was at St. M's. And now. And with, well, perhaps still a thinnest chance it would be all right. She would see him that night or the next morning. There are three thousand colleges in our country . . .

CHAPTER FIFTY

Bobby Arnett tried to assure relatively soft landings for Class IVs likely to be bruised or smashed up in the rough-and-tumble of the college process. It was a matter of professional pride with him, just as important to his professional conscience as the number of Class IVs the school got into elite universities. Often Arnett knew what was happening weeks before his candidates found out. He had buddies, moles, in the admissions offices of the colleges Mathewsians applied to, and the e-mail traffic between them was constant. When reluctant to give him outright facts, they hinted sharply, trusting his circumspection, knowing how valuable was their own college's relationship with St. Matthew's. They would swear him to secrecy . . . *you can't tell him, Bobby* . . . but they expected he would use what he knew when it was helpful to him: to assure soft landings, or, rarely, to hype the excitement in a student the university really wanted. An athlete, perhaps; a cellist; a brilliant minority.

Now he stood on the third floor of Morison, just after six-thirty on a late March evening, self-consciously and embarrassedly catching his breath after the climb up the stairs. He fiddled with his pocket square and tie, knocked on Amanda's door — and heard at once the rasp of a chair being pushed back from a desk. He thought he heard a drawer rumble shut; and then a voice. Be right there, just a minute, be right there. Nowadays you always gave them a bit of time . . .

Usually Arnett would not have visited a girl's, or for that matter a boy's, dormitory. Dormitories depressed him: their fusty smell, their baked heat, their wan décor brought him back to grim memories of his own time at the school. Yes, St. Matthew's was undoubtedly great; all the literature called it a "great national boarding school," and it was famous. But it lived bleakly in his memory as a dark interior place, something like what the Spartans must have put their male children into — icy baths, trundle beds, cruelty, discipline. A joyless place. St. Paul's was vivid New England autumns; Lawrenceville was sweet springtimes; St. Matthew's was endless upstate winter — sallow skins, coughing, people walking like penguins, dark corridors. Look at this hallway, this corridor! A military barracks in Germany must look like this. Or a tomb. He knocked again.

"Hi. I'm so impressed! May I come in? We'll stick something in the door, O.K.? You live well, Amanda. Look at this room!"

Arnett didn't mean it. The room looked like a child's, a child's room in the window of a department store or a room laid out for an ad in a magazine. Everything immaculate, not a blemish or a wrinkle anywhere, everything arranged and arrayed in a strange, pitiless symmetry and order — books, notebooks, cosmetics, lamps, clocks, photographs; a Palm V, upright in its charger, stubby white bottles (he could read the label on one: ginko biloba); pens and pencils. Everything shone and glistened; there was an unnatural cleanliness, a piney, disinfectant smell. The long mullioned window was cracked open an inch or two; the room was unnaturally cool. Over Amanda's desk Arnett saw a Dartmouth poster, a summertime Dartmouth that was lushly green, picket-fenced, green-shuttered — white clapboard buildings arrayed about a village green.

"Who," he wondered, "is the father?"

"Who?"

"The picture of the priest. Are you a Roman Catholic?"

"Yes?"

"Is that guy your priest?"

"No. That's one of the poets we study? Gerard Manley Hopkins."

"Tough life it looks like — for him. He looks tired."

"Yes. The picture was taken just before he died."

"All right, Amanda. Here's a Jeopardy question for you, all right? What were his dying words?"

I am so happy. I am so happy.

"Doesn't look that happy."

"No, not there. But you can't always tell how people feel by what they look like."

The girl looked awful, he thought; gray, drawn, brittle.

Amanda hadn't stood up when Arnett came in, had just sat there with an elbow on her desk. She was wearing a blue jumper over a white turtleneck, the sweater bulky enough to drape her arms and the sleeves bunched all the way down towards the hams of her hands. She had been on the Harnett scale less than five minutes before he knocked, before she had put her things on, and she had been under ninety pounds for the first time, only an hour off the treadmill. She had taken her Celexa, two Xanaxes, a Fiorinal, and a multivitamin with two glasses of tap water. It crossed her mind that, without the water, she could have been under eighty-nine. The Fiorinal was like a punctuation mark, an exclamation point; it made her feel spiky and vivid, like a girl whose gondola has come to a jellied stop at the top of a Ferris wheel. She was poised, giddy but safe, over a sea of flaky light. She caught herself drumming a pen against her teeth.

"Your buddy Toby says you live like a hermit."

"Toby. He thinks he keeps an eye on me."

"Well, you do have a tendency to isolate. I've heard that from a couple of people."

Amanda looks evenly at him. She knows why Mr. Arnett has come. Why make it easy on him?

"All right. I have some fairly definitive news from Hamilton. You're going to like it, all right? You're in! You're in at Hamilton. You're not supposed to know for three or four days. So keep it to yourself. Let me shake your hand."

Amanda manages a smile — almost like a grimace, he thinks.

"It's a great liberal arts college. Ezra Pound went there. Also, I was reading this morning in the Journal, the new C.E.O. of International Cyber, a Cuban guy. Great teaching faculty."

"But I didn't get into Dartmouth. That's why you're here. Everyone knows, when you visit their dormitory room, it's to give them bad news. You're like a Vietnam telegram — Daniella told me that."

This makes it easier. Arnett hates scenes.

"Well, number one, the information is not definitive. It's bad on the surface, not good, but maybe there's a chance down the road. I don't know — but, you know, Amanda, the more I hear about that place, the less I like what I'm hearing. Maybe that's just me. I thought you had a pretty good shot, with your running and your piano video and your new SATs. That was some run-up! Our early read is that they've been very hard on St. Matthew's this year. Almost all our kids. You'll get your letter in about a week — they usually mail to the home, not the school, so alert Mom and Dad. I'm pretty sure it's not good news. Not positive, but . . ."

"I'll e-mail her at the office. She deals with it better at the office. My father wouldn't care if I went to Florida State."

"Hey! You gave it your best shot, all right? Once Dartmouth lets in their geniuses and their legacies and their minorities, there's not a lot of space for normal kids. It's a little school, you know. Big name, little school. There aren't that many spaces. Maybe you can transfer in later. You all right?"

Her heart pounded away as though it would shatter her ribs. She stared at him, arms folded across her chest. Her mouth was open and she touched her upper lip with the tip of her tongue. She didn't seem to him to be tearing up, or getting ready to cry, or anything. Just taking it in. Probably hating the messenger. *He* was the Dartmouth admissions office.

"And, hey, Amanda: Hamilton! And we still have Trinity to hear from. I see their squash team just won a big invitational, in New York. Are you all right?"

"I'm fine, Mr. Arnett."

He touched her shoulder, stood up, and left. It was tough, telling a kid news like this, especially a P.G. They staked everything on their year at St. Matthew's. And he hated it when Class IV girls called him Mr. Arnett. He wasn't that much older than they were.

And yet he felt a lot better for having made the effort to come by and see her. Very few of his Class IV advisees ever S.D.'d. They appreciated it when he made the effort.

Now Amanda took two Klonapins, the very heavy drug Dr. Mitchell had given her mother a couple of years ago — at least that's when they appeared in her medicine chest. Amanda kept them *in reserve*. It was a drug that made you feel like you were walking at the bottom of a warm pool. Her heart was fluttering again, a butterfly beating wildly. By the light from the screen saver she could *see* her pulse, a burble of flesh at the inside of her wrist. It must be going 150 beats a minute, more than it went when she ran. It would be hard even to hold a pen, but the Klonapins would take her down; then she could write in her journal. Mr. Steele had shown the class a Civil War soldier's diary. The last entry said, *"I was killed."* Mr. Arnett is right, my mother will simply have to deal with it.

Her mind wobbled, drifted, but she felt herself sliding towards calm. She was working through it. Give them an hour or so, they work through it. Mr. Arnett had it right.

The building itself was silent. A wind outside, falling and rising, a rasp of rain against the window. To strive ceaselessly, and, after all, you can stand on your head for three weeks; the clamor and tumult, the students rushing forward, masters darting away from you and saying things without meaning, "That's the stuff," and all of them looking over and beyond your shoulder, everything to Measure, Rank, Judge, Compare, Discard.

Outside a dreary drenching rain, the sound both magnified and dulled, beat on the roof of Morison — a rain darkly heralding the ending of winter and the coming of a new season. A fog was settling bleakly about, fitting itself about the school, and on the Seneca, she imagined, the ice that had choked the river was beginning to crack and melt. She could feel the trees in the forest begin to drip. She could hear the dark murmuring of the river.

March 28

Dear Mother and Daddy,

I did not get into Dartmouth. Mr. Arnett has been here tonight in advance of the letter they will send home in a week. Nothing I will write now will mean anything. I won't write anything much. I'm like a priest at a kid's funeral, when he says, there is nothing to say. He means there was something to say, but no one wants to hear it. When I was a little girl you told me "myself" was one word, because you found a letter I wrote that said "I hate my self." Now I make it two words again. You gave me all you could give me, and it wasn't enough.

Love Amanda.

CHAPTER FIFTY-ONE

The rain, soft and warm, sensed rather than heard, bore the faintest aromatic hints of spring, and she was conscious of the yearning voice of a woman, a singer, drifting into her window from another dormitory. She had forgotten Arnett, had written in her journal and put her letter to her parents into an envelope. She remembered holding up her picture of the priest, in Dublin, exhausted and alone and yet bravely at peace in his own abandonment. She had kissed him, and she remembered falling off . . .

Her awakening was abrupt, a sharp awareness of fierce bright cold and light. Late March sunlight, Dr. Passmore observed, is the same light as late summer's — the sun everywhere harshly present, in Morison number 23 casting its flat irradiation everywhere, lighting up Hopkins' face, restoring him. *There lives the dearest freshness deep down things!* — of all Hopkins' lines her favorite. From her pillow Amanda could see a gathering of orange silos next to the photograph: Xanax, Klonapin, Inderal . . . one she couldn't make out. Xantac? Who gave them names, she wondered. Next to them, just unwrapped, lay a math video from an airport mall: IF YOU CAN DO SIMPLE ARITHMETIC YOU CAN DO HIGHER MATH! ANYONE CAN! And in the closet, hanging on a hook on the door was the dress she had worn, five months ago, in her interview with the Dartmouth representative, Miss Cha, the young woman with the two-hand handshake.

She stood and was stunned by her own steadiness and peace. The beating of her heart now seemed remote but steady. On her scale: 89.31. She began to dress herself: stockings, a Navy slip; new cap-toe pumps never worn but sitting since Christmas in a box on the closet floor. A care package: something on Tess's mind. *Have a present, darling!* Lengthwise in the mirror she watched herself brush her hair back, no cowl, no hiding her face, and she fitted over it a velvet black hairband just at the hairline. She saw the merest patch of white flesh over the waist of her slip, still too much of it, lifted her arms into the sleeves of the interview dress. She took Father Hopkins' photograph from the frame, rolled it up and slid it into the pocket of her overcoat. She centered her journal perfectly on the blotter, her letter to her parents on top. She looked again at the admissions photograph of Dartmouth. There was no spring in New Hampshire, someone had told her that; the season went from blazing icy winter to bright green summer, but no spring, when weeds in wheels shoot long and lovely and lush. She took down her worn Penguin Hopkins and wrote on the inside cover: *To Daniella. I Love You. Good luck in all your future endeavors.* She marked and turned down the page bearing the little poem "Heaven Haven" that Dr. Passmore had given them the first time the class met. *I have desired to go . . . where a few lilies blow.*

The rain had scoured the trail of all snow, leaving a glistening surface of marbled ice, of scree, of frozen muddy wrinkles. Puffy plumes of fog, silvery and pallid, rose in wavering columns on either side.

It was terribly hard going, each step having to be measured and calculated, each placement of a foot a taut decision. The last time she had passed this way, she had floated over the trail, carried along in a racing run that lived as a remembered moment of joy, perhaps her only moment of joy, at St. Matthew's. The woods were almost silent; snow lay heavily, everywhere — a tired snow, grainy and porous, its crusts marked here and there by wayward tracks, by bare eddies of brown around the bases of the larger trees.

Amanda left the trail; she began to make her way directly alongside it. It seemed colder, much colder, the lower she descended, the farther she moved away from the school, the closer to the Seneca. You never saw the river until you were upon it; you never heard it.

Now it was before her, below the embankment, the river iced over thinly for almost a third of its width, a cold molten blackness at the center. Along the edge, just at the base of the embankment, a tattered spume had formed after the rain. Now she turned to her left, saw that she could walk quite easily along the top of the embankment; it was clear ahead as far as she could see. Before her, she saw, perfectly framed in memory, Daniella running ahead, effortless, gliding, tumbling finally out of sight. Amanda stopped. Here she slid down to the river, knelt, began a harvest of pebbles and sand, filling the pockets of her navy coat until they could hold no more. It was like filling the pockets of your jeans with rolls of coins. She stood up, moved herself forward, hands extended like an acrobat's on a wire, began stepping out onto the ice, carefully, slowly, making her way to its last thick limit. Into the blackness, under her gaze, seeing nothing but the reflection of her own face, she flung herself forward, sinking down easily and immediately.

EPILOGUE

The St. Matthew's Chapel liturgy had made provision for the death of a student. Hearing, *feeling* the booming resonance of the organ's opening salvo, Joey rose to his feet, lifted to a position, almost, of military attention. He and Tess had been placed in the second pew, exactly where they had sat on Opening Day. Two students sat next to them: Daniella Ben and Toby Carrington, students Amanda was said to have known best.

Joey stared helplessly at the High Cross borne down the long aisle by the crucifer, even less able to master himself here than he had been at the funeral mass at St. Teresa's. In his agony he barely saw the long procession of choristers passing by, the sleeves of their surplices brushing against him. At the end, alone, came Dr. Passmore.

Moving into their stalls behind the altar, the choir began a new hymn:

> *The powers of death have done their worst,*
> *But Christ their legions hath dispersed.*
> *Let shouts of holy joy outburst*
> *Alleluia!*

The powers of death had certainly done their worst. Tess heard: *Lived, Beloved. Died, Lamented. Our Dear*

Amanda, beloved of this school and of the blessed St. Matthew. Since hearing the devastating news, she had governed, almost *rationed* her emotions; and now she sat, tautly swathed in black pashmina, severely erect, looking neither to the left or right. She wore the same tiny ocelot pin she had worn on opening day, but she had allowed herself no other such concession to the awful urgings of her grief and remorse. She was fighting to keep control: but here, at the very heart of the place to which she had sent her daughter to realize a dream, she saw this was a goal slipping hopelessly away. She had watched Joey's helpless tears, the spasms of grief that rocked his body at the Mass at St. Teresa's; they had brought her unbidden a memory of him and Amanda, Joey on his back on the floor of their bedroom, their baby girl held high above his face, her tiny fingers touching his cheeks: Amanda had always adored him.

There had been no homily or eulogy at the mass. She was grateful for this. Tess was far beyond the reach of any phrase of comfort manufactured for the occasion; and how could God, any God, have a purpose in taking Amanda away, her beautiful and only child, her lovely Amanda, to whose promise she had devoted all her own love, all her care? Yet when Dr. Passmore finally rose and made his way to the pulpit, and turned to face them, and when she saw in his face an expression of tenderest compassion, she was thirsty for the comfort he might provide. She trusted him. Had they not worked together towards the same end?

She heard his rich voice, phrases and sentences registering at intervals though she could not fasten fully on his message: "I have loved St. Matthew's all my life and I have loved this girl for the few months we have known her. *Or rather have not known her.* But imagined we did, and took her for granted, simply another

298

one-year student. She was pure, and lovely . . . her silent communion with a poet from another age and with the tender music of a great composer. As wistful and unfathomable as she. We failed her: a more *vigilant* solicitude and kindness we did not have. We did not see her isolation, her fearfulness. Her terror of disappointing our expectations and ambitions for her . . . on the churning little island of ambition we seem to have turned into. Do you bring this virus in, or do we cultivate it here? This lovely child is its most terrible casualty. Do you not remember of the counsel of St. Matthew? *Judge not, that ye be not judged?*"

She had never seen him angry. Hardly anyone had.

"There is consolation for you, Dear Bahringers, and for us." (The headmaster looked directly, searchingly, at Tess). "And yet it must be *earned*. By a lived determination that no such thing ever be allowed to happen: that we choke off and destroy the condition in which it took its nourishment. And no one here will doubt the nature of that condition, who has seen the evidence I have . . .

"But now. God bless you both, God bless our school, and God bless Amanda. May she be forever where springs not fail.

"The School Hymn, All Loves Excelling."

They said their good-byes in the parking lot outside Morison, that place of so many hurried goings and comings, gay promises and trampled expectations. They stood in an awkward cluster: Daniella — whom Tess now addressed by name; the headmaster and Dorothea Rodman; Mr. Arnett — for once silent and subdued; Tess and Joey; Toby. The boy held in his hands a large cardboard box full of the last of Amanda's things, desk and drawer litter that hadn't been packed up.

"May I put it on the back seat, ma'am?"

Tess remembered the boy lifting things *off* the back seat, helping Amanda move in, just six months ago.

Her voice was a voice of desolation, the words crumpled, choked. "Thank you . . . grateful." She saw Toby struggling to control himself, turning away from her so she could not see him cry.

And then suddenly he looked straight at her. "I want you to be proud of her, not just love her, but . . . be *proud* of her. She never complained. About anything."

Soon after they got onto the interstate, Tess managed to lift the cardboard box from the back seat and put it under her legs up front. She began taking things out — photographs, pens, a calculator, a little silver box full of clips; and dozens — so it seemed — of orange pill cylinders ("Amanda self-medicated" was a phrase they'd heard several times). Tess recognized the names of the prescribing doctors, and the medicines they'd authorized, and, sometimes, the circumstances; at least four of them had *her* name, not Amanda's, on the labels. She held up a squat white bottle of *Gingko Biloba: Sharper Memory, Better Retention.*

"She never needed any of that, any of that stuff."

"Don't. Please don't say anything now, please, Joey . . ."

And underneath all these things lay the beautiful journal Tess had given her daughter only ten weeks earlier. Against every instinct she took it up and began reading, starting with Amanda's citation from her poet: THESE THINGS, THESE THINGS WERE HERE, AND BUT THE BEHOLDER WANTING; and then the chronicle of entries, one after another: Amanda's silent, pathetic indictment of her, page after page of it.

This is what I have done, I have done this, I . . .

"Don't read the thing, Tess, read it in a year. No mother could love a kid the way you loved her, you couldn't have given her more, done more, loved her . . ."

She sat crumpled against the car door and the back of her seat. Once or twice Joey saw her turn back a page to read again, heard a stifled, choked sound. He put his hand, palm up, next to her. Finally she took it. In the garage Tess said simply, "I'm going right upstairs. I'm exhausted."

"Don't, don't blame yourself . . ."

"Well, and if not me, who do you blame?"

Joey performed the same domestic duties he had done for twenty years: emptying an ashtray, locking the doors, laying out business papers in his study for the morning, checking the mail. There was an *Architectural Digest* and there were four or five letters, the last of which was addressed to Miss Amanda Bahringer. It bore the return address: Office of Admissions, Dartmouth College, Hanover, New Hampshire, 03755-4030. Joey opened the envelope and read the letter.

His wife was already in bed when he came upstairs. She lay in a way he had never seen: on her back, eyes open and looking up, her head on a single pillow and her arms at her sides.

"Is everything all right? Is Cleopatra O.K.?"

"Fine," Joey said.

"Was there any mail?"

"Nothing important," he answered.